A Walk with Heavenly Spirits

J.E. Grace

This book is a work of fiction. Names, characters, businesses, organizations, places, events, and incidents either are the product of the author's imagination or are used fictitiously. Any resemblance to actual persons, living or dead, events, or locales is entirely coincidental.

All biblical scriptures are from the Holy Bible, New King James Version.

Contents

Chapter 1

It was two years since Allison Stevens had been to her hometown of Rustin, Colorado. She left after high school graduation, due to an unresolved issue with her father. One minute she was in a heated argument and then she was grabbing her suitcase walking out the door, only looking back once, but it was long enough to see the hurt look in her mother's eyes.

She threw her suitcase onto the back seat of Tom's Chevy and got into the front seat. Tom leaned over, gave her a quick peck on the cheek, and then started the car. At that time her heart and mind were a million miles apart.

Tom who was a couple of years older had swept her off her feet. Tall, with gorgeous brown eyes and a voice that dripped like honey, he was always telling her she was the most beautiful girl he ever saw. When he ran his fingers through her long auburn hair, it would send chills through her body and when their eyes met, she felt as though she would melt.

"Tom, where will we go?" Allison asked, now faced with the reality of the hasty decision she had made.

"Collingwood. I've been offered an internship with an advertising firm there. I know you're scared. It's a big step, but you'll see. Everything will work out. We'll get married. Isn't that what you want?" he asked -glancing over at her with his dazzling smile that seemed to make her lose all common sense.

"Yes, of course. But where will we live? Do you have money to get a place? Allison asked, feeling unsure of her future. Doubt was beginning to creep in.

"We'll stay with my brother and his wife until we can get a place of our own. I already talked to them."

"It sounds like you have everything all figured out," said Allison leaning her seat back. "How long will it be till we get there?"

"About an hour and a half," Tom said. "Why don't you get some sleep and I'll wake you when we're there."

"Okay." Allison took one last look out the side window as the highway stretched before her leaving her home behind. Her final thought before her eyes shut was, I will probably never see my parents again.

The years had not been kind to Allison. Tom was not at all what she had expected. He did get his job at Bedford Advertising and seemed to settle in quite nicely, and Allison even managed to get put in charge of the advertising for their magazine. She started to get one pay raise after another and felt she was finally living the life she was meant to live right before the bottom dropped out.

Allison was called into Mr. Bedford's office one day in the middle of June. In the time she had been there, she knew that nothing good ever came from a special meeting with the boss.

"You have been a valuable asset to our company, but with the conflict between you and your husband, due to our company rules we have to let one of you go." Mr. Bedford got up from his desk and came towards Allison. "I hate to have to do this, but we are terminating you."

"I'm not sure I understand why." Allison got up and walked towards the door. "But I'll clean out my desk."

"Stop by accounting and pick up your check and your letter of recommendation before you leave. I wish you the best, Allison."

That was the end of the life she treasured. One-day Allison had a high paying job, a husband she loved and hoped to have children with some day, and then it was all gone.

Chapter 2

Allison's evening started out as it usually did since the divorce. Nothing exciting happened. No friends came by to see how she was doing and there were no messages on her answering machine. She lived an uneventful life.

Allison lay awake in the darkness of her bedroom. Outside the moon was just a sliver in the night sky and there was no wind or sounds to arouse her senses.

She turned over in her large poster bed, pulled the pillows around to cradle her neck, and settled in for the night. It was only in sleep that she hoped to escape the loneliness she felt inside. As she drifted off, she started dreaming.

Allison was engulfed in darkness. The nothingness was almost suffocating. She had no physical body, it had long become unnecessary. Allison floated for what seemed like forever before her Heavenly Spirit communicated with her.

It was the beginning. A time before the universe was inhabited by its many souls, before our generation had made such a mess of things, and before our creator had put it all together; the stars, the universe, and life as we knew it.

The Spirit cautioned her to pay close attention to what was about to unfold before her eyes.

Suddenly, pure energy surrounded her and light illuminated the sky. The first particles of matter appeared like small droplets, exploding outwards creating strings of galaxies. She was in awe as she watched.

Stars were born, surrounded by planets. The beginning of life was taking place, the lower forms of life and then those who came before her.

The Earth appeared to have a faint glow coming from every direction in the heavens, and the entire universe seemed to be the source. She realized she was looking at the life source for all creation.

It was a powerful thing to observe, the universe on its way to growth, and its many extensions of life. How many generations came before her? Would anyone even know they had been here?

She turned over in her bed realizing she was near the edge. She fully expected to hit the floor hard, but to her amazement, she seemed to float. It was as if her body no longer had any weight to it.

She opened her eyes and saw that her surroundings had changed. She was no longer in her bedroom but was somewhere she didn't recognize. She didn't have any feelings of apprehension or fear but a sense of calm and peacefulness. They were feelings she hadn't felt in a long, long time.

During her thirty-three years, Allison had faced many trials, and there were times when she was ready to give up, but a voice inside kept urging her to go on.

When the nudge felt like a warning, she thought it might be her conscience, when in fact it was the Holy Spirit, trying to keep her on the right path. Sometimes she listened and escaped disaster, but on some occasions, her stubborn self-centered-attitude took over, and she had to deal with heartbreak.

Now, she realized that she had never really been alone. God had always been with her, even during the bad times.

She could feel God's presence telling her not to be afraid. He wanted her to look around at all the beauty before her.

As she raised her head, she stared in amazement. The colors of the trees and flowers had a depth she never observed before. She had a strong feeling that everything was connected. Everywhere she looked, there were rivers of living water.

The passage from the Bible about Jesus giving all those who believed in him an abundance of living water that would never run out came to mind. Her feelings of insecurity and loneliness had faded away and peace and warmth that she was not able to adequately describe enveloped her.

Allison sat down slowly on the top of a hill that overlooked a gorgeous valley. Her white gown blew in the soft breeze that caressed her cheek, long light brown hair framed her face, and her blue eyes were wide with wonder.

Immediately, her head dropped, and she began to speak to God. A God she had known for most of her life, but never really understood until now. God hadn't abandoned her. She had left him.

Somewhere along the way, her heart had grown cold, and she had forgotten how to love. She was unable to feel the closeness she had once felt for others. When did it happen? She honestly couldn't remember.

A soft breeze passed across her face. Something had touched her shoulder so lightly that it felt as though a thousand butterfly wings had brushed against her. She called out softly, "I can feel your presence, but I can't see you. LORD, is that you?"

"No dear. I am your Heavenly Spirit, Desire. I know what's in your heart. There is a new desire exploding inside of you wanting to know the truth of our Lord. I'm here to remind you of your past desires and show you what your Lord has promised you in his word."

"Are you talking about the Bible?" she asked.

"Yes. Delight yourself also in the Lord, and He shall give you the desires of your heart. But not all people remember that everything comes from God, and you must put him first. Your

desires have to be in line with what his path is for you. Look off towards the valley, and I'll show you."

Allison watched, and a part of the sky rolled back as if she was watching a movie on a huge screen. The scene opened at work, and her boss had called her into his office. Allison remembered how nervous she had been. She thought she was being laid off. Instead, he had congratulated her on the fantastic job she had been doing.

One of the other workers, Ellen, had taken ill and the company needed to hire a replacement. Her illness was terminal, and Ellen's misfortune had been Allison's gain. Allison was excited at the thought of more money and a better position.

"Do you know what you did wrong and why it didn't work out for you?" asked Desire.

Allison thought for a moment and then replied. "I don't know. I did a good job, followed orders, and I was dependable."

"You did everything right, except show compassion for Ellen. Most of all you did not give praise, to the Lord who had opened up the door just for you. He created the path you were to walk. You sought to please man rather than God."

"I see that now. I have disappointed God with my self-centered ways," said Allison looking at her Spirit with regret showing on her face.

"God has forgiven you. You must learn from your mistakes."

Desire had seen many things through its existence and never ceased to be amazed at the differences within the hearts of those whose prayers and secret thoughts drifted upwards. Once in a while, there had been a struggle between Desire and Conscience within the souls.

When everything was right, Desire and Conscience would band together for the greater good of the Father by keeping the souls on the right path. At that time, there would be a great shout of celebration in the Heavens. Angels would rejoice.

"Did you hear? Yes, another one, LORD. They desire to walk with you!"

Desire remembered the pleas of the little ones most. Their requests were different. They didn't ask anything for themselves, but for someone who meant everything to them. The voices of the innocents hurt most, but Desire knew that the LORD always heard their cries. He would heal their broken hearts.

Allison noticed that the Heavenly Spirit was beginning to materialize. He was tall, had beautiful golden hair, and an angelic face.

"Why can I see you now? she asked.

"You now believe in the blessings of our Lord. Come walk with me."

Chapter 3

"Where am I?" asked Allison.

"You have been allowed into the Upper Realm. God's kingdom is just over the top of Majesty Mountain. Very few living souls have been allowed to see what you see."

"Why did you bring me here? I'm not special," she asked taking in the view before her.

"All God's children are special. He knew you before you were even born and you were given gifts to use to do great things. God wants you to see what you couldn't believe with your own heart."

Allison listened to the words of her Spirit. She knew she had individual strengths, but for a long time, she only felt an overpowering indwelling of weakness. Satan had taken every flaw and led her to temptations that Allison would fail to resist. Alone she didn't stand a chance, but with faith and trust in God, she would be victorious over them all.

"God wants to give you the desires of your heart, but you must follow the path that he has chosen for you. It is not the straight path, and few seem to be able to attain it, especially when they try to do it on their own." The Spirit seemed to float over the ground as he spoke.

Allison remembered some of the times in the past when her path was clouded by fear and lack of self-esteem. No matter what she accomplished, it wasn't good enough and was unable to determine if the direction was from God or not. "How do I know what God's destiny is for me? How do I know who I'm following?" asked Allison.

"You must be patient and wait for doors to open in the direction you want to go. If it's from God, it will never contradict his word. If you feel you can't-do it without God's help and leading, it is something God is calling you to do."

"Am I supposed to pray for direction in everything? I've always tried to stand on my own and make my way," asked Allison thinking about her past decisions.

"Has that made you happy? Have all your plans worked out?" asked her Spirit.

Allison thought for a minute. It seemed like nothing ever worked, and she had spent her whole life trying to be happy, but something always seemed to be missing.

"I was happy as a child. I was close to the Lord then," said Allison unsure of why she had grown apart from of God.

"You have to take that time and bring it into your thoughts when you are feeling alone. You are only alone because you forget God is always with you. Do you put on the spiritual armor of God daily?"

"I have never heard of spiritual armor. What is it?" Allison wondered what it was all about. She was confused.

"Spiritual armor is something everyone needs and has available to them. It is to fight daily battles against Satan. Hasn't Satan tormented or tempted you in some way?" asked Desire.

"Of course, he has. I know that sometimes I feel like it is okay to do something that I know in my heart isn't right. I know that Satan tells lies to manipulate me into going against God, but sometimes it is so subtle that I'm not even aware that he is speaking to me," Allison said as she sat down in the field overlooking the hillside. Her Spirit stood beside her.

"Every day, Allison, you must put on your full armor.

First, you must stand steadfast in the truth of God's word, so you will know when Satan is lying to you.

Second, you must guard your heart against evil. You are protected by the blood of Jesus Christ. Plead the blood over circumstances when you need protection.

Third, you must stand firm in the gospel so you will shine as a bright light to everyone that God puts in your path.

Fourth, you must shield yourself from Satan's doubt, denial, and deceit using your faith, so that you aren't defeated when he attacks.

Fifth, you must keep your mind focused on Christ so that Satan doesn't get a stronghold in your thoughts. You are a child of God saved by grace and salvation."

"Last, you need to know the scriptures, so you can expose the tempting words of Satan when he attacks you. He will quote scripture to you too, but he will twist the truth. You need to know the difference," said the Heavenly Spirit.

"God has given me all these things to fight Satan. I had no idea that he had prepared such protection for me," she said. Allison felt much stronger just knowing she had an arsenal of God's power available to her. Why hadn't she heard of this?

"God wants his children to be able to withstand whatever Satan throws at them. You have to remember you are victorious and with God, there is nothing that is impossible. You need to write these things down and keep them fresh in your mind."

"Will I be able to remember when I go back?" said Allison rising to stand.

"God will keep this visit in your memory. God's word will teach you the rest. Allison, you must be faithful and study his word. God loves you and wants you to know his promises."

Allison strolled along the side of the long valley with Desire and felt such peace. She looked towards Majesty Mountain, and it seemed to shine even brighter than when she saw it the first time.

She could smell sweet spice and floral scents that were exhilarating, and she never felt more alive knowing in her heart that this was her forever home. A song erupted from deep inside of her and found her voice louder, more beautiful than it had ever been. She was singing praises to God.

Chapter 4

Allison awoke with dawn exploding on the horizon, opened her window and for the first time in a long time looked forward to starting her day. She had written down the words her guide had spoken and pledged to start living each day putting them into action. She began by repeating out loud the six parts of the armor of God and started her walk as a spiritual warrior.

She felt confident and decided it was time to follow God's path, not her own. He had given her gifts, and she had spent hours going over what her strengths and talents were.

She was good at serving people, and maybe it was time to help others. She knew that always thinking about herself first never worked in the past, and if she put God first, then she needed to put others first too. She needed to find another job, but where would she look? She decided to start with a prayer.

"Lord, direct my steps today. Lead me to your path and open doors that lead me to the destiny chosen for me. By faith, I have put on the whole armor of God. In Jesus Name, Amen."

Allison took a shower while singing the whole time. She got dressed in a blue blouse that brought out the blue in her eyes, black jeans, and combed out her hair. She was ready to embark on her new day. She opened the front door and took the first step with renewed confidence.

It was a mild, summer day. All along the street in Allison's neighborhood of Collingwood were well kept historical houses with wrought iron fencing or white picket fences.

Allison loved the pastel colors of the exteriors of the homes and the beautifully landscaped flower gardens.

Allison was busy thinking about her experiences with her Spirit and didn't notice that she was coming close to Mrs. Simmons, a woman in her late fifties whom the neighbors felt was ill-mannered.

"Young lady, do you think you can watch where you are going?" said Mrs. Simmons glaring at Allison.

"I'm sorry. I guess I was daydreaming," said Allison stepping aside.

"Daydreaming will only get you into trouble. Try paying attention!" Mrs. Simmons said as she pushed past Allison.

Allison would have been perturbed by the remark, but today was different. Today, she was happy and only felt compassion for the old woman.

Allison continued on her way towards the employment agency. Hopefully, they would find something suited to her. After all, God was helping her now, and anything was possible.

But then she began to worry. *Would anything be available? What if I don't have the right experience?* By the time she reached the front door of the agency, she wasn't sure she could go in.

No! I don't believe you! Go away, Satan. You are lying. I plead the blood of Jesus Christ over you. Be Gone! Allison took a deep breath and stepped inside. *I can do this.*

The interview lasted about an hour, and Allison walked out of the employment agency with renewed hope. Several options had been offered, and she needed to pray for guidance. It was a big decision, and it couldn't be all about the money, but a job she would do with a happy, willing heart. God wouldn't let her down. The answer would come with patience and prayer on her part.

It was late in the evening, and Allison was too restless to sleep. She heard someone or something in her room and threw back the covers, tip-toeing down the hallway. After checking each room and not finding anything, she decided it must have been her imagination.

She got back into bed and thought about how her life had started to change. With her spiritual guide, Desire, she had learned a lot, but she wasn't sure if she was up to all the other guides that were to come.

Forgiveness stood silently in the corner of the room watching Allison. God said this one would be a challenge and Forgiveness would have to be convincing if he was going to change her opinion of herself.

Allison was always unwilling to forgive herself for her past mistakes which led to feelings of guilt and insecurity. Her spiritual life suffered and she had become a baggage junkie over the past few years.

God had clothed her with the robes of righteousness and forgiveness, but she still insisted on carrying all the baggage around from her past. If she could only pack her personal luggage with the love of Jesus Christ, the wisdom and guidance of the Holy Spirit, and the knowledge and obedience of the word, she could have been at peace. She knew she was supposed to be a new person, but Satan had fed her the lies for so long that she was still struggling to regain confidence in a lasting way.

"Allison, don't be frightened. I'm Forgiveness, a Messenger from God. I'm here to help you."

Allison wondered how long her Heavenly Spirit had been watching. This Spirit was going to be hard to face. She had struggled with being able to forgive herself and others that had hurt her. She felt she was to blame for her failed marriage, even though her ex-husband had stopped loving her. She had carried the hurt around; unable to lay her guilt at the feet of Jesus so she could be free. Satan knew her thoughts and entered her mind frequently. Sometimes subtle remembrances would flood her mind until she thought she couldn't bear it anymore.

"Allison, I can feel the hurt you have deep inside. God has blotted out your sins and remembers them no more. You must forgive those who have hurt you. Only then can you truly be healed. You should not keep in front of you what God has put behind him. Forgive others as God has forgiven you."

Allison hung her head and began to weep. Forgiveness put his arms around her holding her close, and she felt a sense of immense peace as a wave of warmth flowed through her entire body. She leaned into Forgiveness and felt like a small child cradled in love.

After a few minutes, Allison opened her eyes and found herself standing on a bluff overlooking the ocean. In the distance was a lighthouse, it's light shining out, bouncing off the water creating a golden glow.

She could smell the crisp ocean air and heard the call of the seagulls as they flew overhead. The sun was starting to set over the water and there was something very familiar about the place, that triggered a memory, one that she didn't want to revisit.

"Do you recognize this place?" asked Forgiveness.

"Yes. It's where Tom and I spent our first anniversary," said Allison as a tear fell from her eye and rolled down her cheek. "Why did he have to leave me? What did I do wrong?" she asked, the emotion rising as she tried to contain the tears.

"He wasn't a believer, Allison. You were not equally yoked. Satan used him to make you suffer and convinced you that it was your fault. You let Satan steal your joy," replied Forgiveness.

Allison thought back to how this used to be her favorite place. She would visit the memory when she was feeling down, and the power of the ocean surf would fill her with renewed strength. She always felt so free and closer to God than she felt anywhere. Then the unthinkable happened. Nothing seemed to matter after that, and all the beauty Allison once loved about the place now only seemed to haunt her.

"How does this place make you feel?" Forgiveness asked.

"That day was one of the happiest days of my life, but then I remember how my marriage turned out and that makes me sad. My happiness was stolen from me, and I'm confused because I don't remember the moment when everything changed. "Why didn't God make things better? Isn't he in charge of my life?" asked Allison.

"God is in charge, but he wants you to seek his help when you face the tough situations in life. He gives all his children free will and the right to choose for themselves."

"Why do I feel like I should have done something? Maybe I could have changed Tom's mind. Maybe I didn't love him enough." Allison stood watching the waves.

"That's just the lies of Satan invading your mind trying to keep you a prisoner. You can't make someone love you. God loves you unconditionally and forever. You are never alone, no matter how many people leave you."

"I don't know if I can forgive Tom. It's been two years, and it hurts as much as it did when it happened, only I don't think of it quite as often as I used to," said Allison as she walked along the edge of the bluff.

"God has forgiven you, Allison, and now you have to honor him by forgiving those that have wronged you. Once you have done that, you will look at things much differently and begin to heal. God wants you to be whole again."

She knew it would be hard to forgive Tom, but deep in her heart, she knew it was the only way to finally be free. She was unsure as to whether or not she could do the task that God called her to do, but her guide told her that God wouldn't have called her unless he equipped her to complete it.

Allison felt a rush of wind that brought a glorious smell that filled her with joy.

She closed her eyes, and when she opened them, she was back in her bed. It seemed like a dream, but she knew the Spirit had been very real.

Tomorrow she would call Tom and tell him she forgave him. She didn't know how he would handle it, as they hadn't spoken since the divorce.

She wanted to grow in her spiritual walk with God, and this was the next step. It wouldn't be easy, but now she felt that with God's assurance, she could be victorious. It was time to get on with her new life and finally break the bonds of Satan.

Allison was beginning to look forward to her visits from the Spirits. Each one brought a word from God and taught her a lesson which she applied to her spiritual journey. Part of it was painful as she faced the mistakes from her past but also gave her great joy to know she could finally put them to rest.

It was the middle of the afternoon when she received the call from the employment office about a job they felt she was a good match for.

She started to hesitate and then agreed to the interview the next day. After all, her last Spirit told her that God would equip her for any challenge that came her way. She knew in her heart, that this was such a time and that God would bless her for obeying.

She was feeling more at ease the past few days, and she knew that reading her Bible and praying for guidance was responsible for the change.

She busied herself completing her household chores and felt a tug in her heart to call Tom. She picked up the phone and dialed the number. It rang a couple of times, and a woman answered.

Allison's first response was to hang up. She mustered up all the courage she had and continued. "Is Tom there?"

"Who is this?" the woman asked.

"It's Allison."

"Hold on, and I'll get him. Make it quick, we were just leaving," the woman said.

There was dead silence on the other end.

"Tom, are you there?" asked Allison. She was beginning to wonder if he would come to the phone.

"I'm here. You were the last person I expected to hear from," said Tom.

"I know, but there is something I need to tell you. Please, just listen," Allison said, trying to keep her voice from breaking up.

"Ok," said Tom.

"I know when we separated I said some things in anger. I just want you to know that I forgive you for what you did. I've changed, Tom. God has shown me how to get past the hurt and go on with my life through his forgiveness," said Allison.

"I'm glad, Allison. I'm sorry too. I know I hurt you, but I did what I felt I had to do. We just weren't right for each other."

"God can change your heart too, Tom. He is real and cares about you," said Allison.

"I'm not into the God stuff, but whatever works for you. Well, I have to go, Caroline's waiting. Take care of yourself," said Tom, the irritation building in his voice.

A part of Allison still had feelings for Tom even though he had broken her heart. She would pray that somehow, he would find his way to God too.

Chapter 5

It had been a couple of days since her phone call to Tom. She felt much better since she had forgiven him and could finally start to put the hurt behind her moving forward with new enthusiasm.

She went for the interview at the Victory Center, and even though she was apprehensive, she accepted the position anyway. She knew God would see her through. God had changed her on the inside, and she was looking forward to helping others in need.

She had been working at the Victory Center for almost a week. It made her feel good being able to help out in the kitchen and the store that supplied the homeless with warm clothing and was amazed at the generosity of the community.

She was busy hanging some recent clothing donations when her new boss, Carol, a petite woman in her late forties entered the room. Carol's short brunette hair was bobbed in a stylish cut, and she wore designer jeans with a matching jacket. She was tall, thin, and carried a clipboard.

"Allison, I just wanted to let you know how pleased we all are with your work and hope you are enjoying being here," said Carol sitting down.

"Thank you. I was a little nervous since all this is new to me, but I enjoy helping the people," said Allison as she took a seat next to Carol.

"We don't have a lot of resources in our small town, and they depend on us for any help we can give them, even if it is just a hot meal or a set of new clothes so they can go for a job interview," said Carol as she glanced at the paperwork.

"I always thought that homeless people were just lazy or that they caused their situation until I spoke to a few of them. They are just like me but have had unfortunate things happen in their lives, some things beyond their control. I can relate to them better now that I have taken the time to listen to them," said Allison ashamed to admit that she had been so judgmental.

"You have the compassionate nature that is needed for this type of work and can be a real help in their healing process. I have a favor to ask you, Allison. I would like you to attend one of our weekly meetings and tell the group a little about yourself and your personal struggles," said Carol giving her a warm smile.

"I don't know if I can do that. I'm not good with groups of people and especially talking about personal things with somewhat total strangers," said Allison shifting in her seat.

"I think you will do fine. No pressure, just pray about it and let me know what you decide. The next group meeting is in two days at 6 p.m.," said Carol. She gave Allison a quick hug before leaving the room.

The struggles Allison had in her past, she had tried to bury and didn't know if she wanted to face them again. *Was this request coming from God? If so, didn't her guide tell her God would not ask her to do anything he didn't prepare her to do?* She would pray for an answer and obey if it was God's will.

Allison clocked out of work at 5 p.m. and headed south on Main street towards the local grocery store. After spotting an open space at the front of the lot, she parked and got out.

Upon entering the store, a friendly clerk uttered a "Welcome to Roger's Grocery."

Allison smiled back at her and went down the aisles placing the needed items into the cart. It had been awhile since she had made an effort to make a home-cooked meal. She needed to change that.

She joined the line that formed at the front of the register. There was a young woman with a small child just ahead of her. She could hear the clerk saying that the woman was short of cash. The woman replied that it was all the money she had.

Allison felt an urgency within her. She knew it was the Holy Spirit. *You want me to pay the extra money for her, but what if I run short before I get paid? What? I need to have faith.* She knew the message was coming from God and she walked over to the woman and handed her a twenty-dollar bill.

The woman smiled and the cahier began bagging the woman's groceries. The woman put the groceries into her cart and waited to speak to Allison.

"I appreciate your help. I don't know how I can repay you. My son has a vitamin deficiency, and it's important that he has healthy meals. My husband left us, and it's been hard coping with everything," she said.

"I'm happy to help out. I'm Allison. I work at the Victory Center during the week. If you ever need help with anything, please come see us. We help with food, clothing, and counseling if you need to talk to someone. Remember, you are not alone," said Allison.

"Jeannie. Thank You so much." She smiled at Allison and reached over touching her hand in a warm gesture.

Allison watched as Jeannie left the store and wondered if she would see her again. Being able to help gave her a warm feeling inside. God would provide for Allison's needs, and she realized there was no need to worry. Worry only replaced faith which was an attack from Satan. She was a child of God, and he had no hold over her any longer. She was growing in her faith.

Chapter 6

Allison prepared her dinner as planned. It felt so good to take the time to cook healthy food again, and she was amazed at how well it had turned out. She hadn't lost her touch.

After clean up, she retired to her big comfortable chair with Bible in hand. Being immersed in the word of God, she didn't notice the presence of a Heavenly Spirit watching her.

The Spirit, Faith, watched from across the room. This young woman had shown significant growth in her walk with the Lord. She was gaining understanding and was implementing everything she had learned during her spiritual visits. Faith was confident that she held great promise. She would lead many to Christ, but she wasn't even aware of it yet. It was God's plan for her life. She was healing, and now she could help others to heal.

Allison could feel the presence of the Spirit. Even though she couldn't see him, she knew he was watching her. She thought about the meaning of faith, a belief in something for which there was no tangible proof, having complete trust. It was the very opposite of doubt. She had learned to accept the spiritual world even more than the real one. This message was about having faith.

A second later Allison found herself standing on a high hilltop overlooking a vast valley. On both sides of the valley, vast armies dressed in battle gear were coming towards each other. The sky was an ominous black, and thunder cracked overhead so loud that she thought her ears would burst.

"Where am I?" asked Allison as her eyes locked on the scene in front of her.

"This is Earth's final battle where the armies of Satan are coming against our Lord," said the Spirit pointing towards the distant armies.

Allison watched in horror as the battle ensued and the slaughter began. Many fell to the chains of death.

"Why is God allowing this to happen? Doesn't He care about the people?" Allison asked.

"This is God's prophesy declared in his word thousands of years ago. Many view his word as a fairy tale and even more fall for Satan's lies and will pay the eternal price."

Just when Allison thought there wasn't any hope for what was happening, the skies began to roll back, and she heard the sound of many pounding hooves.

On each white horse was a saint clothed in a white robe. In front, another figure on a white horse rode downward to meet those on the ground. His eyes were like fire and on his head, were many crowns. He killed the armies with the sword that came from his mouth.

"I know him. Everything is true. Jesus does come to defeat Satan," said Allison.

"Yes, Allison, he comes to save the world. Satan is already a defeated foe. This is his fate. It ends here. The earthly saved were already in Heaven. He spared them from going through all of this."

In an instant, everything faded, and Allison was back in her living room. She was shaking, yet so excited to know Christ was indeed to be the world's final ruler into eternity. She bowed her head and said a prayer thanking Jesus for saving her and everyone on earth who called on his name and believed that he died for their sins.

There was hope, and faith was all she needed to focus her eyes on the heavenly realm. She had a forever home. There was no more doubt about whether or not she was worthy. She belonged to Jesus, and she wept tears of joy.

"Faith, are you still here?" she asked not being able to see clearly.

"Yes, Allison."

"Why do people have such a hard time believing in God?"

"It's hard for them to believe in someone they can't physically see. The world works on visual stimulus and emotion. The scholars of your world go to no end to disprove the existence of a heavenly creator. Man wants to take credit for what lies before him, and some think the world and everything in it just happened randomly. They are convinced they can do anything on their own without God," said the Heavenly Spirit standing quietly beside her bed.

"It's so sad to think that without God, they are lost and have no chance to live an eternal life. Their earthly home is all they have to look forward to and nothing beyond that. All hope is gone for them," said Allison with tears in her eyes.

"That's where you can help. Study God's word and bring it to those that will listen. Greet everyone in love. Love is the beginning of all healing and the Holy Spirit. God will use you to do wondrous things, Allison, beyond anything you can imagine," said Faith as he started to vanish from her sight.

With that, the Spirit Faith was gone. The words and images Allison had witnessed stayed burned into her memory. The picture of the Lord on the beautiful white stallion gave her great joy. She wanted to rush out and scream it to the rooftops, but picked up her Bible instead and opened it to the Revelation of Jesus Christ. The words would have a more profound meaning when she read them this time.

Chapter 7

After Allison's visit from the Heavenly Spirit Faith, she felt a renewed strength within her that seemed to get stronger each day. She was still unsure how much she would tell the people at the shelter about her past. Some of the memories were painful, but she was able to go on knowing her future was much brighter now.

Allison went to work the day of her testimony with an inner peace, even though she wasn't sure what she would say to inspire her audience. She trusted the Holy Spirit to guide her.

She walked into the room taking her place at the podium. A sense of impending fear started to capture her thoughts as she looked out among the sea of faces before her. She said a quiet prayer for God to fill her with calmness. *No, Satan. You can't stop me. I will do this!*

She spoke boldly, "Most of you know me. For those who don't, my name is Allison. I've only been working at the shelter for a short time, but I have grown to appreciate what they do for all of you. I want to give you a little glimpse into what my life has been like and what the Lord has been able to do for me."

"I got married at a very young age to a man I thought loved me. I was very naïve and didn't realize that I chose the wrong person. At that time, I didn't have God in my life."

"My husband left me for someone else, and it took me years to finally understand that I would never heal until I learned to forgive him. That didn't happen until recently. When I turned my life over to God, I began feeling different. I looked at things differently. I had a sense of inner peace that I never knew before," said Allison looking out into the faces of the crowd.

"Just after my husband left me, my father passed away. I couldn't understand why God had taken the two people I loved most out of my life. I didn't realize that Satan was the cause of how I was feeling. Instead, of cherishing the time my father and I had spent together, I focused on the loss. I had trouble working and had outbursts of tears. My relationship with my Mother suffered. I still hope to repair it someday soon. Finally, when I felt I couldn't stand anymore, I cried out to God to take away the pain."

"I was lying in bed trying to sleep and had tossed for hours. I cried until I thought I couldn't shed another tear. Then I felt a warmth come over my body that started at my feet and continued up through the top of my head. Peace came over me, and the tears stopped.

An angel stood at the foot of my bed. I felt the inner warmth like I had been bathed in warm sunshine. The next thing I knew, it was morning, and I awoke with a peaceful heart. The hurt wasn't as bad. I thought of my Dad, and a smile crossed my face. I knew I was healed."

"What I want you to know is that we all face things that we try to cope with on our own, but most times, we just can't. During those times, you need to place it in the Lord's hands and let him carry your burdens. Remember, he will never leave you, nor forsake you."

A young, woman she recognized as Jeanne asked, "How do you know when you are following what the Lord wants for you? It's hard for me to tell?"

"If it's coming from the Lord, he will confirm it to you through verses from the Bible, advice from someone who is grounded in scripture or if it is something you know you can't do on your own. Anything you feel is from God, will never contradict his word," said Allison walking out from behind the podium.

"I have learned through reading God's word that we all fight spiritual battles every day. Satan wants nothing more than to create doubt in your mind and cripple you. You must trust the Holy Spirit to guide your way. God uses any hardships we may encounter to prepare us for a future service or greater blessings. Strong faith comes from believing in God, even in the hard times. You need to seek God, know him, listen and obey." Allison looked out into the crowd waiting for any further questions, but everyone seemed to be rooted in thought. She hoped that the message got them to think about their own lives and how much the Lord could help change their circumstances.

Carol walked up to the front and put her arm around Allison and hugged her. "Let's give Allison a warm thank you for sharing some of her story with you today. Those of you who aren't sure about your salvation or don't have a relationship with the Lord, all you need to do is ask Jesus to come into your heart and repent of your sins. If you have done this, you were saved forever, and eternal life is yours. I pray in Jesus name, Amen."

Allison felt a feeling of gratitude and love from those around her. Many of the homeless came up and hugged her letting her know that her words had comforted them.

She had a new Christian family. Jeanne was among the first to greet her with a hug and words of gratefulness. Her son gave Allison a big grin.

Allison was blessed and amazed at how God was beginning to use her as a witness to his glory.

Chapter 8

So far Allison's journey had been a very enlightening one. She had learned so much from her Heavenly Spirits, but she struggled daily to put her will and desire aside to fulfill the destiny that God had chosen for her.

This particular morning was going to be more challenging than she ever imagined. Now that she was beginning to change inside, she knew there was one thing in particular that God had placed upon her heart. She needed to call her Mother and make amends.

Just thinking about picking up the phone filled her mind with doubt and guilt, of course, instigated by Satan. She was a child of God, and that made her even more of a target.

It was her day off from the center, and it started much the same as any other day. She began by reading her Bible and asking for guidance for her day.

The sun shone brightly through the window warming the side of her face, as she sat with her head bowed in prayer.

"God, prepare me for this day and give me the courage to do what I must do. In Jesus name, I pray. Amen."

A loud knock on her front door broke her concentration. She cautiously made her way towards the door calling out, "Who's there?"

A deep male voice echoed back, "It's officer, Stone. I need to have a word with you."

Allison opened the door. She couldn't imagine why a police officer would need to speak to her.

"Are you Allison Stevens?" Asked the husky, middle aged, police officer.

"Yes."

"May I come in?" asked Office Stone.

"Of course, said Allison as she took a seat on the sofa. Officer Stone sat down in a chair across from her.

"What is this about, officer?" she asked.

"Is your mother, Lucy Stevens?" asked the officer.

"Yes. Is my Mom, all right?"

"A concerned neighbor called the local police when they couldn't get her to answer her phone. Your mother was found this morning unresponsive lying on her living room floor. She has been taken to Rustin Memorial Hospital, and the doctors were able to stabilize her, but she's in a coma. At this point, they are hopeful, but it's too early to tell when or if she will come out of it. Do you have anyone that you can call to be with you?" asked the officer.

"I live alone, but I can call my boss. Maybe she can come over."

"Give her a call. If she can't come, I'll be glad to drop you off over there."

Allison heard what the officer was saying but was she unable to speak. Her life was finally coming together, and she was doing what God meant for her to do, so why was this happening now?

Allison got it together enough to walk over to the phone. She dialed the center. The phone rang a couple of times, and Carol answered, "Victory Center."

"Carol. I have a police officer here with me. It's my Mom. She's in a coma at the hospital in Rustin. The officer doesn't want to leave me alone, and offered to give me a ride if you can't come over right now?" said Allison shifting her weight as she turned away from the officer's view.

"Allison, don't worry. I'll be right over. Have him stay with you until I get there."

"Thanks, Carol. I'll tell him," said Allison hanging up the phone and returning to the living room sofa.

"Officer Stone, she's on her way. I appreciate you staying with me."

"Allison, I know this is hard. How long has it been since you saw your Mother?" he asked, a look of concern crossing his face.

"We had a falling out, and we haven't spoken in a couple of years. We said some terrible things to each other," said Allison feeling a wave of guilt.

"I'm sure if she is like most mothers; she has never stopped thinking about you or loving you. Every family goes through hard times, and we all say things we don't mean sometimes."

"Do you believe in God, Officer Stone? Do you think he forgives us for not respecting our parents?" said Allison wondering if he was also a believer.

"I do, and I know that as long as you confess your misgivings to God and ask forgiveness from the ones you hurt, he will forgive you too. We are all in this world flawed, none perfect. I have seen my share of young kids that have gone off on the wrong path, but sometimes they straighten out and truly amaze me. God doesn't give up on anyone," said Officer Stone.

Allison felt a lot of guilt because the last time they were together she had blamed her mother for her father's death. Allison cringed as she recalled the hateful words she spoken to her. *What if I don't get a chance to ask for her forgiveness? What if I'm too late?*

She heard a car pull up outside and a couple of minutes later there was a knock at the door. Allison answered and was pulled into the arms of Carol who kept repeating that everything would be okay.

Officer Stone waited for the right moment and politely said, "It looks like you are in good hands so I'll be on my way. God Bless," he said.

Carol walked the officer to the door and then led Allison over to the sofa. "Allison is there anything I can do for you?"

"No. Just having you here means a lot to me. I just have to let this all sink in. It's such a shock," she said lowering her head.

"We can go to Rustin tomorrow if you like. I'll have the staff watch the center, and we can go together. Would you like that?" asked Carol. She sat down on the sofa next to Allison.

"Yes. I just couldn't go alone. The doctors aren't sure when or if she will come out of the coma. I don't want to think that she may never recover. There is so much I want to say to her," said Allison as she wiped a tear from her eye.

"Allison, you have to place this in God's hands. He knows what you need without even asking. Everything is according to his time. We'll both pray for her," said Carol looking into Allison's tear-filled eyes.

"I remember when my father died. I didn't think I would ever get over it. I remember that God healed my heart then," said Allison as her voice quivered.

"You never told me about your father. Do you want to share what happened? Sometimes it helps to talk about it," asked Carol wanting to help Allison through the pain.

"My father was a wonderful man. We had our issues when I was growing up, but I always knew he loved me. He enjoyed the holidays and liked to barbecue with family and friends. He was a veteran and went to the V.A. hospital every few months for a check-up. We found out after he died that he had cancer. He never told us," said Allison.

"It sounds like he wanted to spare the family. My Dad was a lot like that."

"A couple of months before he died he went through a significant change in his life. He used to be gone most of the day hanging out with his fishing buddies, but he started spending more time with my mom. He never really discussed God much, but I knew he believed. He started inviting door to door witnesses into the house and accepted their reading material. Mom was stunned," said Allison as she cleared her throat.

"When people are going through an illness they often turn to God for comfort. I've seen it happen many times." Carol moved in closer and held Allison's hand.

Allison took a deep breath and continued with her story. "Some friends of ours saw Dad the night before he died and they said he was smiling and seemed more energetic than he had been in months. Do you suppose he knew he was dying and had made peace with it?"

"It's possible. It does make a difference when you have the confidence of knowing that you will be with the Lord when you die," said Carol getting up from the sofa. "I should be getting back to the center. Would you like me to come back and stay the night with you?" she asked.

"I appreciate you being here for me, but I think I need to be alone for a while. I'm going to call the hospital and see if there is any change in her condition and then try to get some sleep. I want to be rested for our trip tomorrow."

"If you need anything or just want to talk, call me." Carol hugged Allison. "I'll see you at 8 a.m."

"I don't know what I would have done without you," Allison said. Carol walked up to Allison giving her a warm embrace and then left.

Allison grabbed the phone and dialed information asking for the number for Rustin Memorial Hospital. The operator connected her.

"Rustin Memorial Hospital, what room, please?"

"I don't know the room number, but I'm calling about my mother, Lucy Stevens."

"I'll connect you with the nurse that takes care of that floor. Just one moment, please."

Allison waited for the nurse to answer. She had to remind herself that the Lord was with her and that the situation was in his hands. She heard a click, and someone picked up.

"This is Amy. How can I help you?"

"I'm calling about my mother, Lucy Stevens. Is there any change in her condition?"

"I'm sorry, but there is no change."

"I'll be there sometime tomorrow to see her and talk to the doctor."

"Ok, I'll put a note on the chart that you want to speak with him. See you tomorrow."

Allison hung up the phone and felt more helpless than she did her entire life. She decided to make a cup of tea, take a hot shower, and get some sleep, reminding herself that she could sleep in peace even through the bad times because her heavenly father would be watching over her. She refused to let Satan get a foothold.

Chapter 9

It was the middle of the night, and even though Allison believed the Lord was with her, Satan did his best to make her doubt. She had slept for a few hours and awoke startled.

An uneasy feeling came over her, so she reached over and turned on her bedside lamp. It was already 2 a.m. In a few hours, Carol would be taking her to Rustin to see her mom.

Allison was filled with waves of guilt for not being a better daughter. She wished that she had made an effort to call her mom. Satan had begun to infiltrate her mind.

She pulled her Bible out of the bedside table and said a quick prayer for guidance. She opened it up and began to read from John 3:4. "I have no greater joy than to have my children walk in truth."

Allison knew that Satan was the one that was making her feel guilty. She felt the Holy Spirit was trying to send her a message through the passage she had just read.

After all, she knew she had confessed her shortfalls to God. She didn't understand why it was so hard to keep thoughts of Christ first in her mind.

She asked God to comfort her and turned out the light. She needed to get rested for her trip. She was just about to fall asleep when she felt a presence in the room.

She could almost make out the form standing in front of her bedroom window. It was like looking through darkness and having a light in the distance suddenly approach you becoming brighter and brighter. The form seemed to float over the floor as it approached.

Allison called out, "Who is there? What do you want?"

The form stopped in front of her bed.

"Allison, do not be fearful. I am Joy. I am one of your Heavenly Spirits. I need you to come with me."

By now, Allison knew that her spirits always had something important to convey to her. She got up from her bed and held out her hand.

The room was bathed in a glow which seemed to be coming from within Joy. Joy took Allison's hand, and before she could utter another word, they were gone.

They appeared on a rock face overlooking a desert. In the distance, were tall, weathered pinnacles filled with deep crevices where the wind had blown across them. It was dry and windy here. The hot sun from the day had set, and the landscape now was enveloped in the moonlight. The high mesas and plateaus in the distance were just eerie forms that seemed to dominate the skyline.

"I brought you here to show you that a person without God is like a desert, thirsting for the living water that never comes. They run around in all directions confused, but know that something is missing in their life. They live most of their lives in dark places. Christ is the light of truth. God extends his grace and shows us the path to salvation," said Joy.

Joy turned and placed a hand on Allison's shoulder, and a tingling sensation ran through her body. "Allison, God feels your pain as well as your joy. The deeper your walk with the

Lord, the more joy you will have. When Satan tries to get a stronghold on you, your way out is always there from the beginning."

"What do you mean? I don't understand," asked Allison.

"God is always in control. He knows what you need and if you walk deeper with him, the deeper the joy you will have. Joy touched her hand, *"Fill your mind with Christ. He will give you the answer you seek and help you find the narrow path to escape. Satan can't tempt you above what God will allow. Allison, true joy comes with progress towards maturity and when you begin to have a decreasing attachment to the things of this world."*

Allison thought about what Joy had said and wondered if she would ever feel real joy.

"Just when things were going well my mother got sick. I thought now that I follow God everything would be better."

"Allison, the closer you get to God, the more trials and struggles you may have. It's only because of your close walk with God that you can endure the hardships. You need to be joyful every day. Be glad for the day you have and seek each day in ways to glorify him."

In a matter of seconds, Allison was back in her bed. She propped herself up on her pillows and sent up a prayer of gratefulness for her time with Joy. She knew that whatever happened in the next few days she would wake with joy for that day and place the rest in God's hands.

Chapter 10

Allison seemed rested in spite of her lack of sleep. She took a shower and dressed in pale blue slacks and a white sweater. Her overnight bag was packed just in case she would have to extend her stay in Rustin.

It all still seemed like a bad dream. Allison said a quiet prayer for strength to do what was needed. She was just putting her cell phone into her purse when she heard a knock at the door.

She opened the door, and Carol entered. She was dressed in a very fashionable pantsuit and held the keys to her SUV in her hand.

"Are you ready to go? If we leave now, we should be able to miss the morning rush."

"I just have to check to make sure everything is off and grab some bottled water from the fridge. Would you like one?"

"Sure." Carol sat down on the sofa and waited for Allison to return.

In minutes, they had everything loaded into the SUV and were on their way.

Allison sat quietly as the SUV traveled along the freeway towards Rustin. She remembered crossing the Collingwood Bridge, but everything else was just a blur of images that didn't register in her memory. All she could think about was her mom.

"Are you okay?" asked Carol.

"I'm just worried about my mom. I'm not sure what to expect," she said glancing over at Carol.

"I can't tell you that everything will be fine but God will give you the strength you need to endure whatever happens."

"I know that God is with me, but sometimes it's just really hard."

"In about thirty minutes, we should be at the city limits of Rustin. You can help watch for the exit sign for the hospital," said Carol concentrating on the traffic.

They continued along the freeway in a southerly direction. Allison could see the industrial area of Rustin in the distance. In a few minutes, she saw the exit for the city center, then Front Street which led to the hospital parking garage.

Carol pulled off and slowly approached the parking garage. She grabbed a ticket and drove forward to the next level. After finding an empty space, she glanced over at Allison and could see she was lost in thought.

"Allison, do you want me to pray for you before we go in?" asked Carol.

Allison looked at Carol, thankful that she was such a caring Christian friend. "That would be great. I could use some extra strength right now."

Carol bowed her head, held Allison's hands in hers, and softly brought all their concerns to the Lord.

"Lord, we come together before you, to ask that you strengthen Allison. Remind her of your promise that she will never be alone. Give her peace, faith, and patience for you to do your will. We ask in Jesus name. Amen."

Carol opened her eyes and saw a calmness in Allison that wasn't there before the prayer.

"Are you ready to go see your mother?" she asked.

"Yes. I feel better. God is in control and knows what's best. I would be lying though if I said I wasn't hoping for a miracle."

"I know. You have to hang on to your faith. It's what will see you through this." Carol grabbed her purse, opened the door, and stepped out. The parking garage was full of cars, and as she glanced beyond the parked vehicles, she spotted a sign for the elevator to the upper floors.

They headed over to the elevator, got in and punched it for the main floor. The elevator stopped, and the doors opened. As they stepped out, they could see a large reception area straight ahead.

Allison saw a rather tall woman with short brown hair checking over a chart. She saw them approach and laid the chart down.

"How may I help you?" she asked.

"Could you tell me what room Lucy Stevens is in? I'm her daughter, Allison."

"She's in room 208. Last door on your right as you go down that hallway." She smiled pointing the direction out to them.

Allison took a few steps in the direction of the room. She had mixed feelings about seeing her mother. Guilt was trying to creep back, and as soon as her mood started to change, she said a silent prayer.

Allison stood in the doorway to her mother's room. She had not seen her for a very long time and wasn't prepared for what she saw.

Her mother's frail form lay motionless, hooked to monitors that kept track of her vitals. With each beep of the machine, she is reminded that her mother isn't aware of the world she had been so much a part of for so many years.

Allison had heard stories where loved ones actually could understand their families as they spoke to them, even though they were in a coma. She wondered if her mom could sense her presence.

She stepped into the room with Carol right behind her and stood next to her mother's bed. A mask placed over her mother's face provided her with the oxygen vital to her existence. *Would she wake up? Would I have a chance to tell her I loved her?*

As Carol and Allison stood beside the bed, Carol grabbed Allison's hands in hers and started to pray.

"Dear Lord. I bring this prayer to you today. I pray that you give Allison comfort knowing that you are truly in charge. Please place Allison's mother in your loving arms, watch over her, and if it is your will, heal her and bring her back from the darkness. I pray in Jesus name. Amen."

Allison stood at the side of her mother's bed watching.

"Allison, would you like some time alone with your mother? I thought I might get us some coffee from downstairs," said Carol.

"Yes, I think I would. If you didn't mind, I would like some tea."

Carol placed a hand on Allison's shoulder and gave it a light squeeze. "I'll leave you alone then. Be back in a while," Carol said.

Allison could hear the click of Carol's shoes echoing in the hallway and then fading away into the distance. Voices drifted into the room filling the space. She listened to orders given, the sound of carts shoved about, and she felt sadness for the families waiting for any word of encouragement about their loved ones.

She glanced over at her mother and tears welled up in her eyes. It was so hard to fight them back. She knew God was watching over her, but what if it wasn't God's will for her to regain consciousness? She didn't know how she would deal with the reality that she might have to let her go.

Allison decided to talk to her mother even though she wasn't sure she could hear. She leaned over and kissed her mom on the cheek.

She pulled up a chair, and it made a screeching sound as she pulled it forward. She wrapped an arm around her mother's head, stroking her hair.

"Mom, I know I haven't been the best daughter I could have been. I was wrong to blame you for dad's death. I know now that it was his time, but it still hurts. I'm so sorry that I haven't been there for you. I was so wrapped up in my grief that I didn't stop to realize that you were suffering too. I was so unfair and hope that you can forgive me. Mom, I don't know if you can hear me or not, but I love you. Please come back to me."

Under her hands, she thought she felt movement, and it startled her. *Could it be? Did my mother move her hand?*

Allison got up and looked at her mother's face and discovered that her eyes were open. She rushed to the open door and called out for a nurse, "Help, someone, please help me. I think she is waking up."

Chapter 11

It seemed to Allison that it took a long time for any of the nurses or her mother's doctor to arrive. She stood beside the frail body of her mother looking into the eyes that were transfixed on her. She wondered what her mother was feeling, did she have thoughts that were filling her mind or was her stare just an involuntary action?

Allison leaned in closer to her mother, speaking softly. "Mom, can you hear me?" She waited momentarily hoping for an answer, but not expecting one.

Her mother spoke slowly in a soft voice.

"Allison, I'm glad you're here. It's been so long since I've seen you. I'm sorry we parted with harsh words between us. I love you and always will."

"Mom, don't try to talk right now. Save your strength. I realize now that I was just hurting after dad died and wanted someone to blame. Blaming you was wrong. I know that now, and I'm so sorry, Mom. Can you ever forgive me?" *What is taking the doctor so long? I have to do something.*

Allison left the side of her mother's bed and one more time called out for help. She could hear the sounds of equipment being moved around, telephones ringing, and voices calling out, but she couldn't understand what they were saying.

Her mother's voice brought her back to her side.

"Honey, there is nothing to forgive. I did that a long time ago and wanted nothing more than to be able to see your beautiful face. Promise me that you will always hold onto your faith and that you will walk with the Lord. Your Heavenly Spirits will keep you on the right path."

"Mom, how do you know about them? I haven't told anyone."

"I have one here with me now. The Spirit says it's time to go home."

Allison couldn't believe what her mother was saying. *What did she mean, time to go home?*

Allison looked over at her mom. Her eyes were now closed. She leaned down placing her head against her mom's chest to listen to the beat of her heart. She heard nothing. The machine next to the bed showed a flat line.

Allison rushed out into the corridor screaming, "Where's the doctor? My mom's not breathing, hurry!"

From over by the nursing station came a rush of activity. Two nurses grabbed a crash cart, and a doctor followed close behind. They pushed the cart into Allison's mother's room and began to work on her.

Allison stood quietly with tears streaming down her face. *Why Lord? How can you take her away after we finally found our way back to each other?* Allison didn't want to face the fact that the words from her mother may have been the last words spoken between them.

The doctor worked on her mother for what seemed like an eternity. Then as quickly as they entered, the equipment was removed, and they gave Allison the words she dreaded to hear.

"I'm sorry there was nothing we could do. Is there anyone we can call?" asked the doctor.

"No. My friend should be back soon."

"I don't understand what happened, she was awake talking to me a few minutes ago, and then her eyes closed again," said Allison.

"When our loved ones are in a coma sometimes we imagine things because we want them to be better. I can tell you that in your mother's comatose condition there is no way she could have said anything. I'm sorry, Allison."

Allison knew that scientifically what he said made sense, but then God does not work according to science. She knew that her mother had spoken and they were able to tear down the wall they had built between them. She took a moment to catch her breath, fished out her cell phone, and dialed Carol.

Chapter 12

Lucy Stevens had died, and she is headed for her eternal home. She floats above the lifeless form that lay on the hospital bed below.

What a strange sensation looking at what used to house the life that once belonged to her. She wasn't feeling any fear or sadness, but instead, was filled with an immense sense of peace and overflowing joy.

As her Spirit floated above the floor, she saw Allison and was grateful that they were able to fix things between them. She knew that in time God would heal her broken heart.

A bright light was shining and enveloped the entire room in rays of sunshine and warmth. Lucy can hear the Lord's voice calling. A sweet, soft voice. She recognizes it as all his children do and she is slowly pulled up toward the light.

She begins to enter a long tunnel filled with the same light and in no time at all finds herself standing in front of the most beautiful city she has ever seen.

Music rings out praises, and she feels a soft hand grab hers. She looks up, and a smile crosses her face. She is looking into the eyes of her husband who had passed before her. He seems younger, and his face radiates with light. When he speaks, his voice fills her with love. She leans over, kissing him on the cheek.

They walk hand in hand through the high wall of the celestial city. A constant chant of the angels proclaiming the glory of God can be heard coming from inside the gates. The beauty of the Almighty's light shines like a precious jewel in all directions.

Lucy is in awe as she glances toward the Tree of Life, covered with various types of fruit, which grows on the banks of the flowing river that snakes its way through the city.

In the distance lies Majesty Mountain, more majestic than any on Earth. There is no consciousness of time, and she feels an immense peace.

There is light as far as her eyes can see. In the distance, she can make out a sea of saints dressed in flowing white robes. They seem to float above the ground and are all heading in the direction of the center of the city.

Lucy looks over at her husband, her eyes wide with wonder and asks, "Where are they all going?"

He answers, "They are going to be welcomed to the house of the Lord. The feast will begin soon."

Lucy's body, which is a spiritual one now, pulses with excitement and is filled with a love she has never experienced before. As they walk along, the music and voices become clear. Soon, she will be before the Lord and the anticipation fills her with joy.

Chapter 13

It had been five days since Allison's mother died and the funeral is held at a small cemetery next to the Rustin Baptist Church that she had attended most of her life.

It was a fall day with just a slight breeze blowing, but in Allison's heart, a storm was brewing. She knew her Mother was with the Lord but wishes they could have had more time together. There was so much more she wanted to say to her.

Rev. Williams stood reading from the Bible, but Allison barely heard a word. Her best friend, Carol, stood by her side.

The minister closed the service and the people starting to leave went up to Allison to give her their condolences. She was grateful but didn't know any of the people who filed by, but was glad that her mother had all these people that wanted to pay their respects.

Allison's eyes began to well up again, and a tear streaked down her cheek, falling onto the front of her blouse. She quickly took the tissue and wiped it away, trying to get her composure intact. She said a silent prayer for God to give her the strength she needed to get through the day.

Carol leaned in close to Allison, "Are you holding up okay?"

"I knew this was going to be a difficult day for me, but I'm having a hard time believing she is gone," said Allison as she glanced towards the casket, a lump forming in her throat.

"Your mother is with the Lord now, and it will get easier over time. Lean on the Lord for strength and remember you will see her again," said Carol hugging her.

"I know. It's just harder than I imagined it would be," said Allison choking back the tears.

"Are you ready to head back to your mom's house? I know it will be painful because of all the memories," asked Carol.

"Sure. I haven't been there in years, and it hurts now when I say that out loud," said Allison strolling towards the vehicle.

"Don't beat yourself up, you were a different person then, and God has already forgiven you for your indiscretions," said Carol.

They walked towards the SUV noticing that it was the only vehicle left in the parking lot. A slight wind was coming up, and a hint of rain clouds filled the afternoon sky.

As they stood next to the vehicle, an older man walked up. He had short grey hair, a face that seemed to have weathered plenty of life's ups and downs, and dark eyes filled with sadness. He was dressed in a plain blue shirt, blue jeans, and a brown tweed jacket.

"I'm Ernest Tibbs, miss. How did you know Lucy Stevens?" he asked.

"She was my mother. I'm Allison," she said shaking his hand.

"She was a wonderful woman. I took care of her yard. She was always kind to me, and I'm gonna miss her," he said in a low voice. "Will you be staying on at the house? You know if you need me I'd be happy to take care of things as usual," he said as he fought to get the words out.

"Ernest, I'll be here for a couple of days yet, but I'm not quite sure what I'm going to do. If you give me your number, I'll be in touch when I decide."

The old man reached into a worn pocket of his jeans and fished out a piece of paper that had written on it, "Ernest Tibbs, Handyman and a local phone number and handed it to Allison.

"How long have you been working for my mother?" asked Allison noticing his callused hands.

"Nigh on three years. Your mother always invited me to have Thanksgiving and Christmas dinner with her every year. She was a wonderful cook and always decorated her house for the holidays," he said a smile crossing his face as he spoke.

"Christmas was always extra special. Before dinner, she would read out of the Bible about the Lord's birth. She is responsible for bringing me to the Lord this past Christmas."

The man's voice began to break up, and he lowered his head to hide the flow of tears that were starting to take over. He coughed, wiped his eyes on his shirt sleeve, and raised his head before he continued. "She's with the Lord now. I'm sure of it."

"It was nice meeting you, Ernest. We must be on our way. It looks as though it will rain any minute," said Carol, opening the car door. "Can we give you a lift somewhere?"

"Very kind of you, but I just live around the corner," he said. "It was nice meeting ya both."

Allison and Carol watched as the man walked up the driveway heading for the street. Just as they started to pull away, Carol noticed raindrops on the windshield.

She pulled out making a right-hand turn onto the quiet country road. It would take about twenty minutes before they would reach their destination.

With the rain, the view out the window was obscured. It was darker than usual, and the houses they passed were darkened silhouettes.

"Allison, are you hungry? I thought we could stop and pick up a few things from the store on our way. If I remember right, there is one just up the street," asked Carol.

"I don't feel much like eating right now, but a cup of tea would be nice," said Allison giving Carol a forced smile.

Carol waited for the traffic to clear and turned into the parking lot of Baker's Grocery. It was a small mom and pop grocery catering to the locals in the neighborhood.

"Do you want to go in?" asked Carol un-bucking her seat belt.

"If you don't mind, I'll wait here."

"Okay. Anything special you would like me to get?"

"Nothing that I can think of," said Allison as she unbuckled her seat belt and watched as Carol disappeared through the front door of the store.

She sat in the SUV partly bathed in the light from the street lamps. In the partial darkness, she was unable to hold back the tears any longer. Loud sobs escaped her mouth as tears drifted down the side of her cheeks landing on her coat.

Why did God have to take my mom now? Death, it sounded so final. But then, as a Christian, she knew better. It was Satan trying to make her doubt her faith. She had worked too hard to keep strong and prayed for extra strength.

As Allison watched out the window, she saw Carol, shopping bags in both arms, heading toward the vehicle fighting the wind as she crossed the parking lot. She placed the groceries inside and got in.

In the short time, Carol had spent in the store it had grown considerably darker out. Carol drove along the deserted city streets except for passing an occasional person walking their dog.

Another couple of blocks and they would be at the house. Allison knew nothing would ever be the same again. There were so many decisions to make. *What will I do with the house? Should I sell it or relocate and live in it? Would that be too painful?*

Before another thought could enter her mind, Carol pulled up in front of the house at 360 Maple Street that Allison once had called home.

In her younger years, it was a place of love and great joy. Allison felt as though she would never feel joy again.

Carol parked in the driveway, and the sensor light on the front porch blinked on. Carol and Allison grabbed the groceries and walked up to the front porch.

Allison fished the extra key out from under the potted plant where it was kept and unlocked the front door. As she entered she flipped the light switch on.

Carol followed Allison into the kitchen, and they set the groceries down on the kitchen table. They took off their coats, and Carol started putting the groceries away.

"I'll put on the tea kettle," said Allison, filling the one on the stove and placing it back on the burner.

Allison pulled out a chair at the table and sat down. Her eyes scanned the country kitchen that had changed since her childhood. The walls that once were white were painted a lovely shade of aqua, and there were also tiles on the kitchen floor that looked new.

She walked over to shut off the burner, reached into the cupboard overhead, and pulled out two china cups with matching saucers. She remembered the pattern with roses. They were her mother's favorite.

Carol handed Allison a box of tea bags, and she placed one in each cup, carrying them to the table. Carol pulled up a chair joining her.

A whiff of fragrant spice escaped from the teacups filling the air. At first, they sat in silence, enjoying the refreshing flavor of the tea.

Carol was first to start the conversation. "I bought some sliced turkey for sandwiches. Would you like me to make you one?"

"No thanks, I think I'll finish my tea and call it a night. I'll have to check out the bedrooms to see if the beds are made up or not. We might have to move some things around," Allison commented taking a sip of her tea.

"You sit and finish your tea. Which ones are they and I'll take a look?" said Carol getting up.

"The two at the end of the hallway on the left," said Allison.

Allison listened to the sound of Carol's footsteps click as she walked across the hardwood floor that ran the length of the hall and then heard a door open.

Carol returned to the kitchen a couple of minutes later.

"The room is perfect. I'll put my stuff in the last one. Do you need anything before I go to bed?" asked Carol.

"No, I'm just exhausted. I'll set the thermostat and go to bed too. Goodnight, Carol," said Allison wondering if sleep would actually come. Her mind was filled with so many questions.

Chapter 14

Allison went into the guest room next to Carol's. As she opened the door and entered, she stood a moment and then reached for the light switch.

Nothing had changed. The same poster bed with matching mahogany dresser sat where it had always been. Even Allison's favorite pink throw lay over the back of the chair.

She remembered the first day of school, her junior prom, high school graduation and the worst day of her life. *Why did I have to think about that?* She forced the memories down deep. That was in the past, and she should be looking forward.

She slipped off her clothes and grabbed a nightgown pulling it over her head, taking a moment to say a quick prayer, *"Please Lord, let me feel the comfort of your precious peace."*

Allison turned off the light pulled the covers back on the bed and got in taking a moment to position the pillows. She lay in bed staring up at the ceiling thinking over the events of the past few days.

A few days ago, her life was better than she could have hoped. She had a job, loving friends, and her renewed faith had led her in the right direction.

Finally, she had a hope of having the life she always wanted, but now with her mother gone, she would have to make a decision that would affect the rest of her life. *Lord, I need your help.*

With her eyes closed, Allison thought back to her childhood and how happy she had been. But that was before her father died. At the time, she was convinced her mother had pushed him to work harder than he should have, causing his heart attack. She didn't know that he was obsessed with his job and his neglect for his health got the best of him.

Allison sobbed and turned her head into the pillow to muffle the sounds escaping her throat. Her whole body shook as grief-filled her entire being. *Lord, please give me peace. I'm grateful for the chance to finally make things right between my Mom and me, but why do I still have this guilt for not being a better daughter. How could I have been so wrong?*

Allison turned over in the bed, and as she did, a soft breeze blew across her face. She felt a sense of peace and her body began to relax. She could sense a presence, but in the darkness, could not distinguish the Spirit that had floated towards her bed.

The Spirit began to take shape. A golden glow surrounded it, and Allison could start to see faint facial features and long flowing hair.

"Are you another messenger? Allison asked.

"I am Comfort. I heard your sobs."

Comfort floated towards her and placed one of its hands on hers. "I know it's hard to accept that your Mother is no longer with you, but she is with the Lord now. You will see her again."

Comfort removed its hand from Allison's and touched the top of her head. "Sleep now blessed one. When you wake you will have renewed strength and your heart will be at peace."

Allison felt the warmth flow from her head down through to the soles of her feet. A feeling of immense love and peace began to fill her. Her mind became empty. It was if all memories of past or present were erased from her mind and she started to float in a place where pain or guilt didn't exist.

It was early morning when Allison opened her eyes. The sun was shining in through the shades. She squinted, sat up in bed and thought of Comfort realizing she was given the gift of peace

She rose up from the bed and crossed over to the door. Just before she reached it, she stood a moment facing the dresser and picked up a photo of her mom. She smiled and kissed the picture.

"*I love you, Mom.*"

Allison padded across the hall to the bathroom for her shower. She locked the door and turned on the water until it was the correct temperature. She slipped out of her nightgown and stepped in. The warm water sprayed down on her body making her muscles relax.

Finished with her shower, she stepped out and toweled off dressing in her blue jeans and pale blue sweater. As she entered the hall, she was greeted by Carol.

"Did you sleep well? I thought I heard noises coming from your room in the middle of the night."

"I was restless and couldn't sleep, but finally drifted off. I feel much better this morning."

"I know you have a lot to deal with right now. You'll figure it all out. God will give you the strength to deal with everything, and I'm here to help you whenever you need me." Carol walked over and hugged Allison. "I made tea."

"Thanks. A cup of tea sounds good."

Allison was just about to sit down at the kitchen table when the phone rang. She turned and answered it. A man's deep voice that she didn't recognize was on the other end.

"Hello, may I speak to Allison Stevens?"

"This is she. Who's speaking?"

"My name is Arthur Benson. I'm your mother's attorney. I'm very sorry for your loss. I need to get together to discuss her will with you. When would be a good time?"

"Anytime today would be fine, I would like to get as much taken care of before I have to go back to Collingwood," Allison replied.

"I can be there in an hour. I have quite a bit to discuss with you," said Mr. Benson.

"That sounds fine. I'll see you then," Allison said, hanging up the phone.

Allison made another cup of tea and took a seat at the table by Carol.

"Are you sure you are up to this right now? It's been a hard couple of days, and I'm sure he would have understood if you wanted to postpone it," Carol said laying a hand on Allison's shoulder.

"What good would it do to put it off? I would rather deal with it now so I can make plans to go back to Collingwood. I have my job, and I'm sure you need to get back to check on things at the center. I need to figure out what I'm going to do with the house," Allison said taking a sip of tea.

"Well, maybe you're right. You have a lot of decisions to make, but you need to take your time and be sure you are doing what is best for you. Asking God for guidance in everything you do is the best way."

"I did pray last night for his help. In Collingwood, I have my apartment, job, and people I enjoy being around. Here I only have an empty house and people I used to know. I would have to start all over again, and I'm not sure I'm up to it." Allison looked over at Carol.

"You know, sometimes God gives us the hard decisions to take us outside our comfort zone to mold our character and teach us that some choices will be tough ones. If you feel a strong pull towards staying in Rustin after praying for guidance, then you must follow his will for you. That means he has a plan for your life that you aren't able to comprehend, but he knows in advance what is best for you. You know I'll support you in whatever you decide," said Carol.

"I appreciate it very much. I'll see what the lawyer has to say and then pray on it," said Allison as she put her cup in the sink.

Allison knew Carol was right and would do everything she could to follow God's will for her life, even if it was uncomfortable at the time.

Chapter 15

Mr. Benson arrived on time. He was an older man in his mid-sixties, with a round face that had begun to fill with age lines. He graciously offered his hand to Allison and then to Carol and followed them over to the sofa. Mr. Benson took a seat on the couch and Allison, and Carol sat directly across from him in the wing back chairs.

Allison watched as he removed a stack of papers from his briefcase and laid them on the coffee table. She was amazed at the amount of paperwork. *How many assets could my mother possibly have? My mom and dad weren't wealthy people.*

"Allison, you may want to join me on the sofa so I can go over each item with you. I have several places for you to sign."

"Okay," Allison said as she walked over and took a seat next to him.

"Allison, this first set of paperwork is on your mother's property. The house, the furnishings, and her vehicle. They are free of any liens and will transfer to you. I need you to sign all the documents, and if you are married, I will have to add your husband also."

"I'm not married," said Allison, her eyes showing the pain as she fought back the tears.

"Then go ahead and sign each of the pages where I marked with your name and/or initials." Mr. Benson slid the paperwork over to Allison. "Your mother had me keep everything up to date in case anything unexpected happened. She wanted to make sure you wouldn't have any undue stress to deal with," he said as he pushed his body back against the sofa.

Allison finished signing the paperwork and handed them to Mr. Benson. She glanced over at Carol who motioned to her that she was leaving the room. Allison nods, and her eyes follow Carol as she walked down the hallway, wondering if Carol was feeling uncomfortable or just wanted to give her some privacy.

Mr. Benson placed the stack of paperwork face side down and continued on with the next set of papers.

"There is $1000 in checking and $10,000 in savings. Do you have a bank that you would like it transferred to?"

Allison had no idea her mother had that much in the bank. "I didn't even think about bank accounts. I have an account in Collingwood, but since I'm not sure yet what I'm going to do with the house, can I have the name on the account changed to mine until I decide what to do?"

Mr. Benson placed a hand on Allison's. "My dear, take all the time you need. In the meantime, we can close your mother's account and have a new account opened in your name. We can go to the bank together if you like," his mouth formed into a smile.

"That sounds fine. You can give me a call and let me know when you are free. I'll be here for a few more days at least." Allison wondered when Carol needed to leave for Rustin. She would be on her own then.

"I have the title to your mother's car. It is parked in the garage, and the keys are hanging on a hook to the right as you enter. She kept it in good running condition."

"I can't thank you enough for all you're doing for me."

"You mother and I were quite close, and I'm going to miss her. She spoke of you often and only wanted the best for you."

Allison felt her eyes start to tear up and quickly reached over for a tissue from the box sitting on the side table. After wiping her eyes, she turned to Mr. Benson and said, "Is there anything else I need to know?"

"We are done with all the signature pages. Your mother, however, left some money to the church and her handyman, Mr. Tibbs, which I will take care of."

"I met Mr. Tibbs as Carol, and I were leaving the cemetery. He seems like a nice man. He gave me his business card, and I told him I would give him a call if I decided not to sell the house. I'm glad my mother left him something. He said they were close friends."

"They spent every holiday together, and I know he will miss her." Mr. Benson reached over into his briefcase and pulled out the title to her mother's car and handed it to Allison. "Well, I think this about covers everything. I believe your mother's bills and anything else you might need is on her desk in her bedroom. She wanted to make sure I knew where everything was. She didn't have any life insurance. She cashed it in after your father died and paid off the house."

Mr. Benson rose from the couch and placed the signed paperwork into his briefcase. "It was nice to meet you, Allison. If there is anything I can assist you with, don't hesitate to call me." He shook Allison's hand, and she walked him to the door. She watched as he made his way down the porch steps, waving as he got into his car. In a matter of minutes, he had backed out of the driveway and drove out of sight.

Allison was just shutting the front door when Carol entered the room. "Did you get everything taken care of?"

"All but my mom's bank accounts. Mr. Benson offered to go with me to the bank to straighten everything out."

"He seems like a very professional man and sympathetic. I'm sure he will take care of it." Carol walked over and hugged Allison. "I don't want to leave until I know you are going to be okay."

"I am glad that the paperwork is done. I just have to go through mom's bills to see if anything needs to be paid. Do you want to go to the garage with me and check out the car? According to the title, it is a 1998 Buick."

"Sure. Let's see what it looks like."

Allison and Carol walked into the kitchen and out the side door that led into the garage. Allison grabbed the keys to the Buick from the hook and flipped the light switch flooding the garage with light.

In front of them was a blue four-door car. It was clean, without ding or dent, and was a medium size which Allison liked. She put the key into the door and sat down in the driver's seat. Carol walked around and slid into the passenger's seat.

"Well, what do you think? Carol asked.

"I've wanted a car for so long, but I didn't want one this way." Allison became emotional when she thought about sitting where her Mom had sat many times before. She wiped the lone tear from her eyes.

Carol put her hand on Allison's back and said, "I know it's hard, but your mother wanted you to have it."

"I know. I have a lot to do, but I feel drained. I think maybe I'll lie down for a little bit before I start going through some of mom's things to donate to the church."

"Okay. I'll call the center and then clean up while you rest." Carol said as she walked into the kitchen.

After cleaning up the dishes in the sink and tidying up the living room, Carol grabbed her cell phone. After a couple of rings, Mike, her assistant, picked up.

"Carol, good to hear from you, how is Allison doing?"

"Her Mom's attorney came over today to get the paperwork done. She left her the house and some other assets. She has to decide whether to sell the house or move here but she's torn, as she loves her job. I told her to keep praying about it." Carol sat down on the sofa to continue her conversation. "How is everything going there? Any problems I need to know about?"

Carol sensed some hesitation.

"Ken called this morning. It seems there is an issue with the funding for the extra kitchen staff. He said the regular funding isn't enough to cover it."

"I'll most likely head back tomorrow. I'll give you a call along the way. Maybe you can set up a meeting with Ken for the following day." Carol was sure she would be in for a fight. Ken wasn't the easiest person to deal with. "Allison has her mother's car and can come back when she is ready. I'm going to miss her if she decides to stay here."

"We all will," Mike said in a voice that suggested a personal sense of loss. "Well, I'll get back to my duties then. Things aren't the same around here without you. See you when you get back."

"Goodbye, Mike. Thanks for watching things for me. I appreciate it."

Carol set the phone down on the sofa and reminded herself that things at the center were always changing. She was met with challenges ever since she took over as administrator.

First, there was a fight over keeping the center open. The prior owner had somehow made an exclusive deal with the city that the new mayor wasn't willing to honor.

After lots of calls, newly submitted paperwork, and a new plan with existing budget, she had convinced them she could operate the shelter without being in the red. Now, with what Mike told her, it made her wonder what she had neglected to figure into the budget.

No, she wasn't going there, her figures were right on, she had checked them more than once. If someone had got to Ken, who could it be? Was the shelter in trouble? Maybe her fight to stay open wasn't over.

Chapter 16

Allison woke up from her nap feeling very rested. As she entered the hallway, Carol was headed to her room to pack up her things.

"Did you sleep well?" asked Carol.

"I did, and I feel at peace with everything now. I have to tell you something."

"Ok, but I have to start packing to go back tomorrow morning. There's an issue at the center that I have to take care of." Carol followed Allison into the living room and took a seat on the sofa.

"Over the past few months, I have been visited by Heavenly Spirits. They are real, and they have been leading me in my walk with God."

Carol turned to Allison holding her hand. "I knew from the moment I met you that there was something extraordinary about you. I believe in Heavenly Spirits sent by God. I was visited by one once during a time when I felt like I was all alone. The Spirit reminded me that I was a child of God and would never be alone. From that point on, I knew my life would change."

"I knew you would believe me," Allison said.

"You'll be okay when I leave, won't you? Carol asked as she leaned over giving Allison a quick hug. "You know you can call me anytime."

"I'll be fine. I have the banking to attend to and my mother's clothing to deliver to the church. Sunday I'll attend church, and maybe I'll see some people I know." Allison wanted to feel more at ease in case she decided to stay in Rustin.

"I'm sure your mother's church would love to have you. You have to trust in the Lord to get you through the rough times. Over time, things will get easier.

"Well, I have to finish packing if I'm going to be ready in the morning. After, would you like to go out and have a nice dinner?" asked Carol.

"I'd love to. I'll go freshen up."

Allison closed the bathroom door, filled the sink with warm water, and picked up a washcloth from the cabinet. Laying the cloth over her face, she let the warmth soak deep into the pores of her skin and felt a sense of release come over her body.

Allison and Carol had an excellent dinner at a Mexican restaurant a few blocks away. The tacos were tasty, and they topped off their meal with a flan dessert. Since Carol had to get an early start for Collingwood in the morning, they decided to leave for home.

It was around 7 p.m., and the traffic on the streets had begun to thin out. Allison's thoughts wandered to the fact that after tomorrow she would be alone in the house with the task of going through her mom's things. She still wasn't any closer to deciding on whether or not to stay in Rustin permanently.

Allison stared out the window thinking how strange it seemed to be in her old neighborhood. Her mind ran the gamut reflecting on her past. But within seconds she reminded herself that was her former life, and now she was a new person.

Allison glanced over at Carol. "I'm going to miss you."

"We'll see each other soon. If you decide to stay, I'll come visit you and should you decide to come back to Collingwood, your job will be waiting," said Carol.

As Carol pulled up into the driveway, Allison replied, "Thanks, it means a lot to me."

The porch light blinked on lighting their way up the front steps. Allison unlocked the door, found the light switch, and the living room is bathed in brightness.

"Well, I guess I better go to bed," said Carol as she gave Allison a hug. "I have to get up early."

Allison sat down on the sofa. She remembered that it was her Dad's favorite place to sit and she silently talked to him. *Dad, I wish I had done more to make things right before you died. I know now that you were only trying to protect me from heartache and I just couldn't see it. Please forgive me, Dad. I love you.*

A tear formed in the corner of Allison's eye and slid down her face. She quickly wiped it away telling herself that it is too late. There is nothing she can do to change anything. It's time to move on and do the best she can to follow God's path for her now. Only, she isn't sure where it will lead her.

Allison walked down the hallway to her room. As she opened her door, she notices the soft breathing coming from the bedroom next to hers. She stopped momentarily thinking how comforting it is to have someone else in the house. *I don't know why it should bother me. I've been alone for most of my life, but for some reason this time it seems different.*

Allison entered her room, undressed and got into bed. She said a prayer, *"Please God, direct my steps tomorrow and the rest of the week as I do your will for my life and help me to accept it without question."*

As Allison is about to drop off to sleep a soft, sweet voice gets her attention, "Allison, wake up."

As Allison opens her eyes, she can begin to make out the two forms standing at the foot of her bed. One of them is older in appearance, clothed in a head full of grey hair down to his shoulders. The other is taller.

Allison watches with interest as the older spirit begins to speak, *"Allison, we are Knowledge and Wisdom. I am Wisdom. God tells you in the Bible that if you respond properly to the trials of life, you will develop godly maturity and patience. You must keep in mind that suffering is being used by God for your eternal good."*

Allison thinks for a moment and realizes that how she reacts to the trials of life makes the difference in how much suffering she has to endure when she doesn't do the right thing. But, patience is hard to learn. She realizes now that it comes with developing maturity.

Wisdom waits for a response from Allison, but all Allison can manage is to shake her head that she understands. That signals that it is time for Knowledge to speak. *"Allison, God does not want you to be ignorant, lest you sorrow as others who have no hope. Be vigilant in your search for knowledge. It will help you make the right decisions in life and ward off the attacks of the evil one. In all things, seek God's guidance."*

Allison gives each of her visitors a smile and gathers her thoughts.

"I feel so loved by God and will seek daily to walk the path he wants for me. I will pray for guidance in each step I take. I have learned a lot from all my spiritual visitors and feel special knowing God cares for me that much."

As Alison watches the Heavenly Spirits, she can feel rays of warmth go through her entire body. Such a feeling of peace comes over her, and it feels as though she is drifting in a sea filled with more love than she has ever known her entire life. In a matter of seconds, her eyes are closed, and she is fast asleep.

Chapter 17

After lots of hugs and teary eyes, Allison waved goodbye to Carol. The sun had just started to peek out from behind the cloud-filled sky, and it was the beginning of what would be a beautiful day.

She went back into the house and entered the kitchen filling the kitchen sink with hot water. As she washed the plates, she thought about the many items on her to do list. It seemed that as each day passed; the list grew larger instead of smaller.

She finished the dishes and went into the guest room where Carol stayed stripping the sheets from the bed and gathering up the towels from the hamper in the bathroom.

As she entered the laundry room, the phone rang. She set the clothes basket on the top of the washer and picked up the phone. "Allison speaking."

The voice on the other end was familiar, and she recognized it as Mr. Benson's.

"Hi, Allison. Would you have time to go to the bank to set up your account this afternoon? I can come by around 1 p.m."

"That would be fine. I'm just cleaning up from this morning. Carol left for Collingwood today," Allison said thinking how nice it was for him to offer to drive her there.

"I'll see you then," said Mr. Benson disconnecting the call.

Allison hung up and went back to the laundry room. She put the clothes in the washer, added soap, and started the fill cycle. It is nice not to have to go to a laundromat. *This, I can get used to, she thought.*

Allison walked into the living room eying her list that was lying on the coffee table. She sat down, grabbed her pen, and crossed off "go to the bank." The next on the list was to pack up her mother's clothing and other personal items that Allison didn't wish to keep. She made a mental note to pick up some boxes from a nearby store.

She leaned over and picked up her mother's Bible and opened it to the first page and read, *Given to Lucy Stevens by Rev Douglas Williams of the Rustin Baptist Church, 1997. "Awarded for years of dedicated Christian service.*

Allison wasn't aware of how much the church family meant to her mother. She had met Rev Williams briefly at her mother's funeral. She looked forward to getting to know him better and would start by going to church on Sunday.

She entered her mother's room and flipped the light switch. It was the first time since her mother died.

She began pulling out the clothes hanging in the closet and placed them at the foot of her mother's bed. Then she removed all of the boxes from the top shelf.

As she grabbed one of the boxes, an envelope fell to the floor of the closet, spilling the contents onto the floor. Allison picked up the papers, sat down on the bed, and put the documents on the table reaching for the first one.

At a glance, it looked like a legal document. Allison's heart began racing as she read the words. "Birth Certificate. Born to Lucy M. Stevens and Peter Samuel Evans, a boy weighing 8lbs. 10 oz. Samuel Collin Evans. Born Aug.15th, 1970 at Children's Hospital, Denver, Colorado.

Allison couldn't believe what she was reading. Amanda's mother had told her that her baby brother had gone to Heaven shortly after he was born. *Why was there a strange man's name listed as the father?* She was only ten years old when he was born.

There were so many emotions running through Allison, feelings of deceit and years of believing a lie. Is my *brother alive? Did Mom lie to me all this time?*

Allison sat too stunned to move. She spoke out loud to God, "Why Lord? Why did I have to find this now?

Allison heard a knock at the front door and went to answer it. She was greeted by Mr. Benson.

"Please, come in. I'll be right with you. I just have to grab my purse," said Allison.

Allison went to her room and picked up her purse from the dresser, first making sure she had everything she needed to open the account. Allison put on her coat and locked the front door.

Mr. Benson made a left turn into the parking lot at Rustin Community Bank and parked. Before he can open Allison's door, she is already out. They enter the bank with Mr. Benson holding open the door for her.

Rustin Community Bank is a small local bank, and the interior was very warm and inviting. Entering the front door, the teller windows are towards the front.

A waiting area with a dark leather couch, two matching chairs, and tall plants complete the décor.

"Allison, have a seat over there, and I'll let them know that we're here," he said as he walked up to one of the teller windows.

Allison got comfortable on the leather couch. She watched as Mr. Benson approached the teller. In a few minutes, he walked back to join her.

After a short wait, a tall blond woman in her early twenties called Mr. Benson's name, and they were ushered into a back office. As they entered, an older woman with dark hair rose to greet them.

"Mr. Benson, so good to see you," she said shaking his hand. Then she turned to Allison. "And you must be Allison Stevens. So, nice to meet you," she said as she reached out to shake Allison's hand. "Please, have a seat."

Mr. Benson and Allison sat in the two chairs facing the desk. Allison glanced around the office and noticed the photos of what appeared to be a happy family on the bookshelf behind Mrs. Weller. Allison suspects that she was in her late 60's and that the children in the photo are probably grandchildren.

"I'm so sorry for your loss, Miss Stevens. Your mother was a wonderful woman, and we will miss her. I not only knew her professionally, but we were also members of the same church. I will try to make this as easy for you as I can," she said opening a folder on her desk.

"Thanks, Mrs. Weller. I appreciate that," said Allison.

"I have all the paperwork ready. You can have Mr. Benson look it over before you sign. I have prepared a bank statement for your account and made up temporary checks until your bank card is mailed to you. I'll give you a few minutes to look at everything. Any questions let me know." Mrs. Weller left the room, closing the door behind her.

Mr. Benson picked up the first set of papers for the checking account and after looking in his briefcase to verify that the account numbers and amounts were correct, he handed her the paperwork to sign.

Allison signed and gave them back to him. Mr. Benson then handed her the paperwork for the savings account. Allison can't help thinking about her brother who would be eligible for some of her mother's estate. *Will I be able to find him if he's alive? If so, would he want to see me or claim his inheritance?*

Mrs. Weller entered the room holding temporary checks for Amanda's new checking account. "I hope everything was satisfactory."

"Yes. I went ahead and signed all the documents," Allison replied.

"Great. Here are your temporary checks and a slip with the balance in the checking account. Keep in mind that you can transfer from your savings to checking at any time. There is no charge."

"I appreciate it, Mrs. Weller. It was nice meeting you and should I decide to stay in Rustin, I'm sure we will meet again." Allison said.

Mr. Benson stood up and shook Mrs. Weller's hand. Allison rose and thanked her again for taking care of her mother's financial affairs.

They left the office exiting the building. Mr. Benson opened the car door for Allison, and she got in. Mr. Benson opened the driver's door and slid in. Before he started the engine, he looked over at Allison. "Is there anywhere else you would like to stop on the way home? I have time."

"If you could stop at the local market, I would like to pick up some boxes to pack up my mother's clothing so I can take them to the church."

"No problem. It's on the way," Mr. Benson replied.

Mr. Benson drove about three blocks, and she could see Rustin Supermarket on the right. The parking lot was full of cars and people coming and going from the store.

After making a couple of passes around the parking lot, he finally spotted an empty space and parked.

"Would you like me to help you with the boxes?"

"That's ok. I think I can manage," said Allison as she got out. She was just about to enter the front door when an elderly lady walking with a limp addressed her.

"Allison Stevens, is that you?" she asked smiling.

"Yes. Do I know you?" Allison asked, not recognizing her.

"I'm Mrs. Henry. I live next door to your mother. It seems just like yesterday when you would come over for milk and cookies. I'm so sorry about your mom. She was a good friend, and I'll miss her dearly," said Mrs. Henry as she leaned against the shopping cart.

"It's been a long time. Of course, I remember you. Seeing you is one of my treasured childhood memories. I'm staying at the house, and I'd love to visit with you," Allison replied feeling glad that Mrs. Henry was still living next door.

When things seemed strange at home, or she just wanted to get away, Mrs. Henry always welcomed her with open arms. Allison remembered that she never had any children. It was sad as she thought she would have been a terrific mother.

"Well, I have to be going. I have someone waiting in the car for me. I just came in to get some boxes to pack up some of my mom's things. It was nice seeing you," Allison said giving Mrs. Henry a hug.

"I look forward to a visit. Take care of yourself," Mrs. Henry said as she pushed her cart out to the curb.

Allison entered the store and walked up to the cashier. "Do you have any empty boxes?"

The clerk turned towards Allison and replied, "Sure. I'll call produce and have someone bring a few up." She picked up the phone and made the call. "They will be right up," she said as she starting ringing up a waiting customer.

"Thanks," Allison replied as she moved away from the counter and took a seat on a bench by the front windows.

It wasn't long before a young man sporting a produce apron walked over and handed her a few boxes. "If you need more, we have them in the back."

"Thanks," Allison replied as she struggled with the boxes before she finally managed to get a good hold on them. She turned sideways as she exited the store and walked towards Mr. Benson's car.

As she approached, Mr. Benson got out and took some of the boxes from her placing them in the back seat. Allison put the rest in, and then opened the passenger's door, and got in.

Allison watched out the window as he drove along. She is amazed at the diversity of the people in the neighborhood. It had definitely changed.

Chapter 18

It was 6 a.m. when Allison awoke. She had spent a restless night early on and didn't remember falling asleep

She thought about her brother. *What if he is alive? What if I don't find him? What if I do?*

Allison took her morning shower. When she was done, she pulled a sweatshirt and pair of blue jeans from her bedroom closet, grabbed the brush from her dresser, and combed through her hair pulling it back into a ponytail.

Allison entered the kitchen and poured herself a cup of orange juice and sat down at the table. She picked up the phone and called the center. After a couple of rings, Carol answered.

"This is Carol. How may I help you?"

"It's Allison."

"It's great to hear from you. Is everything ok?"

"Do you have time to talk right now? I have something I need to tell you about," Allison asked scooting back in her chair.

"Sure. You know you can tell me anything," said Carol.

"I was cleaning out my mother's closet in her room yesterday, and an envelope fell out from behind one of the boxes. Carol, it was a birth certificate for my brother, but the father's name listed on the certificate is not my father."

"What do you mean it isn't your father?" Carol asked.

"Peter Samuel Evans is the father listed, and my brother is Samuel Collin Evans. I was only ten then, and my mother told me my brother had died. It happened while she was caring for my Aunt Greta in Denver. Now I'm not sure what happened. What if he is alive?"

"I'm sure she had a good reason for telling you what she did."

"I just don't know what to do. If Samuel is alive, he is heir to my mother's estate too. I want to find him," said Allison.

"You need to pray on it. God will tell you what to do. I'm sure your mom's attorney would help you with this. Have you talked to him?' asked Carol as she leaned back in her office chair.

"I thought about calling him, but I wanted to talk to you first. It does make sense when I think back to how my father was acting then. I remember that my Dad kept working late hours and came home really tired. He would sit in his recliner, only getting up when it was time for dinner".

"During dinner, there was no conversation, and when Mom said the prayer, he just sat there with a blank look on his face. They hardly spoke to each other at all. I wondered what was happening to them. The only explanation I can come too is that she had an affair and my dad found out. How could my mother have done such a thing?"

"Allison, we all make mistakes in our life that we are not proud of. She is still your mother, and you don't know what her reasons were for what happened. She may not have lied. Your brother could very well have died just after he was born. Don't jump to conclusions until you check everything out," said Carol.

"My emotions are all over the place. I'll pray that God will tell me what needs to be done. I'm going to give it a few days and then go see Mr. Benson. Maybe he can check into it for me."

Allison held the phone in her hand, and her mind wandered. She felt torn up inside. This revelation of what her mother had done opened up a painful wound. Tom's face appeared in her memory as he was saying he'd had an affair and was leaving her. *Why now, Lord?*

"Are you okay? Allison? Carol repeated.

"I'm here. I was just thinking about when Tom was unfaithful. I can't imagine what my Dad went through and during that time I mistreated him."

"It's going to be okay. None of that was your fault. You were young and rebellious then. Remember God has forgiven you. When your memory conjures up painful images from the past, it's just Satan trying to get a stronghold. I know it's hard, but you must not give in to his lies."

"Well, I'm going to hang up and go finish packing some of my mother's things. Not being around my Mother for the past few years, I had no idea how much stuff she had collected. I'm sure that Rev. Williams can find a family that can use most of it."

"Give me a call anytime you want to talk. Let me know what you find out. I'm praying for you."

"Goodbye. Talk to you soon, said Allison disconnecting the call.

She felt a nudge building up inside of her and the voice of the Holy Spirit telling her to read God's word.

She left the kitchen and sat on the sofa. Picking up her mother's Bible she uttered out loud, "Please, open my eyes to your word and let me see the true meaning of what you want me to know. I place it in your hands, Jesus."

Allison opened the Bible and found herself immersed in the following verses from Romans 8:26, 27, 28. *Likewise, the Spirit also helps in our weaknesses. For we do not know what we should pray for as we ought, but the Spirit Himself makes intercession for us with groanings which cannot be uttered.*

Now He who searches the hearts knows what the mind of the Spirit is because He makes intercession for the saints according to the will of God."

And we know that all things work together for good to those who love God, to those who are the called according to his purpose.

Allison bowed her head, closed her eyes, and said a prayer out loud, "Lord I know that you are wise and know what I need. If my brother should somehow be alive, I will accept whatever the outcome is. My heart is open, and I know that when the time comes, you will supply me with the words I need to say. I pray in Jesus name, Amen."

She opened her eyes and raised her head with a renewed peace. As she packed the clothes into the boxes, she was amazed at her mother's good taste, imagining her mother all dressed up, Bible in hand on her way to church. *Why did I wait until it was too late to share in my mother's life? At least, I was able to tell her I loved her, thanks to a miracle from God.*

Chapter 19

With her mother's things packed up, Allison decided it was time to venture out to the grocery store. She hadn't done any shopping since Carol left.

She grabbed her keys and purse, locking the door on her way out. As she stepped onto the porch, she heard someone call her name. Mrs. Henry was waving at her. Allison walked over to meet her, and as she approached, she could see her coming back from the mailbox.

"Allison, it's so nice to see you again, my dear."

"It's nice to see you too, Mrs. Henry."

"Please, call me Ida, dear."

"Ida, I was just going to the store. Can I get you anything?" asked Allison smiling back.

"I guess I could use a quart of milk. It's nice of you to offer. I feel so relieved with you staying at the house." Mrs. Henry's expression changed to one of sadness as her voice trembled. "It hasn't been the same with your mother gone. She was such a good friend and always checked on me."

"Do you still go to the same church? I'm going on Sunday, and I would love for you to ride along with me."

"I sure do. Your mother and I rode together almost every Sunday. A few times I missed due to my arthritis flaring up, but I made it most of the time. The Reverend preaches a mighty fine sermon."

"I look forward to hearing him. I'll bring your milk over when I get back. It seems strange driving my mom's car, but it's nice to have a car again."

"Your mom would be so happy to see you making good use of it. She loved that car and took good care of it," Mrs. Henry replied as she slowly climbed the porch steps.

"It seems so. If you ever need anything, don't hesitate to ask." Allison answered as she walked over to the car.

She waved at Ida as she backed out of the driveway. Allison glanced back just before she pulled out into the street and saw Ida close her front door. She was glad that Ida still lived next door. It was the one thing that gave some normalcy to being home again.

Allison drove along the city streets and before long pulled up into the parking lot of the Rustin Supermarket. It was around 2 p.m., and the lot wasn't as full as it was on her last visit.

She found a parking spot close to the front of the store. Allison got out walked towards the front of the building and entered. A few shoppers were milling about, but she doesn't see anyone she recognizes.

Grabbing a shopping cart, she made her way down the aisles placing items in as she went along, also remembering to get Ida's milk.

By the time she was done, she had food for about a week, which she felt was enough time to come to a decision about whether to stay or not. Right now, she wasn't any closer to deciding, but she was waiting for God to give her some insight. A part of her wanted to remain, but then part of her felt that it was too painful, and she wanted to return to Collingwood and her familiar life there. She was afraid of change and what the unknown might bring.

She was standing at the check-out line lost in thought.

"Are you ready to check out?" said the clerk..

"Yes, I'm ready. Sorry about that," Allison said placing the items on the counter. Allison thought the young cashier was probably just out of high school. But she was very polite and seemed to know what she was doing. She smiled at Allison as she handed back her change.

Allison pushed the cart through the main doors and out into the parking lot. Just as she was about to reach her parking space, she heard a voice call her name. Allison looked around the lot in all directions, trying to figure out who called her. She didn't see anyone.

She continued to her car and opened the trunk placing her groceries inside. She pushed the cart to the holding area and then entered her vehicle.

She was just about to turn the key over in the ignition when the voice called out to her again. This time, she knew the voice. It was the voice of God.

"Allison, you need to remain here. I have plans for your life, and this is the first step. Don't be fearful, I have equipped you for your journey."

Allison knew she needed to follow God's path he was laying out for her, but she wasn't ready for the change that had to take place first. Allison bowed her head. *"God, I don't know if I can do this. It's painful being here, but I'll try. You know my future, and I trust you."*

Allison turned the key in the ignition, and the car came to life. She carefully checked her side mirror and backed out of the space, continuing through the parking lot until she reached the main street and pulled out into traffic.

Driving the few blocks back home she felt grateful her answer from God had come, but she still felt unsure of what her future held. With God, it could only mean a brighter one filled with change.

Chapter 20

After returning home from the store, Allison took Ida's milk over to her. They had a pleasant chat about Allison's mother, but some of the conversation was very uncomfortable. It was a constant reminder to her that she had not been there for her mother when she needed her most.

Allison left Ida's and walked across the lawn and entered her house. The silence was deafening. *Would I ever be comfortable in this house again?*

She put on the tea kettle and in a few minutes, it whistled signaling it was ready, so she placed a tea bag in the cup. She poured the hot water in and let it steep, as she sat down at the kitchen table to wait.

Bowing her head in prayer, she asked the Holy Spirit to guide her and give her confidence to trust in God for the new life he had planned for her.

Just as she raised her head from the table, a bright illuminated form appeared before her. It seemed to be an angel dressed in a long white gown. *Was it female? Are there even different sexes?* The image began to float until it came to rest in front of her.

The Spirit spoke in a soft voice, but with authority. *"Allison, you need to listen to the voice of the Holy Spirit. You will want to stay away from uncomfortable situations, but some of them will be intended to make you grow in your walk with God. Others will be the wicked spirits trying to lead you astray. Do not be fooled."*

She listened to what the Spirit had to say and tried to gather her thoughts. "I try to follow what God wants me to do, but sometimes it seems impossible. It feels like I'm pulled in all directions."

"In your time of distress, you must call on the Lord. He is always with you. You can have life more abundantly than you could ever imagine. God has a wonderful life planned for you. You just need to believe."

Allison looked into the eyes of the Spirit, and for a moment, she thought she could see into the eyes of God. As quickly as the Spirit appeared, it was gone. Allison felt grateful that God sent all the Spirits to help find her way back to him and finally stay on the right path.

The ring of the phone broke her concentration, and she rose to answer it. A familiar voice on the other end greeted her.

"Allison, how are you?" asked Carol.

"Each day gets a little better. My renewed faith helps see me through," said Allison taking a sip of her tea.

"We have our funding back in place, and I'm hoping that you decide to come back. Everyone misses you."

"God wants me to stay here, but a part of me wants to return to my normal life in Collingwood, but I have to follow the path that the Lord wants me to." With the decision, she would have to turn her back on everything that made her feel safe.

"Take care of yourself. Call me if you need anything. I'm praying that you stay strong and follow what God wants for you, even if that means you won't be coming back." Carol was distracted when the door of her office opened. "I've got to go. Someone just came in, and they look like they need my help."

"Talk to you soon. God Bless"

She sat back down at the table thinking that the timing of Carol's call was strange. She remembered the words of her last Spirit to heed the warnings.

She realized that just because her life seemed settled in Collingwood, it didn't mean that she was living the life that she was supposed to. Sure, she had her Christian friends at the center, a guaranteed job, and felt safe there.

What did she have in Rustin? No friends, no job, and a home she wasn't sure was home anymore. It seemed like there were a lot of unknowns, but then wasn't God supposed to fill in the gaps and provide?

Chapter 21

It was early Sunday morning when Allison awoke to the sun shining brightly through the curtains that draped the windows of her room. To her surprise, she had a restful sleep the night before and with a new feeling of peace, embraced the day with the longing to visit her mother's church family.

She rose up from the bed swinging her petite frame around placing her feet on the floor. She put on her robe and padded down the hallway to the bathroom for her shower.

Allison removed her clothes, reached over to adjust the water streaming down from the shower head, and got in pulling the shower curtain around her. The hot water sent a layer of steam out that soon filled the room. Allison sang praises to the Lord. She was amazed that she still remembered some of the words to the songs from her early years at church.

Done with her shower, she stepped out and dried off putting her robe back on as she made her way into the kitchen.

She put on the tea kettle, put a tea bag into a cup, poured the water to steep, and then walked back to her room to get dressed. She had about an hour before it was time to go over to see if Ida was ready to go.

She sat down on the sofa in the living room and opened the bible saying a prayer for the Holy Spirit to lead her to the scripture he wanted her to read. In a few minutes, she felt a strong urge to open to Romans 12: 5 which read, *So we, being many, are one body in Christ and individually members of one another.*

Allison continued reading Romans 12:6 *"Having then gifts differing according to the grace that is given to us, let us use them; if prophecy, make us prophesy in proportion to our faith.*

God was trying to make sure she remembered to use the gifts that she had to witness to others. Also, to remember that she was a member of God's family and connected to all his children everywhere.

Just then, she heard a light rap on the door and got up to answer it. Ida stood there dressed in her Sunday best, which also included a very stylish hat. "Are you ready to go, dear?"

"Come in. I just need to grab a coat, and we're on our way," said Allison as she opened the hall closet. She walked over and picked up the Bible she was reading earlier, along with her purse.

Allison followed Ida down the front steps locking the door behind her and made her way to the car. She opened the passenger's door so Ida could get in and then walked over and opened the driver's door. They talked as they waited for the engine to warm up.

"I can hardly wait to introduce you to all the church members," said Ida."

"I look forward to meeting everyone. Rev. Williams talked a lot about my mother's love for the church and how important she was to everyone there," replied Allison smiling at Ida.

"She sure was. We all miss her. I'm hoping you decide to stay here. It's nice knowing you are right next door. It makes this old lady feel safe."

"God answered my prayers, and he wants me to stay in Rustin," said Allison. "It will be hard to leave the job I love and the wonderful people I work with in Collingwood though."

"Change isn't easy. Since God wants you here, he will open doors for you, Allison."

Allison put the car in gear and pulled out into the street. "I know. I trust God to guide me in the right direction," said Allison as she drove along the city streets of Rustin. "I've only been to the church once, and I'm not sure I know the way."

"Don't worry dear, I can direct you. When you get to the Rustin Supermarket, you need to make a left on Ellison Way and then a right on Oak Grove. It will be about a mile out on your right," said Ida.

Allison drove along past the supermarket and made a left at the light which was just turning green as she approached. The supermarket lot was occupied with only a few cars. As she drove through the stop light, she put on her turn signal and got over in the left lane.

"How far is Oak Grove?" Allison questioned.

"It's only a couple of blocks. You turn left at Rustin Wheel & Tire. My husband wouldn't take our car anywhere else."

It wasn't long before Allison spotted the tire shop and slowed down to make her turn. Just as she was passing, she saw a woman with her young daughter in tow. The little girl was jumping up and down giggling as her mother tried to hang on to her hand.

Allison's heart became heavy as she thought of her mom. When she was young, she used to take walks uptown to the ice cream shop and playground during the summers. Allison's mom would push her on the swing. She always wanted to go higher, but her mom still kept her at a safe height.

In a few minutes, they were pulling into the Rustin Baptist Church parking lot. It was full of cars, and people were heading towards the front steps of the church.

As Allison parked the car and helped Ida out, she heard a voice calling from behind her, "Allison Stevens, is that you?"

She turned around and faced a woman approximately her age with long brown hair and sparkling brown eyes. A smile spread across her face as she spoke. "It is you. I bet you don't remember me, do you?"

"I'm sorry. Your voice sounds familiar, but I just can't place you," said Allison.

"We used to be neighbors in High School, but I moved away my last year. I know it's been a lot of years, but I would know you anywhere. You haven't changed much, just a little older. I'm Violet Henderson. My parent's and I lived in the green two-story Victorian across the street. It's so good to see you again. How are you, Mrs. Henry?"

"I'm fine dear, nice to see you," said Ida giving her a smile.

"I can't believe it's you. How have you been? When did you move back?" asked Allison.

"I've been back about three years now. I work at the courthouse here in Rustin. Our old house was empty when I moved back to town, so I bought it. You'll have to drop by sometime soon so we can catch up."

"I sure will. I guess we better get going or we'll be late for church," Allison said, as she hooked her arm in Ida's and walked with her up the steps.

As they entered the church, Allison could hear soft organ music playing and saw people taking their seats. Ida led them to a front pew.

"I have to sit close, dear. I can't hear as well as I used to," said Ida.

Rev. Williams was a couple of pews over shaking hands with members of the congregation. When he spotted Allison, he politely excused himself and walked over to where she was sitting.

"Allison, so glad you could come. If you don't mind, I would like to make an announcement introducing you to everyone."

"That's fine. I'm looking forward to your sermon," said Allison as she shook hands with Rev. Williams and then he left taking his place at the pulpit.

"Welcome everyone. I'm pleased to see so many smiling faces here in the house of God today. Before we get started with our hymns, I would like to welcome Allison Stevens, the daughter of one of our departed members. Allison, will you stand please." Allison stood and then sat back down. "Thank you so much. We all remember her mother, Lucy, a wonderful woman of God. Her help with our fundraisers and overseas missionary work will not be forgotten. She was always willing to give to others with no regard for her own needs. She is missed but resides with the Father now. Amen."

"Greta, if you would play for us. Let's sing one of Lucy's favorite hymns, "In the Garden.""

Mrs. Henry removed a hymnal and opened it to the song sharing it with Allison. As they both sang the words, Allison, couldn't help but think that there were so many things she didn't know about her mother but the words she sang made her feel closer to her somehow.

The voices of the congregation echoed throughout the little church and filled the air with sweet melodies that rang up into the heavens. When the song ended, Rev. Williams began his sermon, which Allison found to be very comforting. It almost seemed as if it was directed at her. Maybe it was God's way of getting her attention.

When Rev. Williams made the altar call, Allison felt a firm tug pulling at her heart. It was as though God wanted her to re-dedicate herself to him.

At first, she was reluctant to go in front of all the people she didn't know, but the pull was so intense that she couldn't fight it any longer. As the organist played the soft sweet melody, it was like a soothing river of healing waters to her ears.

Allison slowly rose from the pew and smiled at Ida. Ida leaned in and said in a soft voice, "Would you like me to go up with you, dear?" Allison nodded her head, yes, in response.

Ida took Allison's hand and followed her to the front of the pulpit, and they both knelt down on the carpet. Allison closed her eyes and could sense that others were joining her.

"Father, these children of God knelt before you, are here to proclaim their dedication to you. If there are any with unforgiven sins, let them confess them and know they will be forgiven. We know Lord that you died for the forgiveness of all our sins and through your resurrection and grace we are heirs to everlasting life. I pray in Jesus name, Amen."

Allison stayed bowed down with her eyes closed. She said the prayer along with Rev. Williams and felt a rush of warmth flow all through her entire body. Then at the top of her head, ever so lightly, came a touch. She knew in her heart that it was the touch of Jesus.

She could hear Rev. William's voice off to the right of her, so she knew he didn't touch her head. It was a touch she would never forget. Tears of joy filled her eyes and rushed down her face.

Allison could hear some shuffling of feet around her and opened her eyes. People were getting up and taking their seats, some stopping to hug other church members.

Rev. Williams walked up behind her placing a hand on her shoulder. "Allison, your mother would be so proud of you. She talked about you all the time, and it was evident to me that she loved you very much."

"I know. I wish things could have been different between us."

"God has forgiven you. He needs you to go on with your life and walk the path he has chosen for you. I do hope you decide to stay in Rustin, but I know you have to do whatever God leads you to do," he said.

"I've been struggling with that. I do like Rustin, and God has pressed it upon my heart to stay here," replied Allison.

"We have a great Bible Study Group that meets every Wednesday. It is part bible study and also a support group for members who have lost a loved one. Brett Collins is our group volunteer leader. He lost his wife, Vicki, from cancer a year ago and is a single father. We would love to have you if you're interested," said Rev. Williams.

"I guess it would give me a chance to get to know some of the church members. I'll give it some thought. What time do they meet?" asked Allison walking along with Rev. Williams.

"We start at 7 p.m. and usually finish up around 8:30 p.m. There's Brett now. I'll introduce you."

Chapter 22

Allison turned around, and her eyes met Brett's. A beautiful smile began to form on his face that sent tingles through her. Brett was handsome, with hair a warm shade of brown. He was broad shouldered, tall, and appeared fit. Clutching tightly to his hand was a small girl with curly auburn hair. She had a fair complexion which was set off by the most beautiful green eyes Allison had ever seen. The girl hugged her father's waist as they stood next to Rev. Williams.

"Brett, this is Allison Stevens. She's Lucy's daughter. I invited her to join our Bible study and support group."

Brett reached forward to shake Allison's hand. "Nice to meet you, Allison. I do hope you will join us. I don't know what I would have done without the group. It has been a blessing in a rather dark time in my life," he said his eyes looking down at the young girl beside him. "This is my daughter, Ebony. Honey say hello to Allison."

A soft sound escaped Ebony's lips as she whispered, "Hi."

"Hello, Ebony. You're a beautiful girl," said Allison as she reached over to shake Brett's hand. "It's nice to meet you Brett, and I'll think about joining the group."

"Mrs. Henry. How have you been?" asked Brett.

"Better now since Allison is staying next door. She's such a help. So much like her mother," said Ida giving Allison a warm smile.

"Ida, are you ready to go home?" asked Allison.

"Yes, dear, I think I need to lie down. It's been a full day." Ida reached over and shook hands with Rev. Williams. "I enjoyed the message."

Brett and his daughter stood talking to Rev. Williams as Allison and Ida walked toward the front door. Allison loved the fact that the first single man she had met in Rustin was a Christian man.

Ida and Allison walked together to the car. Allison felt blessed to have someone like Ida as her friend. She helped to fill the void left by her mother.

They walked to the car and got in. Allison turned the key, and the engine fired up. After a minute or two to warm up, she backed out of the parking space.

The church parking lot was empty now except for a few cars. She maneuvered the car out into traffic and drove along the same route she followed earlier.

"I enjoyed church service today. I think I will give the Bible Study Group a try," said Allison.

"I'm glad you enjoyed the service, and the group is a good idea. We can always use support from other Christians. It can get pretty lonely sometimes."

"How long has it been since your husband died?"

"Ed passed away about eight years ago." Ida's voice began to quiver, and Allison knew it was hard for her. "We were married over forty years, and I still miss him every day."

"I can't imagine losing someone after being together that long. How do you make it through every day?"

"That's where the Lord comes in. Just knowing that I have a home in heaven with my Ed, is all the comfort I need. We will be together again someday. When I get sad, I think of Ed and what he would want for me. He would want me to live the rest of my life in joy with the Lord looking out for me."

"I wish I could have met him," said Allison watching for the traffic signal up ahead.

"I wish you could have too. Ed would have liked you."

"Do you feel up to having lunch with me?" I have everything for sandwiches in the frig, and I made potato salad last night."

"That would be lovely. Your mother and I used to have lunch together most Sunday's. We used to eat, read the Bible, and pray for each other and those in need that we knew."

Allison and Ida had a lovely lunch followed by a short Bible reading. Ida bowed her head and prayed over both of them before going back to her house.

Allison enjoyed the time they had spent together and the apprehension she felt about staying in Rustin was beginning to fade. The Lord had led her to a loving church family.

Chapter 23

It was a new week, and a month had gone by since Allison had moved back to Rustin. Time had seemed to fly by, and she was starting to feel more and more like she was home for good.

Her mom's possessions had gradually been emptied out of the house. She had donated most of her mother's personal things, except for a few items she just didn't want to part with.

She had purchased a few pieces of wall art, a recliner, and a new television. She enjoyed watching Christian shows and felt their words of encouragement helped ground her in her faith even more.

She had managed to gain enough courage to go to her first Bible Study Group on Wednesday and really enjoyed it. Everyone was so open and empathetic. As each person told their story of their personal struggle, she realized that there were others who suffered much more loss than she had.

Brett told his story to the group that night. Allison's heart ached as Brett spoke about how his wife, Vicky, had died of breast cancer after such a long fight. She could hear the hurt Brett felt down deep in his soul. Coping with not only his loss but that of the loss of a mother for Ebony, was at times, unbearable. Ebony, even though she was young, was still old enough to remember her.

Brett told the group about the struggles he went through trying to be both father and mother to Ebony. At the end of his testimony, it was apparent that his ability to cope came from group support and his faith in God. He let everyone know that the whole experience that started as resentment and blaming God for taking Vicky ended in acceptance and healing. His healing was slow, and he was still growing as a Christian. Every day was a struggle, but now he felt he could face whatever challenged him.

Allison came away from the first meeting that night with a stronger faith in God's promises. As Brett had said just before she left the meeting, "Everything is possible with God. We just need to hold tight to his promises."

The ringing of the telephone stopped Allison's train of thought, and she answered it.

"Hello."

"Hi, Allison. How are you?"

"I'm fine Mr. Benson, just a little surprised to hear from you. Is something wrong?" asked Allison, wondering if there were outstanding bills that she didn't know about.

"Not at all, I wanted to see how you were getting along and wondered if you had come to a decision whether or not you are going to keep the house. If not, I have a client that's a realtor. She could help you with the sale."

"I am keeping the house. My place is here in Rustin. I do have another matter I would like to discuss with you. Would you have time to see me sometime this week?" she asked.

"I have some free time towards the end of the week. Why don't we plan to meet at my office on Thursday at 1 p.m., but if something comes up, I'll give you a call. Will that work for you?"

"That' sounds fine. It shouldn't take long. I just have a document for you to look at," said Allison.

"I'll see you then," said Mr. Benson.

God had answered Allison's prayers about whether or not to try to find out if her brother was still alive. A part of her was excited knowing that she might actually have family out there somewhere, but then doubt crept in and tried to dissuade her from going forward.

Satan was still trying to enter her thoughts, but now she knew how to make him flee from her. She knew that fear didn't come from God and that she had freedom in Christ. She could imagine all kinds of outcomes, but then that too was a source of fear. She was stronger than that now.

Allison put on the tea kettle to heat while she folded up some laundry from earlier that morning. She stopped briefly and walked over to grab the remote putting the television on a Christian music channel. The house filled with the sounds of praise music and Allison hummed along to it. She could feel the presence of the Lord and his love lifting her up.

She had learned to distinguish the Holy Spirit's voice that grabbed her attention at times when she least expected it. It led her in the direction that the Lord wanted her to go and she began to willingly obey.

The kettle whistled, and she stopped what she was doing and walked into the kitchen to retrieve it from the burner. She grabbed a tea bag and poured hot water into a cup, adding a couple of spoons of sugar, and stirred. She brought the tea to her lips and gently blew to cool it and then took a sip.

A light rap on the door got her attention. She walked over and opened the door. Ida was standing there holding a plate of freshly baked cookies.

"Hi, dear, I thought maybe you would like some oatmeal raisin cookies. They are hot out of the oven. They were Ed's favorite."

"Hi, Ida, come in. Would you like a cup of tea?"

"I'd love one," Ida replied as she walked into the living room.

Allison took the plate of cookies from Ida and set them down on the kitchen table and took out another teacup placing it on the counter. Ida sat down at the table.

"You have done a great job with the house. It's neat as a pin. Your mother would be so happy to know you are here."

"Ida, God wants me here, and even though I'm scared, I know that he will open doors for me," said Allison making Ida's tea and placing the cup on the table.

"Thanks, dear. You are making an old woman very happy with your news. I know you might not understand why God wants you here, but over time he will reveal his plan to you. You just have to be patient." Ida took a sip of her tea. "How do you like the Bible study and support group?"

"I enjoyed it. At first, I was nervous, but when Brett talked to us about his loss and struggles, I seemed to relax. He has a way of explaining his relationship with the Lord that makes you want to have that kind of relationship too," said Allison.

"Yes, it has been hard for them both. Vicky was a wonderful mother. Her family meant everything to her. In her last hours, she tried to explain to Brett that she was going to be with the Lord and that he would send his comforter to heal his broken heart. She made sure he knew that she didn't want him to be alone, and that one-day God would send him someone to love."

"She sounds amazing. How long were they married?" Allison asked as she took a bite of cookie.

"Not long. Five years or so, I think, but they loved each other very much. Brett needs to find love again, and little Ebony needs a new mom."

"I'm not sure he is ready for that yet," said Allison.

"Well, I should be getting home. Time for my afternoon nap. I seem to get tired earlier these days," Ida said as she got up and moved towards the front door.

Allison walked Ida to the door. Ida turned and gave Allison a pat on the shoulder. "You and Brett would make a lovely couple you know. You should give him a chance. Really, get to know him. I think you will like what you see."

"Oh, Ida, I'm not looking for a permanent relationship. I've got so much to get settled in my life. I would like to continue a friendship with Brett though."

"You know that's how the best relationships start. Ed and I were friends for over a year before we finally tied the knot. You may think you aren't interested right now, but God might just have other plans for you." Ida stepped out onto the front porch. "See you later, dear."

Ida slowly made her way across the lawn. She stepped up onto her porch pausing briefly to wave to Allison.

Allison waved back and was glad that Ida still lived next door. A gentle soul that always put others first and was becoming quite the matchmaker. It's as though she knew what God wanted for Allison before she did.

What would tomorrow bring? She didn't know. Would she find out Brett was the soul mate God had intended for her?

Chapter 24

It was a mild day as Allison drove through town to Mr. Benson's office which was located about a mile from her house and an easy commute.

The traffic was typical on a weekday. The local fast food places were packed with people getting a quick lunch before heading back to work, and people were strolling along the tree-lined sidewalks enjoying the day.

Allison maneuvered her car through the intersection at the corner of Page and Main Street and headed up the block before turning into the parking lot. At this particular time of day, the lot was relatively empty.

Allison turned off the car's engine, unbuckled her seat belt, and got out locking the door behind her. Her brother's birth certificate was securely tucked away in her purse slung over her shoulder. She was dressed in a pink sweater and a pair of black slacks.

As she approached the front entrance, she could see Mr. Benson standing just inside the door talking to a beautiful young woman. Allison opened the door and entered the building. Mr. Benson and the young woman glanced her way.

"Allison, it's so nice to see you again," Mr. Benson said smiling. "I would like you to meet my daughter, Jennifer."

"Nice to meet you, Jennifer," said Allison shaking her hand. "Your father has been so helpful. I don't know what I would have done without him."

"He does enjoy helping people. Well, Dad, I have to be running. See you later at dinner," said Jennifer giving her dad a quick peck on the cheek.

"See you at dinner, dear. Love you."

"Love you too Dad," said Jennifer as she exited the building.

"Well, I have to admit I'm a little more than curious about why you're here," said Mr. Benson as he headed to his office with Allison close behind.

Allison entered the office and took a seat in front of the massive desk which was piled high with folders. It was apparent that he was a busy man.

"Would you like some coffee, Allison? I just brewed a fresh pot."

"I'm fine. Thank you."

"What can I do for you?" asked Mr. Benson leaning back in his chair.

"I need you to take a look at this document. I want you to find out if my brother is alive or not," said Allison as she passed the birth certificate over to him.

"I wasn't aware that your mother had any other children."

"My mother told me that she had a miscarriage while she was in the hospital in Denver. I didn't think anything of it until I found this document in my mother's closet," she said handing it to Mr. Benson. "As you can see, the person listed as his father is not my father. What if she didn't miscarry, but gave him up for adoption? I remember my mother going to stay with my aunt during that time and there seemed to be tension between my parents. It was right before I left home." Allison took a deep breath and waited for Mr. Benson to comment.

"You do realize that if your brother is alive, that he could decide to challenge the will. That could make things difficult for you. Are you sure you want me to look into this?"

"I have to know the truth," replied Allison.

"I'll get started right away," said Mr. Benson. "I'll either be in touch or Jennifer will as soon as I know something definite. My daughter has decided to join my practice, and I couldn't be happier."

Allison rose from her seat and shook his hand. Not wanting to get her hopes up, she would put it in God's hands and wait for the outcome, even if it led to disappointment.

She walked out and got in her car. She started the engine and drove towards the Rustin Supermarket to do some grocery shopping. Carol would be coming with her things from the apartment, and she wanted to return the favor by cooking her a nice dinner. Maybe she would invite Ida over also. She was sure Carol would enjoy her company.

After a quick shopping trip, Allison arrived home. She put away her groceries and turned on the local Christian music channel taking a few minutes to gather her thoughts.

With Carol bringing her things, the move to Rustin seemed more permanent. She was about to close one chapter in her life and embark on a new one. *What would it bring?* She would have to gather all the strength she had within her to do the Lord's will. A voice within her echoed, "Remember, you are not alone."

Chapter 25

Allison awoke to the sound of birds singing and the early morning sun shining through the curtains. She rolled over and smiled happily knowing that Carol would arrive later that afternoon. She couldn't wait to see her.

Allison reflected on her Heavenly Spirits and wondered if she would ever see them again. The visitations had stopped once she received the message from the Lord telling her to remain in Rustin. Maybe there were no more messages for her. *Do I have nothing else to learn? That can't be.*

She had grown in her spiritual walk and was gaining the confidence she so desperately needed. She couldn't wait to talk to Carol about her experiences.

Allison took a quick shower and dressed in a blue long-sleeved shirt and blue jeans. After getting a cup of tea, she decided to take a walk out in the backyard and sat in a lounge chair. She glanced around thinking back to times she had spent with her mom and dad. Most of them were happy times. Some, not so much.

At the back of the yard was a small gazebo. Her dad had built it as a Mother's Day present. Those were the good times before he started spending more and more time away from home.

Thinking about the yard and the fact that she was keeping the house, made her realize that she should probably give Ernest a call to set up a time for him to do the yard work.

She got up and went into the house. It was 9 a.m., and she picked up the piece of paper she had tucked away in the kitchen drawer and carefully dialed his number.

A man's voice answered, "This is Ernest."

"Hi, Ernest. It's Allison Stevens."

"Well, Hi, Allison. Nice to hear from ya. How ya been?"

Allison took a seat at the kitchen table. "I'm doing much better. I just wanted to let you know that I'm keeping the house."

"That's good. You mother would be so happy to know you are staying here," said Ernest.

"The reason I'm calling is to set up a time to have you do some yard work for me."

"When would you like me to do the work? I can come most any time," Ernest replied, taking a minute to wait for an answer.

"Just give me a call, so I know you're coming. That way I'm here to make a check out for you before you leave."

"Okay. I just knew God wanted you here," said Ernest.

Allison could hear the click on the phone notifying her that he had hung up. *What a sweet man. Strange how he seemed to know Allison's path too.*

Allison's circle of Christian acquaintances was growing. God let her path cross with just the right people, and they were ready with guidance, uplifting conversations, and support. Her fears of not having any friends in Rustin were squashed. God again was providing for her needs.

Allison spent the rest of the morning and early afternoon cleaning house and preparing food. She had talked with Ida, but she had declined the invitation to come to dinner. Ida wasn't feeling well, so Allison told her she would check in on her later.

Allison had just entered the house when she heard a vehicle pull up in the driveway. She glanced out the kitchen window and saw Carol exiting and heading up the walk to the front door.

Allison rushed out the door wrapping her arms around her. Carol returned the affection by giving her a long hug.

"Allison, you look great. Rustin must be agreeing with you," said Carol standing next to her SUV.

"I am starting to feel comfortable here, but I still miss you and all my co-workers at the center," replied Allison.

"I know. Everyone misses you too, but we are only a short drive away," said Carol as she grabbed her overnight bag from the SUV and followed Allison into the house.

"Would you like a glass of iced tea and relax a bit before we unload?" Allison asked getting glasses out of the cupboard.

"That sounds great. The traffic was pretty heavy all the way here. Everyone heading out for the weekend," Carol said taking a seat on the sofa.

Allison took the pitcher from the refrigerator and poured them each a glass of iced tea and joined Carol on the sofa, taking a sip as she sat down. She handed the other one to Carol.

"I have dinner planned and thought we could spend a quiet evening at the house and catch up if that's okay with you?" asked Allison.

"That sounds great. I have until Sunday afternoon before I have to drive back, so I'm leaving Saturday up to you. I would like to see more of Rustin though." said Carol stopping briefly to take a sip of tea. "Have you spoke to your attorney yet about your brother?"

"I met with him and gave him the information on Thursday. His daughter has joined as his partner so she will be assisting him. I'm excited but nervous about what he will find," said Allison getting up to refill their drinks.

"It sounds like you will know the truth before long and you can put it to rest. In the meantime, you just have to place your faith in God and not worry about it."

"I know. I'm trying to remember to do that, but sometimes it's hard when I've been used to relying on myself to figure everything out. The truth is, it never worked out that well for me anyway."

"How is your neighbor, Mrs. Henry? She seems like a lovely person. Of course, I only met her the one time, but I could see the love of Christ shine through her."

"She insists that I call her Ida and we've become close friends. I invited her over for dinner with us so you could become more acquainted, but she isn't feeling well today. I told her I would check on her later," said Allison worried about her. "She has been there for me through the hard times after I first got here and is always ready with a word of support just when I need it."

"Well, shall we unload the car now? I'd like to take a shower before dinner if that's okay. I need to relax those driving muscles," said Carol glancing over at Allison, waiting for a response.

"We can put them in the corner of my room for now, and I'll unpack them later. While you shower, I'll run over and check on Ida."

Carol got up from the sofa and started towards the door with Allison right behind her. Allison latched the screen door in the open position for easy access.

Allison felt like a failure. All of her worldly things just barely filled up the back end of Carol's vehicle.

No! Life wasn't measured by possessions accumulated while on Earth. Again, Satan was trying to feed her lies. The treasures she would store up in Heaven were the important ones. Living her life for God, having faith, following her destined path; that equaled a full and successful life.

Chapter 26

With the vehicle unloaded and the boxes moved to Allison's room, all that was left to do was start dinner. She had thawed out some pork chops earlier and just had to pop them in the oven and set the timer. Carol was taking her shower, so Allison decided to walk over and check on Ida.

Allison crossed the front yard making her way up the porch steps. She reached Ida's front door and made a succession of four loud knocks. No answer. Maybe Ida was in the back of the house where she couldn't hear the door. She knocked again and waited for a few minutes. Nothing.

Allison had a bad feeling. She turned the door-knob and pushed inward. The door popped open, and she entered the living room which was lit by one small table lamp.

She continued through the house reaching the kitchen. It was spotless. Ida was an excellent house-keeper and liked everything kept in its place.

Allison walked cautiously down the short hallway, glancing at the photos proudly displayed on the walls. It looked as though many generations of Ida's family had been photographed over the years.

She called out as she pushed open the door to one of the bedrooms.

"Ida, its Allison."

From one of the other bedrooms, she heard a muffled whimper. At first, she wasn't sure she had heard anything at all, but then she heard it again. She continued in the direction of the sound.

She opened the first door on the right. It apparently was Ida's hobby room. An old Singer sewing machine sat in the corner with patterns and bolts of fabric piled on top. Ida was not there.

She closed the door and continued to the last bedroom. When Allison opened the door, she saw Ida lying on the floor next to the bed. She moaned as Allison knelt down on the floor next to her.

"Hold on, Ida. I'm going to call 911. Help will be here soon," said Allison grabbing a pillow from the bed and placing it under her head. She reached up for the phone resting on the nightstand next to the bed and dialed 911. The dispatcher answered, and Allison gave her the address and returned the phone to its cradle.

Allison turned back to Ida, "Ida, can you hear me? Is there anything I can do for you?"

Ida's eyes opened. She glanced up at Allison and spoke in a low voice. "God is going to take you on an amazing journey. Give Brett a chance. He's the one God sent for you."

"Ida, it's okay. Don't try to talk right now. Save your strength," said Allison leaning over Ida.

"I can see Ed. He's come for me. It's time for me to go home."

Ida's eyes widened. She was staring at something by the doorway, and a beautiful smile crossed her face.

"Ida, hold on. They will be here any minute. You're going to be all right. Just hold on," said Allison as a tear escaped her eye and made its way down across her cheek. She said a silent prayer for Ida, not wanting to lose her friend. Ida was like a mother to her now.

As Allison held Ida's hand, she could hear the loud wail of the ambulance outside. Then Ida's hand went limp in hers. Ida closed her eyes, and Allison knew it was for the last time. She had crossed over to her resting place and had joined her husband and family members that had gone before her to the arms of Jesus. A sense of loss enveloped Allison, followed by joy for Ida. She would miss her.

Allison went to meet the paramedics. They were just coming up the front steps as she opened the door.

"She's inside," said Allison. She could see Carol walking towards her and waited on the front porch.

"What happened?" asked Carol as she walked up the steps.

"The paramedics are inside with her now, but I think she is already gone. She said she saw her husband, Ed, and that she was going home to be with him."

Carol walked up and placed her arms around Allison. They stood there just holding each other.

That night after dinner, Allison sat on the sofa with Carol next to her, neither one moved. Heads were bowed in prayer, each calling on the Lord in their individual way.

A couple of days later, Ida was laid to rest next to her husband. The service was performed by Rev. Williams, and there were many of the church congregation in attendance, as Ida was a friend to many. She was a helpful counselor and wise beyond her years. It was evident that everyone would miss her.

With Ida gone, Allison realized she would need the support group at church more than ever. *What would happen to Ida's house now? Did she have living relatives?* Ida never spoke of any.

Allison would have to fill her hours leaning on the Lord and immerse herself in the word. She couldn't stop thinking about Ida's last words to her, that Brett was the one God had chosen for her. *How could Ida possibly know that? Would God make it known to her?*

Chapter 27

Allison had a heavy heart. With Ida gone, she was once more feeling very alone. Ida had been a great friend and a godly woman, with much wisdom.

She couldn't help smile to herself though when she thought about Ida and her husband reunited in Heaven. That of course, brought back the memory of her mother's passing. Every unfortunate circumstance somehow seemed to have a silver lining when it came to the Lord's plan. Life was full of surprises.

Allison's thought about Brett. *What if he is my soul mate?* Ida seemed sure of it.

Today was Wednesday and her weekly Bible study group. She would have to see Brett again. *What if he had no feelings at all for her? What if he did?*

Allison had put off confronting one major area of her life. A job. She had been in Rustin for several weeks and the money her mother left her wouldn't last for long.

She had been growing restless, and it wasn't like her not to be productive. It was time to contact the employment agency and see what opportunities were available. Deep down in her heart, she knew the Lord would lead her in the right direction. After all, when he closed one door, he would always open another.

It was around noon, and Allison decided to call Carol before making lunch. A couple of rings and her familiar voice came through the line.

"Victory Center, Carol speaking."

"Carol, its Allison. Do you have a few minutes to talk?" asked Allison sitting down in a chair at the kitchen table.

"Hi. I've been wondering how you've been. It's so good to hear from you."

"I'm doing pretty good. I'm calling to see if I can get a letter of recommendation from you. It's about time I start looking for another job."

"I can get one ready and put it in the mail today. I'm sure that you'll find something. You know God has the perfect job waiting for you, right?"

"I know. I'm just nervous not knowing what it might be. I'll let you know when something comes through for me. Talk to you later. Thanks."

It was past lunchtime, and Allison's stomach gave a rumble. After going through her cupboards, she finally decided on a bowl of chicken noodle soup and a sandwich.

While it was heating, she went into the living room and put the television onto the Christian music channel. Instantly, the house was filled with worship music, lifting her spirits and she began to sing along as she stirred her soup.

After eating, Allison decided to go out into the backyard and check on the flower garden. Ernest had done an excellent job in keeping the yard mowed, and the bushes trimmed but didn't know much about flowers.

She opened the gate that led to the backyard. She seemed to feel more at peace there. I suppose it was because most of her happy memories happened in this very place.

With the onset of winter, the flowers that once were beautiful now were in their dormant stage. Since coming to grips with staying on at the house, she couldn't wait for Spring, knowing that the yard would be alive with splashes of vibrant color and the bird-houses that her mother had placed around in the backyard would be filled with new life. She wondered how different things would be then. Instead of looking forward with apprehension or fear, she now felt confident that God was in control. Things could only get better.

She took a seat in a lawn chair, leaned back, and took a moment to feel the peacefulness. Thoughts of her brother filled her mind. She wondered if he were alive, what was his life like? Was he married? Did he have a family? So many unanswered questions plagued her mind. If it were God's will, she would find out soon.

Allison sat quietly looking up into the sky. Knowing she had been into his realm and close to God made her smile. There was comfort in knowing that God was very real.

A dog barked a few houses down. It was getting late, and she needed to do a few things indoors before getting ready for the Bible study group.

As she shut the backyard gate and went around to her front porch, she glanced towards Ida's house out of habit. Her eyes filled with tears and sadness remembering that she was gone. *I miss you, Ida!*

Allison spent the next hour tiding up her house. The clock in the living room chimed out five o'clock, and she headed to her bedroom to get dressed. As she walked down the hallway, she stopped momentarily to glance at the framed photographs that graced the walls of the hall.

The first one she noticed was her mom and dad on their wedding day. Then there was one of Allison as a new born, and her favorite; Allison and her dad in the backyard during one of their many barbecues. These were fond reminders of the happy times.

Allison entered her bedroom and pulled a blue dress from the closet. Modern, but not too revealing. She wanted to make the right impression on Brett. *What am I thinking? It's just a Bible study group. It's not like a date or anything.*

Deep down, she knew she wanted to go on a date with Brett. She would like to get to know him better. Also, Ebony. It must be so hard for Brett raising a young girl without a mother. *Who would talk to her about all the questions a young girl would have?* Maybe Brett's mother would be there for her. Allison sure hoped so.

Allison pulled her coat from the closet, grabbed her purse and Bible and headed out the door. It was a crisp afternoon, and there wasn't a cloud in the sky.

Allison opened the door to the Buick and buckled up. She placed her purse and Bible on the passenger's seat next to her before starting the engine. In a few minutes, the car was warmed up and ready to go, and she carefully backed out of the driveway and on to the city street.

Just as she came to an intersection, the light turned red, and she came to an abrupt stop. A red muscle car, possibly a Camaro, pulled up right behind her.

She checked her mirror as the car seemed a little too close. She could see a young man in the driver's seat, probably in his early twenties and couldn't believe the look he had given her. She turned her head and waited for the light to change and reached over making sure the doors were locked before she continued down the street.

Allison had just turned off on Oak Grove. The car was still following close, and then it hit her bumper hard jerking her head forward.

She sped up a little. The other car sped up too and then hit her again causing her to lose control and veer to the left. She quickly jerked the wheel back to the right just in time to avoid an oncoming car. *Why is he trying to force me off the road?*

Allison began to pray out loud. "Lord I don't know what the person in the car wants. I'm afraid, and I need your protection now. Please guide my car and let me get to the church safely."

She continued down the street and made a right turn towards the church. She quickly checked her mirror for the car that had been following her. It was rapidly gaining on her again.

Allison wanted to turn into someone's driveway and rush to their front door for help, but then she didn't know anyone, and she could be placing herself in further danger.

She checked once more to see if the car was still approaching and saw that it was almost upon her. The vehicle came up quickly behind her hitting her bumper again.

The driver yelled some profanity at her that she couldn't quite make out. The next thing Allison knew, she was spinning toward a ditch. The front of her car came to an abrupt stop, resting on the base of a tree.

Dazed, blood dripping down across her face, she raised her head up, looking into the crazed eyes of a tall stranger.

The young man jerked open her door shouting, "Give me your money, bitch. Make it quick. I won't tell you again," he said pointing a gun at her head.

Allison retrieved her purse which now was lying on the floorboard next to her feet. She pulled it up into her lap, and her assailant quickly grabbed it pulling the money from the inside and tossing her purse at her.

His dark, cold eyes met hers. He stared at Allison and calmly cocked the hammer on the gun and pulled the trigger. The hammer clicked. Allison jumped. Nothing. He pulled the trigger again...nothing.

The next thing she heard was his quick footsteps retreating, and then an engine started up, and the car sped away. *Thank you, Lord, for sparing my life. Lord, I don't know what to do. I need help!*

Allison sat shocked at what had just happened. She wasn't sure if she was able to walk or what damage had been done to her car.

She carefully pushed open her car door and turned in her seat. She was still a little dizzy, so she took it slow. Hanging onto the car door, she tried to stand up but had to sit back down quickly. The pain was unbearable.

She grabbed her cell phone and called the church, but there was no answer. She was about to dial 911 when she heard a car approaching. *No, Lord, please don't let him come back.*

She sat with her head against the steering wheel, pain entering her body from her head and back.

"Allison, is that you?" said the man's voice that sounded like it was coming from miles away.

"Who's there? Help me?" said Allison.

Chapter 28

Allison blinked her eyes, and when the haziness cleared, she was looking into the familiar dark brown eyes and beautiful smile that belonged to none other than, Brett Collins.

"Allison, can you hear me? I'm calling an ambulance. Hold on, helps on the way," said Brett as he removed his hand and dialed 911.

"Brett, don't leave me," Allison pleaded, just before everything went black.

Brett sat on a chair next to Allison's hospital bed. Even though he had just met Allison recently, he felt an automatic connection to her. He hadn't felt this way about anyone since Vicky died and wasn't even sure if he was ready for a relationship yet. After all, Brett had Ebony to consider. The last thing he wanted was for her to get hurt.

Allison opened her eyes and could see the faint outline of a man sitting beside her bed, but couldn't make out who it was.

She lay still, waiting for her fuzzy vision to clear. The man had his head bowed down, and his eyes were closed. Allison had the impression that he was deep in prayer. *Is he was praying for me?"*

Brett opened his eyes to discover that Allison was awake. He got up and stood, reached down, and took her hand in his.

"You're at Rustin Memorial Hospital, just rest, I'll call the doctor." Brett reached over and pushed the button to call the nurse.

In a matter of minutes, a young, blonde-haired nurse entered the room. "What can I do for you?" she asked.

"I just wanted to let the doctor know she's awake," said Brett.

"Thanks. I'll let the doctor know right away," said the nurse as she left the room.

"Brett, why am I here," asked Allison trying to sit up in the bed.

"You were in an auto accident and have a concussion. The doctor wanted to keep you for twenty-four-hour observation to make sure there weren't any other complications," said Brett, his voice laced with concern.

"Oh, now I remember. It was awful. This man kept following me and ramming my car. He pushed me off the road and then robbed me. He had a gun and went to shoot me, but for some reason, the gun didn't go off. I thought I was going to die," said Allison. Her voice shaky and coming out in spurts.

"I'm sorry. I didn't know. The police need to be notified," said Brett.

"Was my purse in the car? I think he threw it back at me after he took the money," asked Allison, worried that the man had her address.

"Your purse is in the drawer next to your bed. Your identification is still in it. I had your car towed to the garage for now until you decide what you want to do later," said Brett giving her a gentle hug.

"How can I ever thank you? I don't know what I would have done if you hadn't come along when you did," Allison said glancing up at Brett. Tears began forming in the corner of her eyes, and one slid down across her cheek.

Brett was about to answer her but was interrupted by her doctor.

"Allison, you are one lucky young lady. Your x-rays came back fine. No internal injuries or broken bones. You have a concussion and some strained muscles. I'm going to release you this morning and I want you to follow up with your regular doctor in a week."

"I don't have a local doctor. I just moved here recently," replied Allison.

"The receptionist will set up an appointment. In the meantime, get some rest," said the doctor. He patted her on the arm and left the room.

Allison was lucky. The incident could have been much worse. Again, God was watching out for her, and in time she would be as good as new.

"Brett, please don't call the police. I just want to forget this whole thing. I'm going to be okay, and as far as the money goes, it can be replaced. I'll probably never see the person again," said Allison as she pulled the covers away from her body and swung her legs over the side of the bed.

"But, what if you do. I don't think you should let this go. What if the next person isn't so lucky? Can you live with yourself knowing you didn't do anything to stop him? You should at least report it and let the police do their job," said Brett.

Allison could see the concern on Brett's face. Maybe she wasn't thinking clearly. Perhaps she should at least report it.

"Okay. You can call the police. I'll give the officer my statement."

"I think that's the smart thing to do. You still have to deal with the insurance company, and they will want to know what happened."

"Of course, you're right. I hadn't thought about that," said Allison opening up the cabinet beside the bed. She found her clothes tucked away inside. "I'm going to try and get dressed," said Allison waiting for Brett to leave the room.

"Can you manage on your own or do you want me to ask one of the nurses to help you?"

"I'll be fine. No need to bother the nurse."

"Be careful. I'll be back in a little bit," said Brett. "Is there anyone you need me to call?"

"I should still have my cell phone. I'll go ahead and make the call when I'm done dressing," said Allison. She needed to talk to Carol. She was the closest person she had to family now.

Brett smiled at Allison, pulled the curtain around her bed for privacy, and left the room. She could hear the heels of his shoes making contact with the floor as his footsteps vanished down the hall.

She took Brett's advice and gave her statement to the officer that came to the hospital before she was discharged. She wasn't looking forward to having to pick the man out of a line-up, that is if they were lucky enough to apprehend him. She was doubtful as he was probably long gone by now.

Chapter 29

Brett was kind enough to drive Allison home from the hospital. He even helped her to the couch in the living room and insisted on fixing her a cup of tea before leaving.

Allison couldn't remember when she had a man show her such warm attention. Even Tom, early on in their marriage wasn't that attentive. She thanked Brett for all his help and promised to take it easy. He said he would call and check on her and for her not to hesitate to call him if she needed anything.

With Brett gone, Allison, started thinking about the young man who had robbed her. She wondered what had happened in his life to cause him to take the path he did.

Allison tried to pull herself up into a sitting position, but the soreness of her muscles made her cry out in pain. It would be awhile before she would be pain-free. She decided to give it a second try and this time hung onto the side of the couch, pulled herself around, and then stood in place until she got her balance.

She ambled into the bathroom, got a washcloth and ran it under some warm water. She squeezed out the excess and began patting her face.

As she glanced into the mirror, she saw a nasty bruise just above her left eye. She knew it was only superficial and that it would eventually heal. What worried her, was getting past the memories of the incident..

She had to keep focused on getting better. She had to forgive the man who robbed her before she could heal. From reading her Bible, and her spiritual visitor's messages, she knew it was her first step.

She wanted to move on with her life, but she knew it wouldn't be easy. Every time a car door slammed outside, she jumped. If she heard a man's voice outside, she worried it was him coming back for her.

Her human emotions tried to control her. But she had to lean on God for strength and put the situation under constant submission.

She was just coming out of the bathroom when the phone rang. It took her a little longer to get to the kitchen to answer it. When she picked up the receiver, all she could hear was heavy breathing.

She was stunned and for a moment stood there motionless unable to speak. Finally, she found her voice, "Hello, who's there?" she asked.

No one answered so she hung up the phone. Maybe just a wrong number. After all, it was unlisted and not many people had it.

Still uneasy from the phone call, Allison pulled back the kitchen curtains and looked outside. It was early afternoon, and the neighborhood appeared quiet. The street was empty, except for an occasional person walking their dog.

Allison felt that her imagination was running away with her and said a prayer. *Lord, I know I have nothing to fear. You are always with me, but I need your help. I don't want to live in fear, and I know it's not your way. Please help me to forget the pain from this circumstance and help me to move on. I pray in Jesus name. Amen.*

Allison opened her eyes, raised her head, and was grateful for the closeness she felt. With God, all things were possible, and she knew God would turn her grief into good. She would come through a better person than she was before.

The ringing of the telephone brought her back to the present time. She walked over to grab the phone, hesitating for just a moment before picking it up.

A deep male voice echoed through the receiver, and she began to relax.

"Allison, it's Rev Williams. How are you feeling?"

"I'm feeling a little better. Still very sore though," Allison said. She was touched that Rev Williams would take time out from his busy schedule to check on her.

"I know this might not be the right time to discuss this with you since you are recovering from your accident, but I wondered what your plans are as far as finding a job here in Rustin. I have something that I'm hoping will interest you."

"I plan on looking for a job as soon as the doctor releases me. What did you have in mind?" Allison couldn't imagine what he might suggest. She didn't think that the church could afford to hire anyone full-time.

"With the passing of Mrs. Henry, I found out from her attorney, that she left her house and a large sum of money to the church. We can afford to do our addition now," said Rev Williams.

He took a moment to gather his thoughts and continued. "The plans are to construct another building adjacent to the church that will be used as a rescue center for the homeless. We want to help broken families with clothing, jobs, temporary housing, and food."

"That sounds like a wonderful idea. Ida would be so pleased. She loved her church family very much," said Allison, as she fondly remembered the time spent with her at church. Allison was glad that Ida's last gift would be put to good use.

"Allison, I know you worked at the center in Collingwood before moving here, and God has put it upon my heart to offer you a position at the church. You are the perfect person to help run the new center. Maybe your friend, Carol, would be willing to help you in a consulting capacity. What do you think?"

"She will be here sometime this evening. She insisted coming to help with my recovery. I'll ask her about it, and when we come to church on Sunday, it will give you an opportunity to speak with her," said Allison. Her mind was spinning. She was excited about this new opportunity but was uncertain if she had the experience needed for such an important position.

"Are you sure you are up to coming to church? I'll understand if you need to skip a Sunday or two. I just want you to get better."

"The support of my church family will help me heal. I'll see you Sunday."

"I'll talk to you more about everything after church service. Take care of yourself. God bless," said Rev Williams.

Allison replaced the receiver back in the cradle and walked over and sat down at the kitchen table. She had to take a minute for everything to sink in.

With the expense to repair her car and the money that was stolen, she knew she would need a job soon. Not only did God answer her concern before she even prayed over it, but gave her the opportunity to serve in her church to help those less fortunate. She was amazed at God's goodness and most of all his timing.

Chapter 30

It was early Friday evening when Allison heard a car pull up into the driveway. She walked over to the living room windows and pulled the curtain back so she could see out. Carol was shutting her car door and heading for the front porch.

Allison opened the front door and greeted her.

"It's so good to see you," she said ushering Carol into the living room.

"It's good to see you too. How you feeling?" asked Carol putting her suitcase down.

"I'm doing better. Just a lot of soreness that will eventually go away, at least no broken bones. God was looking out for me," said Allison. She couldn't wait to tell her the news. "Why don't you put your suitcase in your room and I'll put some water on for tea."

"Sounds good," said Carol as she disappeared into the guest room.

Allison put water on and pulled out a couple of cups. She went back into the living room and sat on the sofa waiting for the kettle to signal the water was ready.

Carol walked back into the living room and took a seat next to Allison.

"Well, all settled in. How are you doing, really?" asked Carol with a concerned look.

"I'm not going to lie to you. This whole ordeal has taken its toll on me. When the phone rings I question who is on the other end. If a car door shuts outside I jump, wondering if it's him coming back-that maybe he found out where I live. I hate living in fear. I know I'm not supposed to give in to the fear, but it's so hard to control," said Allison shifting her weight on the couch.

"I haven't been through anything like this, but I can only imagine what you are going through." Carol reached over and put a hand on Allison's shoulder. "I'm here to help with whatever you need."

"Thanks. You can't imagine what a relief it is to have you here," said Allison as her eyes began to tear up. "I do have some good news. Rev Williams called and offered me a job. Ida left her house and some money to the church, so now they can afford to build their center."

"That's great. Every city needs resources. It seems to be an on-going problem everywhere. What will you be doing?" asked Carol.

"I'm not sure yet, but he wanted me to ask if you would be willing to work in a consulting capacity for the project. I don't feel that I know enough to tackle a project of this size by myself." Allison heard the tea kettle whistle and started to get up to fix their tea.

"Let me get it. You rest," said Carol. She left the room and in a few minutes returned with two cups of tea, handing one to Allison. "I'll have to check my schedule, but if I can find the time, I would love to help out."

Allison smiled at Carol. "I appreciate any help I can get. I'm assuming that I will be helping the Administrator. I think that could be Brett. He's been doing all the accounting for the church and running some classes."

"I notice a change in your expression when you say his name. Is there something you're not telling me?" asked Carol.

"Not anything to tell, even though Ida was convinced that he is my soul mate. Brett's wife died a year ago from cancer, and he has a daughter, Ebony, who is four years old. It's sad. Ida told me all about it."

"It must be hard being a single father raising a girl. I bet she misses her mom," said Carol taking a sip of her tea.

"Ida said it was hard on both of them. He teaches the Bible Study group at the church. Ebony, is a little shy, but is probably still having a hard time adjusting."

"Well, you never know what God has in mind. He seems to be working in your life, even in spite of the difficulties you have had. God doesn't promise we won't have problems, just that he will be there to see us through them," said Carol.

Allison jumped, reacting to the ringing of the phone.

"Would you like me to get that for you?" asked Carol.

"Thanks," said Allison. She watched as Carol left to answer it. Allison could hear her saying, "Just a moment. I'll get her."

"Allison, it's Chief Stanley, from the Rustin Police Department. He wants to talk to you." Carol took the cell phone over and handed it to Allison and then sat back down.

"Allison speaking."

"Allison, I know you are probably still recovering from your accident, but is there any way you can come down to the station. We think we have the person that robbed you and I need you to identify him. Is that possible?"

"I have a friend here that can drive me. When do you need me there?"

"As soon as possible. I know this is hard for you, but there isn't any other way. You are the only person who saw him," said Chief Stanley.

Allison took a deep breath. She couldn't believe that they might have him.

"Carol, could you drive me down to the Police Department?" asked Allison.

"Sure. Whatever you need," said Carol getting up to put her cup in the kitchen.

"I'll be right there. Where do I need to go?" asked Allison.

"Just check in at the front desk, and they will page me. I appreciate your cooperation," said Chief Stanley.

Allison set the phone down on the coffee table and started to sob.

Carol sat down and wrapped her arms around her. "It's going to be all right. I'm going to be right there with you. You can do this."

Allison wiped the tears from her eyes and got up off the couch. "I'm going to wash up a little, and then I'll be ready to go."

Carol was waiting by the door when Allison entered the living room. She grabbed her coat off the coat rack and with her purse in hand followed Carol out the door locking it behind her.

On the way to the police station, Allison sat quietly in the passenger's seat dreading the fact that she might be face to face with the person who had caused her all the pain. *How will it make me feel seeing him again? God, please give me the strength to do what I have to do!*

In what seemed like a matter of minutes to Allison, Carol was pulling up in front of the Rustin Police Station. They got out and walked towards the front doors of the building.

As they entered Allison glanced around the modern facility. In front of them was a large counter. An officer stood behind it, and he glanced up as they approached.

"I'm Allison Stevens. I'm here to see Chief Stanley," said Allison, her voice breaking up as she tried to calm herself. Carol placed a hand on her shoulder for support and Allison smiled at her in appreciation.

"I'll let him know you're here," said Officer Ross, picking up the phone to page the Chief. After completing the call, he hung up and told them to have a seat, and Chief Stanley would be right with them.

Allison and Carol sat quietly as their eyes wandered around the sterile facility. An officer walked a handcuffed young prisoner through. As he passed them, he gave them a menacing look. Allison quickly looked away wondering what the man had done.

The officer punched in the code, a door opened, he went through with his prisoner, and it slammed shut behind them. Allison was lost in thought when Chief Stanley approached them.

"Allison. Chief Stanley. Will you please come with me?"

Allison and Carol followed him through a hallway into a small corner office. Allison glanced at the walls that were covered with awards for distinguished service.

Office Stanley motioned for them to have a seat.

"Allison, in a few minutes, I am going to take you down to a special room. You will be able to see the suspects, but don't worry, they won't be able to see you. There will be a group of five men, holding numbers. I just need you to tell me if you see the man that robbed you. Take your time and make sure you have the right person. It's critical. Do you understand?"

"I do. Can my friend come in with me? I would feel better with her in the room," asked Allison shifting in her seat. Carol looked over and gave her a nod in agreement.

"That'll be fine. I want you to be as comfortable as possible. I know this is difficult," said Office Stanley rising from his desk. "This way."

Allison and Carol followed the Chief. They took a couple of turns down the long hallway and then he opened a door and motioned for them to enter. The room was empty except for a few chairs.

As Allison and Carol stood in front of a giant window, the lights flashed on, and they could see five men entering in a line. They were asked to stand to face the officer and were each holding a number in front of them. One, in particular, stood out, and she knew right away that he was the one.

His eyes seemed to lock onto hers, even though she knew it was impossible for him to see her. The room began to spin, and she felt as though she was falling down a dark tunnel. She thought she would retch at any moment and beads of sweat appeared on her forehead and hands. Just before everything started to go dark, she heard a voice that sounded as if it came from a long way off.

"Allison, maybe you should sit down a moment. Chief, could someone get her a glass of water?" asked Carol as she helped Allison to a chair.

The Chief used the phone inside the room, and in a couple of minutes an officer entered and handed Allison a glass of water. Allison started to get her bearings and brought the glass up to her lips, taking a slow drink of the liquid.

"Thanks, Carol. I'm starting to feel better now," Allison said as she leaned back in the chair.

"Did you see him? Is that what happened?" asked Carol.

"Yes."

"Just take a breath and when you are ready, let me know which one he is," said the Chief.

Allison got up from the chair and took another look at the men. There was no doubt, the robber was there.

"Number two," Allison said as she looked away.

"Thanks. I have a paper here for you to sign stating that the person who caused your accident and robbed you is number two, Romero Rodriquez. That's all I need for now. We may have to contact you when he goes to court, in case you have to testify. Follow me back to my office, please."

Allison still stunned from the ordeal followed Chief Stanley back to his office. Carol followed close behind. The Chief motioned for them to have a seat and handled Allison a clipboard with a paper on it for her to sign.

She looked it over and then signed her name to the bottom. *What would happen now? Will I be forced to see him again in court?*

Chapter 31

The last couple of days with Carol had been great. They spent the time catching up on everything. Allison loved having someone close to talk to again.

Carol had spent part of Saturday cleaning house for Allison and then had gone to the store to stock up on groceries until Allison's car was ready and she was able to drive again. It had been in the garage now for over a week waiting for the bodywork to be done.

Allison had found out that the repair bill wasn't as much as she expected. The body man was a member of the church, and he gave her a discount on the bill. Another blessing from God- she was sure of it.

"Dinner will be ready in about an hour," said Carol putting the chicken in the oven to roast.

"Thanks so much. I haven't had much of an appetite, but I'll try to eat something," Allison said. Hopefully, by the time it was done she would feel more like eating.

There was a knock at the door. "Do you want me to get that?" Carol asked.

"Sure," Allison said, wondering who the visitor could be.

Carol walked over to the door and opened it. Outside was a tall man with the most gorgeous eyes she had ever seen, holding a bouquet of beautiful flowers. Beside him stood a small girl who clung tightly to him.

"Is Allison here? I'm Brett, and this is Ebony," he said.

"Come in," Carol said as she opened the door wider.

Brett and Ebony made their way into the living room. He handed the flowers to Allison. "These are for you, something to cheer you up."

Allison took the bouquet of flowers from Brett and admired the bright colors and then handed them to Carol to put in a vase.

"How sweet of you, they are beautiful. Thank you," Allison said.

Brett took a seat in the recliner and Ebony hopped up in his lap, clinging tightly to his neck. "I hope I'm not intruding. I was in the neighborhood and thought I would stop by and see how you are doing."

"I'm feeling much better, and I have Carol here to help me. Carol was my boss at the center in Collingwood," Allison said shifting her weight on the couch and rearranging her blanket.

"I'm glad you have someone to help. Have the police had any leads on the person that robbed you? I sure hope they find him," Brett said.

"The police have the robber in custody. Carol took me down to identify him. It was hard for me to look at him, but at least he couldn't see me behind the glass. Chief Stanley said I may have to testify at his trial. I'm hoping he pleads guilty and it doesn't come to that," Allison said her voice trembling as she spoke.

"I know this is hard for you. You went through a traumatic experience, and it isn't something you can forget easily. Put it in God's hands. Everything will work out in the end. You just have to have faith," Brett said smiling at Allison.

Carol sat quietly listening to Brett's concern. She glanced at Brett and when she saw the chance, joined in the conversation. "I'm so glad that Allison has a church family to help her through her ordeal. It was nice to meet you and Ebony," Carol said.

"It's been nice meeting you too. Allison, if you need anything don't hesitate to call. I hate to rush off, but I really must be going. I have a meeting with Rev Williams this evening." Brett said getting up.

Carol rose from the sofa and followed him to the door.

"See you soon," Brett said. Ebony turned back and did a wave goodbye to Allison and Carol.

Carol shut the door and winked at Allison.

"What?" Allison said.

"You didn't tell me he was so good-looking," Carol said.

"Nothing is going on between us. Brett's just a friend, okay," Allison said. Although she thought it would be awesome if it turned out to be something more.

"From where I was sitting, I saw the way his eyes light up when he talks to you, and his daughter is so adorable. You could do a lot worse," Carol said.

"I can't deny that I like him, but we haven't known each other very long. If God decides he's the one for me, he will bring us together. In the meantime, we're just friends," said Allison pulling up the cover that had slipped off her lap.

"Well, I think God has definite plans for the two of you. Maybe Ida was onto something when she told you he was your soul mate," Carol said as she left the

J.E. Grace

room to check on dinner. The aroma of roasted chicken filled the kitchen indicating that it was close to being done.

Allison threw the cover off and slowly stood up. "I'm going to go wash up a little," she said. "I forgot to check the mail today. Do you think you could check it?"

"Sure. I'll be right back," Carol said placing plates and silverware on the table and then went outside to check the mail.

Carol reached in pulling a couple of envelopes out of the mailbox. The top one caught her eye. It was addressed to Allison and was from Dutton & Ellis Law Firm. She hoped it wasn't bad news.

When she came in from outside, Allison was already sitting at the kitchen table. She walked over and placed the envelopes on the table.

"You have something from Dutton & Ellis Law Firm. Do you suppose he found some information on your brother?" Carol asked as she put the food into bowls and set them on the table.

"That's not Mr. Benson's firm. I have no idea who this is?" Allison said as she opened the envelope. As she opened the letter, a check fluttered down onto the table upside down. When she turned it over, a gasp escaped her lips.

"What is it, Allison?"

"It's a check from the law firm. I can't believe the amount. Can you read the letter? I'm too flustered." Allison asked.

"Okay," Carol said picking up the letter.

Dear Allison, the enclosed check is from Ida Henry and was to be sent to you after her death. She wanted you to know that she always felt like you were a daughter to her and since

154

Ida had no children of her own, she wanted to help make it easier for you. Sincerely, Stephen Dutton.

Tears streamed down Allison's face. "I never imagined she would do something like this. Carol, the check is for $25,000," Allison said.

Carol got up from the table and hugged Allison. "You know she wouldn't have done this unless she loved you. You made her last day's happy ones, and she is just returning the favor. Think of all the good you can do with it," Carol replied.

"Yes. I'll have to pray on it and see what God wants me to do. I can't believe it. In just a few weeks, I have a new home, a new job, new church family and now this. I feel so blessed." Allison sat there staring at the check unable to believe her good fortune.

"It makes the bad incident not so significant, doesn't it? God turns everything bad into good. You never know what he has planned. We should probably eat before it gets cold," Carol said as she passed the vegetables to Allison.

They filled their plates, and Carol said a prayer. "Dear Lord, we come before you today humbled by your goodness. Thank you, Lord, for this meal we are about to partake in and for your gift of loving friends. I pray in Jesus name, Amen."

Allison raised her head feeling like her heart would burst with joy. She felt so blessed and amazed at how far God had brought her. She was eternally grateful for his love, blessings, and salvation. Now it was up to her to share her good fortune with others. *She wondered where God would lead her.*

Chapter 32

It was early Sunday morning when Allison awoke to the noise of water running in the shower.

She would have to get moving if she was going to be ready for church. It gave her a sense of joy having someone to go with her, and it filled the emptiness she had since Ida passed away. Carol was always ready with an encouraging word.

The shower shut off. Allison could hear Carol as she padded across the hall. A soft knock on her door and her sweet voice rang out, "Allison, are you awake? Do you feel well enough to go to church?" Carol asked waiting by the door for a reply.

"I wouldn't miss it. I'm getting up now," Allison said as she lifted her body up and swung her legs over the side of the bed. It took a minute or two to get her bearings. Despite her good intentions, her body ached in rebellion, but she was determined to honor her God today by attending services.

As she was coming out of her room in her house-coat and slippers, she passed Carol. "I'm going to take my shower, and then we can have a bite of breakfast before we leave," Allison said.

"I'll go ahead and mix up some pancake batter and dress after we eat," Carol said as she made her way to the kitchen.

As Allison closed the door to the bathroom, she could hear Carol bustling around the kitchen. It saddened her knowing that Carol was leaving today.

Allison was enjoying her company and wasn't looking forward to being alone again, but then with the new job on the horizon, she would have plenty to fill her empty hours.

Allison dropped her robe and kicked off her slippers. She reached over, turned on the faucet and entered the shower letting the warm water cascade over her. The water helped soothe her aching muscles. She wondered how long before she would be back to normal again.

Turning off the shower, Allison grabbed a towel and dried off. It was painful rubbing her skin. She put her robe back on and opened the bathroom door entering the hallway. Carol was just finishing up the batter as she joined her in the kitchen.

"There's hot water if you want a cup of tea," Carol said as she dropped some pancake batter onto the grill. "Pancakes will be ready in a minute. Hope you're hungry."

"I'm starting to get my appetite back. Guess that means I'm getting better," Allison said as she put her tea bag in the cup to steep.

It was around noon when Rev. Williams finished his sermon, and the church members started to file out of the church, stopping briefly to shake hands with other members or give a warm embrace. The power of the Holy Spirit was evident throughout the church, and it gave Allison a warm feeling of belonging.

The sun peeked out from behind the clouds as people made their way to their cars for the drive home. Children ran along in front of their parents, meeting up with their friends, and their laughter filled the air.

Allison stopped on the front steps of the church to take it all in, while Carol stayed inside to talk to Rev. William's about consulting on their upcoming project.

Allison knew in her heart that this was the beginning of the rest of her life and knowing how great and abundant God's blessings could be, it would be nothing short of miraculous. Finally, she understood the great love that her mother had for her church family and in a short time, had come to love them too.

Lost in the moment, Allison didn't hear Carol come up behind her. "You look deep in thought. Is everything okay?" she asked.

"Just thinking about how blessed I am and that this place is starting to really feel like home," Allison said smiling at Carol. "Did you get everything worked out with Rev. Williams?"

"I did. The project sounds exciting, and it's so wonderful that you get to be a big part of it. I'm so happy for you."

"At first, I was a little overwhelmed and doubting that I knew enough to handle it. Rev. Williams is convinced that I'm the right person for the job though," said Allison as they continued down the porch steps and across the parking lot.

"God chose you for this, Allison, and he will equip you. Then, of course, you have me to help out too. How can you lose?" said Carol. A giggle escaped her lips as she put her arm around Allison.

Allison and Carol stopped at a small cafe for lunch on their way home. They entered and instantly felt like they had stepped into the past. The décor was right out of the fifties.

Their eyes took in the brightly colored neon lighting and below the counter graced with bright red Formica tops, were matching chrome seats. Across the sides of the room were booths covered in the same red vinyl and at each one was a mounted jukebox. The floor was covered in black and white checkerboard patterned tiles.

They took a seat in a booth, and within a few minutes, a waitress in a red uniform with a white apron approached.

"What can I get for you to drink," she asked. "We have a root beer float that's on special, and I highly recommend it." Her hair was pulled back into a stylish ponytail which made her fifties look complete.

Allison looked at Carol and winked. "What do think? Should we split one?"

"I can't remember the last time I had a float. Why not," Carol said.

"A root beer float coming right up. What else can I get you?" asked the waitress.

"I'll have a cheeseburger and fries," said Allison.

"The same for me," Carol said. She reached over and put a quarter in the jukebox and picked out a song. A few seconds later, "Ain't That a Shame" began playing. "I just love the old songs, but then I guess it's a little before your time."

"It is, but I remember this one. It was one of my Dad's favorites."

Allison looked around the diner as they waited for their lunch. The place was pretty full.

159

In a corner booth was a man and woman with two young children. The younger one, a little girl, probably around five-years-old, waved at Allison and smiled as she sipped on a thick chocolate shake. Allison smiled and waved back. It reminded her of when her mom used to take her to the Green Parrot Soda Shop for milkshakes as a child. Those were fond memories, and she held on to them tightly.

Their food arrived a few minutes later. They spoke briefly about Allison's job, and Carol's involvement in the project between bites of food, which they decided was excellent and made a mental note to come again.

After paying their bill, which Carol insisted on taking care of, they walked to the SUV which now was in a sea of vehicles.

They got into the vehicle and buckled up. Carol started the engine, backed out, and drove toward the exit. She was just about to pull out into traffic when Allison's cell phone rang.

"Hello, Mr. Benson. Yes, I'm free tomorrow. See you then," Allison said. She disconnected the call, replacing her cell phone in her purse.

"I can't believe it. It's a miracle. My brother is alive, and Mr. Benson knows where he is."

information about your brother, Samuel. You can decide what you would like to do after you hear it," he said, opening a folder on the top of his desk.

"Your brother is still living in Denver, Colorado. His father owns Evans Auto Repair Service, and Samuel works part-time for him. His mother, Maggie, was the bookkeeper for the business for years until Samuel was around 17 years old. His mother passed away due to a losing battle with cancer." Mr. Benson looked up from reading and pulled out another form from his folder before continuing.

"Samuel took his mother's death really hard and started hanging out with the wrong crowd. His father did everything he could think of including counseling, but nothing seemed to help. Samuel has quite the rap sheet-assault, theft, carjacking and finally a botched robbery. He drove the getaway car and spent three years in prison before being paroled."

It wasn't what she wanted to hear. Allison sat in shock trying to absorb it all. "What has he been doing since he got out?"

"According to the other information I was able to locate, he did a complete turnaround. It seems while he was in prison he started corresponding with a counselor from one of the local churches. He participated in a Bible study class the counselor ran at the prison. When he got out, he became a church member and helped out with their outreach program." Mr. Benson glanced up to see Allison wiping the tears from her eyes. "I know this is a lot to take in, but I think it would be worth it to give Samuel a chance to get to know you," he said.

Allison took a deep breath and replied. "I do want to see him. Can you contact him? Maybe we could meet here at your office the first time. I would feel more comfortable. After all, he is a complete stranger to me."

"Why don't you think about it and let me know when you want to hold the meeting. Then I'll call Samuel and get it set up." Mr. Benson closed the file folder, rose from his desk, and followed her to the door. "Everything is going to be fine, Allison." Mr. Benson hugged her and walked to the front door with her, opening it for her to exit.

"Thanks. I appreciate all you have done for me. I'll be in touch soon," Allison said, before turning away and walking out the front door.

Allison continued across the parking lot until she reached her car. She stood by the door in a trance-like state for a few minutes before unlocking it and getting in.

Her brother, Samuel, had a troubled past. He made some wrong choices in his life which cost him dearly. Her heart went out to him. They had one thing in common. They thought they could live their life without God, and it didn't sound like it worked out any better than it did for her. The only bright light in all of it was that God was there to pick up the pieces and set him on the right path again.

Excitement started to build inside her. She had a brother. The only living family left. She wanted him in her life, but it would have to be his choice.

Allison drove through downtown Rustin turning onto streets one after the other until she found herself back in her driveway. Her mind had wandered, considering all the possibilities of a relationship with her brother. If he indeed was a Christian, she couldn't imagine him not wanting to see her. She wondered what his father had told him. Did he know he was adopted? She hoped so. Otherwise, it could make for an uncomfortable situation.

She exited her car and walked up the front steps of her house. She put her key in the lock and entered just as the downpour came. She hung her coat and umbrella on the coat rack just inside the front door and laid her purse on the coffee table.

She went into the kitchen and put water on for tea, meanwhile picking up the phone to call Carol. After a couple of rings, Carol answered.

Allison told her all about her visit with Mr. Benson, stopping only momentarily to retrieve the whistling kettle from the stove. She poured the water into a cup and put a tea bag in to steep.

"Are you going to try to meet with him soon," Carol asked.

"I'm going to call Mr. Benson tomorrow and have him set something up as soon as possible. I can't wait to meet him. I wonder if he will resemble my side of the family or look more like his Dad," said Allison, taking a sip of her tea.

"Be sure and call me after you meet. I can't wait to hear all the details. I see a bright future for you."

"I will. I'll call you soon," Allison said, putting her empty cup in the sink.

"How are you healing up? Almost back to normal?" asked Carol.

"I'm a lot better. I have a doctor's appointment at the end of the week, and I have a feeling he will release me. I'm hoping the planning stages of the new project are completed soon so I can start work," Allison said, looking out the kitchen window. The rain pelted the window with large drops before sliding down the window pane.

"Talk to you later. Take care of yourself," Carol said.

"You too."

Allison's stomach churned reminding her that she had skipped lunch. She pulled out the fish she had purchased the day before and placed it in an oven dish with some seasoning and turned the oven on. While she waited for it to reach the correct temperature, she got out some fresh vegetables and placed them on to boil.

While dinner was cooking, she decided to watch the Christian music channel while she relaxed. A smile crossed her face, as she turned up the volume to enjoy her favorite Christian singer, Evan Storm.

She had been introduced to his music by Carol when she worked at the center and had been listening to him ever since. His band was called Joyful Noise, and he sang a mix of old gospel and new Christian rock. Her favorite was, "Can You Find a Way," which was playing.

Evan Storm's voice was deep and his smile was warm. It was apparent that he was filled with the love of Christ and was one of the best Christian singers she had ever heard. She wasn't a so-called fan, as far as following him online. She was never into that sort of thing.

Allison's was interrupted by the buzzer on the stove indicating that her fish was done. She poured the water off the vegetables and made herself a plate, deciding to eat in front of the television to catch the next show. A television evangelist was talking about, "The Greatest Gift-Love.

Love-that was something Allison had learned that with God was unconditional. She realized that she was finally open to having a relationship and for the first time in a few days, she thought about Brett. She wondered what he was doing. *Was he thinking of her? Did he feel a stirring within him like she did when they were together?*

Allison finished up with dinner, washed the dishes, and decided to call it a night. The rain had subsided to just a light drizzle. She could hear it as it dripped along the roof, while she lay in her bed thanking God for her many blessings. She didn't know what tomorrow would bring, but with God, she knew she was ready for anything.

Chapter 35

The sun was just breaking over the Rockies when Samuel opened his eyes. He glanced out the large windows that provided a view of the Rockies and surrounding meadow and glanced at the fresh layer of newly fallen snow that graced the landscape.

Samuel stretched and threw off the covers, glancing around the room that was his growing up. It had been a couple of years since he was home, but everything was just as he remembered.

His room still had tell-tale signs of his youth, from the model airplanes hanging overhead to the model cars that filled the shelves over his desk. The baseball bat and glove still hung on the wall next to his high school Player of the Year plaque, and his guitar sat in the corner. He thought back to the time he wrote a song for his mom and sang it to her. She beamed with pride as she listened. She was his biggest fan.

Those were the good times, the days when his Mom was alive and well. But, Samuel didn't want to think about it. That was a painful memory of his past and the road he had traveled after that had turned his life into a living hell.

He had made his peace with God, but would forever be sorry for what he put his dad through at a time when his life was painful enough as it was. He would live the rest of his life trying to make it up to him.

Samuel thanked God every day for the outreach worker that had helped turn his life around. He had fought with him trying to turn him away, but the man was determined not to give up on him.

Samual had repaired his relationship with his father, and it was good again. His father had always been there for him, even during the times when he didn't appreciate it.

Samuel got out of bed and padded across the rug covering the highly polished wooden floor of the log house. He grabbed some clothes from his suitcase and went into the adjoining bathroom to shower.

He placed his clothes on the rack on the inside of the door, walked over and adjusted the water for his shower and got in. He let the hot spray cover his body, and he felt his tight muscles begin the ease up. As he scrubbed his body, his deep voice rang out with God's praises.

He was finally walking the path God had chosen for him. He was fortunate and brought many young people to the Lord with his music and words of inspiration. His father was proud of him. He only wished that his mother was alive to share in his joy. His mom didn't know sickness or pain anymore. God held her in his arms.

He was just getting out of the shower when he heard a knock on the door.

"Samuel, you about ready to eat breakfast? I know after your long drive, you have to be starving," Peter said.

"I'll be right out." He could smell the scent of coffee that crept through under the door.

He grabbed his razor and made a few swipes over his face clearing the stubble from the past couple of

171

day's growth. He put on blue jeans and a blue flannel shirt, rubbed some gel into his long black curls, and gave his reflection in the mirror a once over. His whirlwind performances left little time for shaving, but then with his schedule it rarely did. At least now, he had a couple of weeks break to spend with his dad until his next gig in Wyoming.

He opened the door of the bathroom crossing through his bedroom and entering the hall leading to the rest of the house. As he came into the kitchen with its high wood beamed ceiling, he saw his father taking the bacon out of the frying pan placing it on plates. Next to it was Samuel's favorite omelet and country fried potatoes.

"Well, Dad, it looks like you outdid yourself today," said Samuel.

His Dad grabbed the plates and placed them on the island and sat down next to Samuel. "Do you want to say the blessing, or should I?" he asked.

"Go ahead," Samuel said, bowing his head.

"Lord, thank you for this breakfast we are about to partake of and especially for bringing Samuel back to me for a visit. Bless his work Lord as he gives you all the glory. I pray in Jesus name. Amen." Peter looked over at his son, with a big smile on his face. "It's good to have you home, Son."

"It's good to be home, Dad. It's been far too long. I'm sorry I couldn't be here sooner, but at least I'm yours for the next couple of weeks. By the time I leave, you'll be ready to have the house back to yourself again," Samuel said, a laugh escaping his throat.

"Not a chance. We better eat this before it gets cold, after all, I did make your favorites," Peter said taking a bite of omelet.

"It's awesome, Dad," said Samuel placing another bite in his mouth.

They sat on the stools eating their breakfast and watched the snow fall outside. Winter in the Rockies could be brutal, but then Samuel was convinced it was the most beautiful place on earth. He had missed the home that contained the two-story A-Frame house and the Evans Auto Repair Service Shop. Most of all he missed getting his hands dirty helping his Dad repair automobiles.

His Dad was one of the best auto mechanics around and was highly respected in the community. The past couple of years he had slowed down some though, due to problems with his legs. The cold was starting to bother his arthritis, but he wasn't willing to quit, so he decided limiting his work during the winter would solve the problem and with the addition of a new heating system, it kept the work area toasty.

Samuel was happy that his dad had finally taken his advice. Samuel made a good living, and he always sent him money to help out. Of course, his dad would call and try to tell him that he didn't need it. Samuel kept giving it to him anyway.

They were just finishing up their breakfast when Peter's phone rang. He picked up his plate placing it in the sink to wash and then answered the phone.

"Hello, Peter, speaking," he said.

Peter stood holding the phone with a puzzled look on his face. "Okay, I'll let him know. Call me back later this afternoon after I talk to him," Peter said, hanging up the phone. He stood there wondering how best to tell Samuel.

"Dad is everything all right?" asked Samuel. His dad acted like the wind had been knocked out of him.

He couldn't imagine what could have shaken him up this bad.

"Son, let's have a seat in the living room. There is something that I need to talk to you about."

Samuel followed his dad into the large living room. Across one wall was a gigantic stone fireplace and overhead hung a five-point trophy buck. Samuel remembered the year his dad bagged that one. He was thirteen, and his dad had bought him his first rifle.

In the middle of the room hung a chandelier made of deer antlers and two matching lamps that were placed on end tables surrounding the oversized dark brown leather sectional.

The tall windows wrapped around the room providing fantastic views of the mountains. Across from the sofa facing the grey and white stone fireplace that reached from floor to ceiling, was a pair of matching brown leather chairs. Samuel had fond memories of curling up in one of the chairs as a young child, while his mom read to him.

Samuel and Peter sat in front of the fireplace. His dad who was jovial earlier was now pensive.

"Samuel, your mom and I have never lied to you about being adopted, and we always knew that sometime in the future someone from your biological family might contact you. That call was from Mr. Benson in Rustin. He's an attorney representing Allison Stevens," Peter said. He took a deep breath and continued, "It seems that your biological mother passed away. Allison ran across your birth certificate, and since you are a legal heir, she had her attorney try to find you. He wanted to know if you would be willing to go to Rustin to meet her."

Samuel was stunned. He never thought of his biological mother very often. Now she had died, and he had a sister. His mind was doing cartwheels, and his thoughts became jumbled. He gave himself a minute to clear his head before he spoke.

"Dad, did you know she had a daughter?" Samuel asked.

"Lucy mentioned her once, but she was graduating from high school and was leaving for college. By that time, we came to our senses and realized what a mistake we had made. We agreed that we would never see each other again. It's a mistake I have lived to regret the rest of my life. I hurt your mother deeply, but being the Christian woman that she was, she forgave me, and we put it behind us," Peter said. He couldn't hide the shame from Samuel. I was written all over his face.

"When did you find out about me?" asked Samuel. He was trying to piece things together. He knew he was adopted, but neither one of his parents had shared any details with him.

"It was almost a year later when Lucy called me one day at work. She was very distraught. Her conscience wouldn't let her keep the secret from her husband any longer, and she finally told him about us." Peter hung his head barely able to go on. His voice cracked as he continued.

"She was having a difficult time with her husband. He was working long hours and becoming less and less interested in their marriage. She was beginning to think he might be having an affair of his own. Of course, that wasn't the case."

175

"Lucy was eight months pregnant. She said I was the father and she had told her husband. He went into a rage and stormed out. She went to stay with her sister here in Denver, and when it was time, she checked into the hospital." Peter glanced over at Samuel and could see the confused look on his face.

"I went to see her. She had thought about keeping you but didn't think her husband would ever allow it. She said she couldn't give you up for adoption like he wanted her to do unless it was to me. I hesitated even bringing it up to your mother, but I didn't want to lose you. Your mother and I could never have children, and you were an answer to our prayers. Your mother accepted you as her own and never looked back. She loved you the moment she saw you." Peter waited patiently to see what Samuel would say next.

"Dad, I'm glad you stepped up and did the right thing. I have no regrets being raised by the both of you. I had a loving home. We all make mistakes and I know I wasn't the son you expected either. I know Mom loved you and she loved me with all her heart. Do I wish I could have met my biological Mom? Of course. But back when I was a teenager after mom died, I felt like my whole world ended. I know I should have let you help me, but I was so angry. I was angry at God for taking her away from us," Samuel said his voice strained. It was still hard to talk about his mom even now.

"Dad, you've always been there for me. I'm a Christian now, and God has been good to me. If my sister wants to see me, I'll meet with her, but I would like to have you there with me. I know it will dredge up old memories, and if you can't, I understand," said Samuel.

176

"If that's what you want, Samuel, you know I'll be there," Peter said.

"Thanks, Dad. It means a lot to me." He got up from his chair and placed his arms around his dad. "I guess you can go ahead and set up the meeting. The sooner, the better. I want to enjoy some time with you before my next show," Samuel said.

His dad smiled at him, patted him on the shoulder, and made the call.

Chapter 36

Allison was just leaving her Bible study group when her cell phone rang. She stopped momentarily in the corridor of the church and grabbed a nearby chair.

"Allison speaking."

"Hi, Allison. Mr. Benson. Do you have a few minutes to talk?"

Allison knew it had to be news about the meeting with her brother. She took a deep breath and answered, "Yes, go ahead." She leaned back against the back of the chair and patiently waited for his reply.

"I got a call today from Peter Evans. Your brother wants to set up a meeting as soon as possible. Peter will be joining him. How does Friday afternoon sound? That will give them a couple of days to prepare for the trip."

Allison was stunned. "I'm surprised to hear back so soon, but that will be fine. What time?"

"How about 4 o'clock. Does that work for you?

Since Allison knew she didn't have any plans for that time, she agreed. With the meeting all set, she disconnected the call and placed her cell phone in her purse.

She continued to sit in the chair glancing out the windows of the church. Only two days and she would finally be able to meet her brother. Also, she would get to meet the man that her mother had an affair with. She didn't know what she would feel when she saw him. After all, he was the one who contributed to the problems between her mother and father. She had to find a way to forgive him if she wanted a relationship with her brother.

While she sat absorbed in thought, she didn't hear the sound of soft soles on the carpet approaching her.

"Allison, are you okay? I thought you left already," said Brett, concern lacing his voice.

"I'm fine. I just had some surprising news, that's all," Allison said, as she got up from the chair and faced Brett. She loved the fact that he always had this tender side to him. He was so willing to help another in need.

"If you want to talk, you know I'm always here for you," he said.

"I know."

"Can I walk you out, I'm just leaving too. I have to pick Ebony up before I head home," Brett said walking towards the door.

Allison walked next to Brett, and when they reached the front door, he politely held the door open for her. They walked in parking lot engaged in a conversation about the study group. The small group had grown to over twenty-five, and more people were joining.

When Allison got to her car, Brett turned to walk away but stopped abruptly. Allison had unlocked her door and was about to get in.

"Allison, I hope this isn't too forward, but I wondered if you would go out to dinner with me."

Allison was taken off guard and at first, didn't quite know what to say. She turned to face him and replied, "That would be nice."

"Would tomorrow evening be too soon? I know a restaurant I've wanted to try out. Seven o'clock?"

Allison had butterflies in her stomach, and all of a sudden seemed to lose her voice, but mustered up enough to answer.

"That would be great."

"I'll pick you up around 6:30. See you then. Have a good evening, Allison," he said as he walked to his car.

Allison got into her car, started the engine and let it warm up, leaning back in the seat while she thought about the date. *Why, yes?* Now she would have to go through with it, w*hat if they didn't have enough in common? What if they did and it led to a more serious relationship?* She didn't know if she was ready for a commitment or if she could even make one.

Since her car was warmed up, she put it into gear and exited the lot. Through the headlights, she could see a dense fog building outside as she drove. She still wasn't comfortable driving at night, especially when she had to pass the place along the road where the incident had occurred. *How long would it plague me? Would I eventually be able to pass by without the memories rushing back to haunt me?* No, God would heal her from it. She would trust in his word.

She came to a stop light, and while she waited, she turned on the radio to a Christian station. She hummed as she drove the final couple of miles to her house. It still seemed odd to call it her house. Allison always thought of it as her mom's.

The town seemed quiet for 8 o'clock at night. Only a few customers exited the supermarket.

Rustin was a town she had lived in while she was growing up, yet now, people passed her every day, but there were so few that she knew. Of course, the town had grown while she was gone, with more businesses replacing the mom and pop stores that she remembered.

It was time to make new memories, and she would try her best to do just that. She would start with her brother. *What was he like?* At least they would have their faith to bring them together. God would be the center of their relationship, so how could it go badly?

Chapter 37

Allison tried to busy herself with menial tasks while she waited for the clock to tick down. Nervousness became her enemy. She tried her best to calm her nerves, but for some reason, her body wouldn't listen.

She had an hour left until Brett would be there to pick her up. She must have tried on every outfit in her closet before finally settling on a cute conservative blue dress with a matching jacket.

She gave her house the once over and thought of Ida. Ida would say, "A house can be tidy, but one wants to know it is lived in." A smile crossed her face as fond memories ran through her head. Ida was one in a million.

The house seemed too quiet. Allison went over and turned the television on the Christian music channel, and gospel sounds filled the house. Christian music always lifted her spirits.

Her nerves began to calm down, and she said a silent prayer for God to give her a sense of calm throughout her evening. It was the first date in a very long time. When was the last time?

It was a chilly Autumn day, and the leaves outside were beginning to turn beautiful colors of yellow, brown and golden orange. She never tired of looking at them. As she looked out the window, she saw a young boy ride by on his bicycle followed by another boy. It seemed as though they were in a race.

It had been a long time since she had ridden a bike. She remembered the one her Dad had bought her for her sixth birthday. It was pink and had leather streamers hanging from the handlebars.

Her father would push her from behind, and she sailed along not realizing he had let go. Just knowing he was back there gave her the confidence to go on. She smiled as she realized her Heavenly Father was a lot like that. He let her experience life on her own but was always there even when she didn't know it. He was there to pick her up when she fell.

Allison was reminiscing and almost didn't hear the knock on the front door. She left the room and went to answer it. When she opened the door, Brett was holding a bouquet of flowers.

"You look nice. These are for you," Brett said handing her the flowers.

"Thank you. I'll put the flowers in water, and then we can go," said Allison walking into the kitchen. She got a vase from under the sink, added some water and carefully placed the flowers inside. She had wondered if the blue dress that hugged her curves was the right choice. But then Brett said she looked nice.

Allison went back into the living room, grabbing her coat and purse. She followed Brett outside to his car. He went around to the passenger's side and held the door open for her before going around to the driver's side to get in. He was not only handsome but a gentleman.

"I made reservations at Gino's so we shouldn't have to wait long to get seated. I hope you like Italian food," Brett said, as he backed out of the driveway.

"It's one of my favorites. My dad used to take me to a small Italian restaurant for my birthday every year after I turned thirteen. I've loved Italian ever since."

Allison sat looking out the window. Gino's was just across town, and they sat in silence as Brett drove, only making eye contact a couple of times.

Brett signaled to turn right and pulled into Gino's parking lot. The lot was starting to fill up. A few couples were exiting their cars and making their way inside.

Gino's was a mom and pop restaurant that had managed to stay afloat even after the giant chains like Olive Garden opened in Rustin. Gino's had captured the heart of most of the locals, and they were loyal customers. They wouldn't dream of going anywhere else. Not only did Gino's have the best Italian food, but also the best customer service in town.

Allison's eyes widened as they exited the car. She realized that she knew the place. She had many birthday dinners there. The outside had changed a little over the years. The building had a bright new coat of paint, an addition of canopies over the front windows, and a new sign. She was sure it was the same place though. She couldn't wait to see what they had done with the inside.

"Brett, I can't believe it. I think this is the same place my dad used to take me," she said as they walked towards the front door.

"I hope it's okay, then. I know how hard it is to lose your dad. I lost mine when I was around sixteen. You can never fill the hole in your heart that they leave," he said opening the door for her to enter.

"Its fine," she said walking up to the counter next to Brett. "They were all good memories."

The restaurant interior was much different than she remembered. The ceiling had been lowered using drop panels held in place by wooden beams. The walls were a golden tone, and the carpet was light brown and plush. All the tables were covered with red linen tablecloths, and in the center of the table, candles glowed. It had more of a romantic ambiance to it than what she recalled.

"Mr. Collins, your table is ready," said the hostess. "Please follow me."

Bret had Allison go ahead of him, and when they reached the table, he pulled out a chair for her before taking the seat directly across from her. They were lucky enough to get a table facing the front windows that looked out into the courtyard.

In a matter of minutes, a waiter came to their table. "What can I get you to drink?" he asked.

"Just water for me," said Allison.

"Same for me," Brett added.

"Is the restaurant different than you expected?" asked Brett.

"They must have done a remodel since the last time I was here, but I like what they did. It looks great," Allison said. She didn't remember it having a courtyard either, so that must have been part of the remodel.

"Should we check out the menu?" Brett asked. "I've heard that the Rigatoni is good." Brett picked up the menu and looked through the listed dishes.

Allison picked up her menu. There were so many items to choose from. She finally decided to ask the waiter what the nightly special was.

The waiter returned and held a pad to take their order. "What can get you this evening?" he asked as he patiently stood next to their table. Another waiter hurried through holding a heavy tray filled with platters of hot food. He stepped aside to let him pass.

Brett motioned for Allison to order first.

"What is your nightly special or what do you recommend?" asked Allison looking up at the waiter.

"I would highly recommend this evening's special, "Rigatoni with Pomodoro sauce. If you like shrimp, I would recommend that you add that as well."

"I would like an order with the shrimp, please," replied Allison.

"I'll have the same, thank you," Brett said handing him the menus.

The waiter wrote the order on his pad, collected the menus, and smiled before walking away.

With their orders out of the way, Allison glanced towards the table closest to her. A couple stared dreamily into each other's eyes as their hands lightly touched. It was apparent that they were very much in love. A yearning for a real love like that stirred inside her.

"Well, we will be working together soon. I was so surprised when Ida left money to the church. Now we can do the expansion that is so badly needed," Brett said.

"I was surprised too when Rev. Williams asked me to be a part of the staff. I was waiting for my release from the doctor, so I could start job hunting. Now, I won't have to."

"I understand that Carol will be helping as a consultant. She will be a big help to us, but I'm surprised she has the time."

186

"She has been a good friend," said Allison taking a sip of water.

The waiter brought the meal. Allison and Brett talked in between bites of food and when they were just about finished, Brett, leaned in toward Allison.

"Do you have plans for the rest of the evening, or would you like to watch a movie at the house with Ebony and me?" He smiled at Allison waiting for a reply.

Allison thought a moment before answering. "I would love to?" She couldn't refuse when those dark eyes seemed to make her melt, and his voice made her feel so safe.

Chapter 38

Brett pulled up in front of a two-story house in one of the best neighborhoods in Rustin. The home was nicely landscaped and had a circular driveway.

He put the car in park, got out and went around to the passenger's side to open the door for Allison. He led her up the front steps, holding the front door open for her to enter.

Brett's home was very organized in spite of the fact that he was a single father with a young child.

Allison sat on the leather sofa facing the fireplace and watched the flames as they bounced and flickered while she waited for Brett to check on Ebony.

"Well, it seems like she is out for the night. I'm sorry she won't be able to join us. My mom is lying down with her," Brett said.

"Does your mom live here with you?" asked Allison.

"Yes. After my wife died, I was going through a difficult time. My mom was living alone in a house much too big for her after my dad died, and it just seemed like the logical solution. It's worked out well for all of us," Brett said taking a seat next to Allison on the sofa.

"Can I get you anything?" Brett asked.

"I'm fine, thanks. Dinner was wonderful. I had a nice time," Allison said leaning back against the sofa. "You have a beautiful home."

"I can't take credit for the decorating. That was all Vicky. I haven't had the heart to change anything. I felt it would be better for Ebony leaving things the way they were," Brett said. His eyes held sadness when he spoke of her.

All through the room, Allison could see touches that were female inspired. From the decorated photo frames that housed what appeared to be vacation photos at the beach, to beautiful wreaths that seemed to be homemade. Her presence was everywhere. Allison wondered if it were possible for Brett to be open to another serious relationship. Maybe she wasn't realistic, but only God knew what was in his heart.

"Blame it on my counseling, but I haven't been able to stop thinking about the day I found you deep in thought after our bible group, and you didn't want to talk. Do you feel comfortable talking about it now?" Brett asked.

Allison was taken by surprise. She needed to talk to someone, but was Brett, the right person? If they were going to have a relationship she had to trust him. He wasn't there to judge her. She knew that in her heart. If they began a relationship, she would want him to meet her brother.

"Brett, there are some things about my mom you don't know. Rev Williams doesn't even know. I was having a hard time coming to grips with the truth."

Allison spent the next half hour pouring her heart out about her mom's secret, her brother, and the upcoming meeting, in between moments of tears. Brett sat silent and let her talk.

"I can't say I understand what you have been going through, but I do know that God is there to help you during your time of difficulties. Maybe, he even arranged for you to be able to meet your brother. His ways are beyond what we can comprehend, but they always are in our best interests," Brett said putting his arms around Allison and holding her close.

Allison leaned into him, and it seemed a natural act. He was reliable, safe, and comforting. It's the first time she had been able to let go of her fear of getting close to someone again. God was beginning to heal her, and she liked how it felt.

Allison eyes now held the light of hope. She had found someone to trust with her heart, a godly man.

It was around 3:45 p.m. the next day when Allison pulled up in the parking lot of Mr. Benson's office.

She got out of the car and walked up to the front doors of the building. The receptionist greeted her as she entered and told her that Mr. Benson was waiting for her in his office.

Allison dressed in a blue sweater, and grey slacks, topped off by her high heeled boots walked towards the office. She unbuttoned her coat and pulled off her scarf before entering.

"Allison, have a seat. Your brother and his father just called. They had to make a quick stop and are running a little late, but should be here anytime." Mr. Benson called his secretary. "Jennifer, hold all my calls. When Peter and Samuel Evans get here, direct them to my office," he said hanging up the phone. "I'm sorry to keep you waiting. How are you holding up?" he asked.

"I'm nervous but excited. I'll be glad to get it over though, whatever the outcome, so I can go on with my life," Allison said getting comfortable in the chair while she's waited.

"To put your mind at ease, when I spoke to Samuel and his father, Peter, they were very gracious and seemed excited to meet you as well. I think this will be good for all of you. If you will excuse me, I need to make a couple of quick calls while we wait."

"Sure. If you can tell me where the restrooms are, I'll be right back," Allison said getting up.

"Just down the hall, the last door on the right," said Mr. Benson.

Allison hung her coat on the back of her chair and laid her scarf on top of it before opening the door to leave.

She walked down the hallway and entered the bathroom. She went over to the large mirror hanging over the sink and checked out her reflection. Her stomach was doing flip-flops. *God, please give me the strength I need to go through this. I know you are with me. I trust you.*

Allison got a paper towel and ran it underneath the cold water. She ran it around her neck enjoying the coolness. She took a deep breath and walked out of the restroom back into the hallway.

She approached the office and slowly opened the door. When she faced the two men seated before Mr. Benson, a gasp escaped her throat. It couldn't be.

Chapter 39

Allison stood there unable to speak or move and couldn't believe what her eyes were taking in. Could that be her brother sitting next to the older man with graying hair? Maybe it was just a coincidence-maybe he just happened to resemble him, but those grey eyes were telling her different.

"Allison, come in," said Mr. Benson.

Allison came into the room and took a seat just across from Samuel and his father. She sat, stunned.

"Welcome, everyone. Allison recently inherited some property from her mother's estate. Per her request after we found out she had other living relatives, she wanted them to be included as heirs," said Mr. Benson. He looked over at Allison, "Allison, if you would like to explain your intentions, I'll turn it over to you."

Allison was still shaken and wondered how she was going to go about finding out if her suspicions were correct or not. She glanced over at Samuel and Peter.

"I had you come here today so we could meet and get to know each other. Samuel, I would like to put your name on the deed along with mine as the owner of the house passed on to me by my mother. It's not much, but I want to be fair," Allison said wondering what his response would be.

"Allison, I appreciate the offer, but I'm going to have to decline. I've had a good life with my mom and dad. I have a very successful career, and I don't need the money. I haven't had any contact with my biological mother, and you have more claim to her estate than I do. I'm happy with just getting to know you."

Allison had to know what he did for a living. It would clear up her suspicions. Now was the time to ask.

"If you don't mind my asking, what is it that you do?" Allison asked feeling uncomfortable as she waited for his response.

"Not at all, I'm a Christian singer. You may have heard of me if you listen to Christian music. Our band is Joyful Noise, and I go by the stage name of Evan Storm."

Allison's heart raced inside her chest. Wow, her brother was Evan Storm, her favorite Christian singer. What were the odds?

After she composed herself enough to speak, she said, "I wondered when I first walked in but thought maybe you just happened to look like him. I listen to your music all the time on the Christian music station," said Allison.

"Well, since we don't have any changes to make to the deed, I guess we can wrap this up so you can go and get acquainted," said Mr. Benson. He got up from his desk and shook hands with Samuel and Peter. He hugged Allison and opened the door for them.

Allison looked up and said, "Thank You."

"You're welcome, Allison. Glad I could help."

Allison, Samuel, and Peter walked out to the parking lot together.

The wind had come up since they had entered the building and Allison quickly put her coat on buttoning up as they walked. She placed her scarf back around her neck.

"Allison, we would be honored if you would join us for lunch. We would like to spend some time with you if you don't have any other plans," said Samuel. Peter nodded his approval.

"I don't have any plans and would love to. I can follow you. Where would you like to go?" Allison asked. She was feeling more comfortable now, and there was so much she wanted to know about Samuel.

"We passed an Italian restaurant on the way here. I think it was Gino's. Would that be okay?"

"That's fine."

Samuel and Peter walked over to their Ford pickup and got in. Allison got into her car and started it up, and a few minutes later she was following them across town.

Allison's mind was racing. She was almost too excited to contain herself while driving. She took a breath and thanked God for all the blessings in her life. Now God had returned her brother to her, and she had a real family again.

The lunch with her brother and his father went amazingly better than she could have ever hoped. Samuel's father reminded her a lot of her dad. He had graying hair, a positive outlook, and pride of his family. She could sense the great love he had for his son, and his faith in God.

Samuel talked about how his father and mother had prayed for him to find God, and that when he hit rock bottom, he had turned to Jesus for salvation.

Peter told her about his auto repair business and how Samuel had been a great help until his career took off. She could see he was very proud of the man he had become.

They exchanged addresses and phone numbers and agreed to get together again. Allison had an open invitation to join them in Denver anytime. She promised to come for a visit before Samuel went back on the road.

Allison gave them both a hug, which they eagerly returned. With smiles on their faces, they went back to their truck, waving as they got in.

Allison got into her car. Started it up and headed for home. She couldn't wait to tell Carol about their meeting.

Her head was still reeling. She finally had most of the answers to the questions that had weighed heavily on her mind. God was good. He provided blessings that seemed to keep running over.

Chapter 40

It had been a few days since the meeting with Samuel and his father. If she wanted to see Samuel before he left on his tour, she had to make the arrangements soon.

She picked up the phone and called the number he gave her.

"Hi Mr. Evans, it's Allison, I hope I'm not calling at a bad time," she said.

"Please, call me, Peter. What a nice surprise," he said.

"The reason I'm calling, is I wondered if it would be a good time to come for a visit. I could stay a couple of days if that's okay. I know Samuel has to leave soon," said Allison. Allison wondered if it might be awkward staying at the house with them. Even though they were no longer strangers, she didn't know what to expect. She had only been to Denver once to visit her aunt, and she imagined it had changed a lot over the years.

"That sounds wonderful. I know Samuel will be pleased. He hasn't stopped talking about you since we were in Rustin. Be sure and call when you get into town so Samuel can meet you. When will you be here?" said Peter.

"I'm leaving the day after tomorrow and should be there by early afternoon. See you then," said Allison hanging up the phone. Now all she had to do was pack. The GPS she bought for the car would take her on the shortest possible route.

Her thoughts wandered to Brett. She hadn't spoken to him since the meeting. She missed him, which surprised her. They weren't in a relationship, but she had grown close to him in the short time they had known each other.

It was 3:30 p.m. when Allison gathered up some clothes for the washer. While they washed, she grabbed a sweatshirt and made her way out to the backyard.

She went to her favorite spot-the gazebo- and sat looking up at the sky. It was a cold, cloudy day, but inside her heart, the sun was shining.

Alison bowed her head and spoke to God. He would always come first in her life. She had learned some valuable lessons from the Heavenly Spirits and the Holy Spirit that dwelt inside of her. Through reading God's word, she had become strong and felt she could face most anything.

God, thank you for bringing Samuel and his father into my life. And also, Brett. I promise to ask for your guidance in all things instead of going forward blindly. Thanks for sending your Heavenly Spirits to counsel me, and to help me get me on the right path. I will honor you in everything I do, and if I fall, I know you will be there to pick me up. I will try each day to become the best follower of Christ I can be. In Jesus name. Amen.

Allison raised her head up, and a soft breeze blew leaves from the trees around her. She watched as they floated to the ground. It was getting closer to winter. Soon the trees would be bare, waiting for the rebirth of spring.

She took a few minutes to speak to her father.

Daddy, I met my brother a couple of days ago. You would have liked him, Dad. I didn't think my heart would ever heal when I lost you and Mom, but now I'm not alone anymore. I still miss you every day, but God is with me, and I understand how Mom had such strong faith. I don't know if you made things right with God before you died, but I have to believe you did.

With a chill in the air, Allison rose from the gaze-bo and went back into the house. She walked over and took the phone from the receiver in the kitchen and dialed Brett's number. A few seconds later, a small, girl's voice answered.

"Hello. Who is this?' asked Ebony.

"Hi Ebony, it's Allison. Is your Dad there?" asked Allison.

"He's in the shower. Do you want me to go get him?"

"That's okay, honey. I'll call back in a little bit."

"Okay," said Ebony. Allison heard the clank of the phone as she hung up.

Allison started her dinner. She would have time to eat before she called Brett back.

She set the timer on the oven and went into the living room to read her Bible. The bible class was studying John 14 about walking in the fullness of the spirit.

Jesus had referred to the Holy Spirit as another helper. When she felt helpless, she knew the Holy Spirit was there to lend her a helping hand and strengthen her when she needed it. *Why has it taken me so long to realize it?*

Allison was deep in her study when the timer for the oven went off. She put her Bible down and went to retrieve her dinner.

She placed her dinner on a plate, grabbed herself a glass of milk, and bowed her head to pray. *Lord, bless this food I'm about to eat. Let all the glory go to you for everything in my life. With you all things are possible. I pray in Jesus name. Amen.*

She finished her dinner in silence, grateful for how her life had turned out so far. She had many friends now that God had sent into her life and she was thankful for them. When she needed support, they were always there for her.

She was just finishing up her dishes when her cell phone rang. She walked over to the table, picked it up. Carol's sweet voice rang through on the other end.

"So good to hear from you, how are you?" asked Allison. She took her phone and walked over to the couch and sat down.

"I'm good but busy. Our new funding went through, and we are swamped with applications. There is more of a need than I even expected," said Carol. "We will be processing forms for quite a while."

"That's great, can't wait until you come here to help us get our program going. Brett said it will probably be another week or so before they break ground for the new building. We will be working out the other details for administering services before it's done," said Allison.

"Speaking of Brett, how is it going between you? Anything you want to tell me about?" asked Carol teasing.

"We're just friends right now. We went to dinner this last week at Gino's and then over to his house. We were supposed to watch a movie with Ebony, but she fell asleep," said Allison.

"Dinner and his house, huh! Sounds like more than just friends to me," said Carol.

"I'm taking it slow. Brett hasn't given me any inclination that he wants anything more. His mom lives with him and takes care of Ebony while he works," said Allison. "It's an arrangement that's worked out well for both of them."

"How did your meeting go with your brother?" asked Carol.

"It went great. You won't believe it. Do you remember the music cd you gave me of Joyful Noise?"

"Yes," answered Carol.

"The lead singer, Eric Storm, is my brother. It's his stage name," said Allison, the excitement rising in her voice.

"What! Wow! I can't believe it. What's he like? Is he as handsome in person?"

"He is, but he is so down to earth, and you can just see the light of Jesus shine through him. His dad, Peter, was so sweet and reminds me of my dad. I'm leaving tomorrow for a visit," said Allison.

"God is sure working on you, girl. Can't wait to see what he does next. I have to run. Give me a call when you get back."

"I will. Love you."

"Love you too. Bye," said Carol hanging up.

Allison disconnected the call and placed her phone on the coffee table. Could Carol be right? Could her relationship with Brett be changing and moving towards a romantic one?

Chapter 41

Allison talked to Brett later that afternoon. He was happy for her and told her to drive safely and to have a great visit. His last comment before hanging up surprised her. He said he would miss her.

Allison hoped that during her visit, she would have a chance to ask Peter some questions about her mom. There were still some things she would like to put behind her. It might be difficult though talking to him with Samuel there. She didn't know what he had told him.

She plugged in her destination to map her route on the GPS. It would take around two hours to get there.

Since it was October, there was a good chance of a freak snowstorm, so she packed some heavier sweaters and jeans. She had loaded emergency supplies- water, food, blankets, and a first aid kit. When she checked the weather channel, it said that Denver already had a few inches on the ground, but that the roads were clear.

That night Allison went to bed early to get a good night's sleep. It was her first road trip, but she was confident everything would be fine.

Sometimes, she looked into the mirror and hardly recognized the woman looking back at her. She was more confident, loving, and had a renewed sense of faith.

She fluffed up her pillow, turned on her side, and smiled. *So, Mom. Now I know how you coped with all your trials. I understand where your faith came from and how in spite of things, you always seemed happy. It was your faith in God!*

Lord keep me safe tomorrow. Guide my path. Give me the right words for the day and in everything may I remember to give you the honor. In Jesus name. Amen.

She had just finished her prayer when she felt God talking back to her. *What? Don't ask me to do that, Lord. How can I help him? I know he needs you, but how can I help after what he did to me? Okay, Lord, I'll try. I know you will be with me.*

Allison went to sleep that night knowing she had a difficult job ahead discussing God's will for her with Samuel. *Would he understand and be willing to help?*

It was 6 a.m. when Allison's alarm clock signaled it was time to get up. She took her shower and dressed in a warm sweatshirt and jeans.

She entered the kitchen and filled her travel mug with the hot tea she had brewed earlier.

She did a double check to make sure everything in the house was turned off and that the door to the garage was locked. When she was sure everything was secure, she put on her jacket, grabbed her purse, mug, and suitcase and headed for the door.

As she opened the door, she felt a cold blast of air hit her. The temperature had dropped down during the night, and there was no sun out yet to help take the edge off.

She maneuvered her way down the front steps and set her mug on the roof of the car while she placed her suitcase in the back. She made a second trip back to the house for the pillow and blanket she had sitting on the sofa.

Locking the front door after her, she walked to the car and placed the items on the back seat next to her suitcase. Okay, suitcase, check-blankets, and pillow-check. Food and water on the floor-board of the back seat-check.

With the knowledge that everything she needed was in the car, she started it and let it warm up. She turned on the defroster to clear the condensation from the window. There was only one stop to make. She needed gas for the trip.

Allison stopped at the Rustin Quick Stop and topped off her tank. The gas station was filled with motorists getting their daily coffee fixes and gas before heading to work. She had to wait in line to pay for her purchase. When the transaction was completed the cashier flashed her a smile and said, "Have a nice day."

Allison replied, "Same to you," as she continued out the door.

She walked across the parking lot dodging cars coming and going. One driver did an annoying honk as she waited for the vehicle to pass. She didn't let it get to her, but continued to her car and got in.

She exited the lot pulling out into the street. After a couple of blocks, the traffic thinned out some, and she entered the exit merging onto the freeway.

Allison reached over and turned on the radio, and within seconds soothing Christian music filled the inside of the car. She smiled later on when they played Joyful Noise's latest release. She would never hear the band's music again without feeling a great sense of warmth and love fill her.

She glanced at the landscape as she traveled along the freeway. The scenery had changed a little now from Rustin's valley landscape and started to show part of the incredible Rocky Mountains.

Allison loved the mountains. Majestic and tall rising above the landscape, their peaks dotted with a powdering of freshly fallen snow, always made her feel closer to God. She couldn't wait to get to Samuel's. They lived on the outskirts of town so she would be able to enjoy the outdoors and was looking forward to afternoon walks.

As she got closer to Denver, the traffic became more intense, and she had to keep a close eye on the road. Her GPS warned her of the turnoff onto Grandview Avenue, and she started to merge, coming to a stop at the light. She did a right-hand turn, went down about two blocks, and parked next to "Milo's Bakery."

Allison grabbed her purse off the seat and got out. The bakery was a quaint place with bright blue colored shutters on the windows and a front window stenciled with pictures of bagels, donuts, and cups of steaming coffee. It was perfect to get a cup of tea and call Samuel to let him know she had arrived.

Allison opened the door and entered. Inside people were milling around. Some were ordering their selections, while others were seated at the tables. There was a garden area in the back that seemed to be almost full. She hoped that she could still find a seat there.

"Good morning. How may I help you?" asked the cashier. She was an older woman, probably in her sixties, and had a beautiful smile. She made her feel welcome.

"I would like a cup of tea and one of your blueberry scones, please," Allison said when she finished reading the overhead menu.

"That will be $4.69. Is that for here or to go?" asked the cashier.

"For here," replied Allison as she opened her purse and pulled out a five-dollar bill laying it on the counter. She waited while the cashier got her order ready.

The cashier brought her order, took the money and returned Allison's change to her. Allison thanked her and made her way outside to the garden area. At the back, she found an empty table and took a seat.

The air had a crispness to it but wasn't too cold. The sun was out, and the warmth hit her face as she sipped the warm tea. She took a bite of her scone, which was delicious.

She set her teacup down and fished her phone out of her pocket dialing Samuel's number. She took another sip of tea while she waited for him to answer.

"Peter, speaking," he said.

"Hi, Peter. It's Allison. I'm at Milo's Bakery on Grandview Avenue," said Allison.

"I'll send Samuel right away. He should be there in a few minutes," Peter said. "See you soon," he said before hanging up.

Allison disconnected the call, finished her tea and scone, and twisted through the crowd now gathered inside the bakery until she was outside. She got into her car and waited.

Chapter 42

Samuel pulled off the road and continued down Vista Way. About halfway down he made a sharp left and pulled into the parking area in front of a large two-story log home and shop with a sign that read Evans Auto Repair. Allison pulled in behind him and parked.

Allison was taken in by the view and the rustic look of the log home. Its reddish wood held a brilliant sheen, and her eyes rose to the second-floor decks above. A set of stairs wove its way to the ground below.

A sense of peacefulness enveloped her as she got out. The ground had a light sprinkling of new snow, and her boots sank in as she made her way towards Samuel's truck.

"Did you have a good trip?" asked Samuel hugging her.

"I did," she said hugging him back.

"Where's your luggage and I'll carry it in," asked Samuel walking towards her car.

"It's on the backseat on the driver's side."

Samuel retrieved her luggage, and they walked beside each other up the steps leading to the massive front door.

As they stepped inside and entered the foyer, Allison was in awe at how beautiful the place was. The odor of fresh pine and coffee filled the air. Samuel set her luggage down.

"The guest room is upstairs. When you're ready, I'll show you to your room. I know Dad is excited to see you again. You're the first visitor we've had in a while."

Just then, Peter, hearing voices, made his way into the foyer.

"Wonderful, you're here," he said walking over and hugging Allison.

Allison hugged him back and smiled. She pulled off her coat and gloves, placing them on the coat rack by the door and removed her boots.

"Well, let's go into the living room," said Peter leading the way.

Peter took a seat on the sofa and Allison, and Samuel got seated in the armchairs by the fireplace.

Allison admired the gorgeous grey and white river rock stone fireplace reaching from floor to ceiling. A crackling fire danced inside filling the room with warmth. She had no feelings of being uncomfortable as she thought she would. The home was warm, inviting, and felt filled with love.

The Evans had impeccable taste, from the natural wood of the walls encompassing the home, to the accessories that completed it. She couldn't help but feel drawn to the chandelier hanging over the sectional. It was made from antlers, and there was a lamp on each end table that matched.

"Peter, your home is beautiful. I love the cabin feel and all the natural wood. There is only an occasional log home where I live. There are mostly, historic 1800's homes in the downtown area. Granted, they are lovely, but I prefer the rustic look," Allison said shifting in her chair as she made eye contact with Peter.

207

"I'm glad you like it. It's been my home for over thirty years. My wife, Maggie, loved it here," said Peter with a sad look in his eyes.

"If you don't mind my asking, what was Maggie like," asked Allison. She was curious what kind of person raised her brother.

"She would have loved you. She had an outgoing personality and faith that was unshakeable. Her only regret was the fact that we couldn't have children. She had so much love in her heart to give, and I know it saddened her every day."

"When your mother contacted me to take Samuel, I couldn't believe our good fortune. Then I got worried about how Maggie would react to having a son that wasn't technically our own. Being the good Christian woman that she was, she forgave me and fell in love with Samuel the moment she set eyes on him. We brought him home and never looked back. He is the love of my life," Peter said smiling at Samuel.

"What about you, Allison. Did you have a good life with your parents?" asked Peter.

"Yes, for most of it. My dad was a loving and gentle man. My mom also had unshakeable faith, but I can't understand why she lied to me about Samuel. Now, I realize that because of her faith, she felt ashamed and didn't want me to think badly of her. I can't imagine the pressure she was under at the time. It had to be so hard to give Samuel up," Allison said as her eyes began to tear up. "I'm just glad that she thought enough of you to ask you to take him and that Maggie was okay with it."

"Your mother was a good woman. We weren't together very long, but I had a lot of respect for her.

She asked God's forgiveness for her mistake and tried to do the right thing," said Peter. "I'm grateful every day for Samuel."

"I saw my father a few months before he passed away. He had just built a gazebo in the backyard for my mother. It was her favorite spot, and I got the feeling that things were good between them again. They seemed more like the parents I grew up with. I think my father must have regretted asking her to do something she didn't want to do," said Allison.

"I'm glad that they had a good life in the end. With forgiveness from God, anything can be whole again. I know God healed our marriage and made it better," Peter said. "Well, anyone ready for lunch? I've got a large shrimp salad in the refrigerator. Are you okay with shrimp? I do have meats for sandwiches if you would rather have that," asked Peter.

"Shrimp salad sounds wonderful," replied Allison.

"Great. Let's head to the kitchen then."

They gathered at the kitchen table and passed the shrimp salad around, followed by fresh French bread and ice tea. Allison, Samuel, and Peter bowed their heads in thanks, while Peter said the prayer. "Dear Lord. Please bless us as we partake of this meal. Thank you, Lord, for bringing Allison into our lives and reuniting our family. Help us each day to walk on your chosen path for us. To you only goes the glory. I pray in Jesus name. Amen."

They spent part of the afternoon catching up on lost time and getting to know each other better. Not only had God brought her back to her brother, but he was part of a family who knew and praised God. She felt blessed and knew her mom was smiling down from above.

After lunch, Samuel, asked Allison if she wanted to take a short walk around the property. Peter left to take a nap while they were gone.

Allison and Samuel stepped off the front porch. The sun was shining overhead, and the snow glistened in the distance laying in small mounds along the side of the pathway leading out into the meadow. As they walked, Allison took a moment to gaze at the aspen trees now powdered with fresh snow.

"It must have been wonderful growing up here and getting to see this every day," Allison said as the sound of their boots crunched the snow below their feet as they walked.

"It was great. It was like having a giant playground. When friends came to stay the night, my dad used to come out here with us and built a bonfire and told us stories. We camped in tents overnight. It was awesome. There is something just a little farther up the road I would like to show you if you're up to it," said Samuel grabbing Allison's hand is his.

"Sure. Lead the way."

Chapter 43

Samuel led Allison around a bend in the path. They walked hand in hand for a few more minutes and then the trail opened up in front of a flowing creek.

Aspen and cottonwood trees lined the body of water on both sides, all dressed in the fall colors of orange and yellow. Along the creek, a sparse layer of snow lined the edge of the creek bank. Beyond in the distance, Allison could see the mighty peaks of the mountain range, covered with swatches of snow.

The air was crisp, and she drew in a breath of the clean air. She could hear the flow of water as it swiftly ran across the rocks.

She glanced to the left and was surprised to see a treehouse in a nearby tree. A ladder going up the tree, complete with climbing rungs all constructed from wood, gave access to the structure.

"How are you at climbing? Samuel asked, flashing Allison a grin.

"I'm okay. What's up there?" asked Allison walking over to the tree to get a better look.

"Come up and see," he said.

Allison moved out of the way as Samuel climbed the ladder. He waited at the top to make sure Allison was behind him. Allison reached the top, and Samuel pulled her up onto the platform.

She entered the tree house. Inside was a bench that wrapped around one side. As she glanced at the wall, the photo of a woman caught her eye.

"Is that your mom?" Allison asked.

"Yes. This was my special place when I was young. Anytime I needed to be alone to think something out, I came here. After my mom died, I spent a lot of time here. I didn't want to cry in front of my dad, so I came here instead. My dad and I built this when I was ten."

"When did you find out you were adopted?" asked Allison.

"It was a few months before my mom died. She wanted me to know the truth, and it was easier with the both of them to explain it to me. They offered to take me to see your mother, but I didn't want to see her. They were my parents, and that was all I needed. Now I wish I would have gone," Samuel said. He took a minute to gather his thoughts and continued. "After mom died, I felt God was punishing me for not seeing my real mom. I felt like that was why he took my mom away from me."

"Did your dad help you understand?"

"He tried but I wouldn't listen, and then I started hanging out with a bad crowd at school. I did manage to graduate by the skin of my teeth, but after it was party time. I was never home. The next thing I knew, I was sitting in jail facing a prison sentence. It broke my dad's heart. He was still trying to cope with losing my mom."

"What changed everything for you?" asked Allison. She was curious to find out what got him on the right path.

"I had been in prison about three months. The reality of knowing that this was my life for the remainder of my sentence began to sink in. It was hell. I felt in my heart that I didn't belong there, but I didn't know what to do with the time. I was seeing a counselor, but I wasn't cooperating." Samuel ran his hand through his hair pushing it out of his face. "Then I had a visit from a counselor from the Prison Outreach Program through a local church. He brought me a bible and a couple of magazines on salvation. At first, I was turned off. I didn't want anything to do with the God thing."

"Did you talk to him?"

"I was filled with hate and threw them at him. He just stood there not saying a word. He left them on the floor where they landed and turned to face me. He left his card and said when I wanted to talk to give him a call. He said there was nothing I did in my past to keep God from forgiving me and that he loved me. Then he walked out."

"Did you read what he had left? Obviously, something happened to change your life," said Allison. She wanted to know if God had spoken to his heart or if this counselor had led him back to Christ.

"Like I said, I had a lot of time on my hands. In my lonely cell, reading was the only thing to occupy my time. One night, I got this urge to read one of the booklets on salvation that he left and it got me thinking. My mom and dad were Christians. I was raised in the church, so I had some exposure to God and Jesus. There was a prayer for salvation in the back of the book, and I decided that I wanted to change my life. I asked for forgiveness and agreed to turn my life over to God. From that day forward, I was a model prisoner and even led a couple of other prisoners to Christ."

"So, what do you do now when you're not touring?" asked Allison.

"I work in the Prison Outreach Program through our local church. I wanted to help pass on the gift of salvation to other prisoners that have lost their way so that maybe they can help others. It is liberating knowing you make a difference and the glory all goes to God. Without him, I couldn't do it." Samuel reached over and placed his hand on top of Allison's and gave it a light squeeze. "Well, should we get down from here. We probably should be getting back."

"Okay. I think my legs are going to sleep. Is it my imagination or is it getting colder in here?" said Allison getting up from the seat.

"You know, I think you're right. Guess I'm not as young as I think," Samuel said laughing.

Allison climbed down from the tree house with Samuel right behind her.

They made their way back to the house, and after removing their boots which were covered in snow, they entered the living room. Peter was laying on the sectional watching a Christian movie on the television.

"You're back. How was your walk?" Peter asked.

"Great. I showed Allison my old tree house," Samuel said.

"It was great, and a beautiful spot," Allison said as she stood by the fire to warm up.

"The weather forecast predicts another two or three inches of snow tonight. I went ahead and put your suitcase up in the guest room while you were gone," said Peter getting up from the sectional.

"I'll show you to your room. There are fresh towels in the bathroom if you want to freshen up," said Samuel walking towards the staircase.

"A hot shower sounds good right now. Thanks," said Allison as she followed Samuel to her room.

Samuel opened a door at the top of the stairs on the left. It was a big room very well decorated. The walls had been painted a pale green. A large wooden poster bed was in the middle of the room with two matching nightstands.

Across on the other wall was a huge armoire, as well as, a regular closet. There was an adjoining bathroom with a large corner garden tub that had a window that looked out towards the mountains. Candles lined a shelf behind the bathtub, and there were more on the counter by the double sink. Across the room was an enclosed walk-in shower.

"I'm going to take a shower too," said Samuel as he walked out the door shutting it behind him.

Chapter 44

With her shower done and dressed in loose fitting slacks and a casual shirt, she unpacked her clothes and headed downstairs. As she entered the living room, Samuel was placing some logs on the fire.

She walked up and stood next to him by the fireplace. He was comfortably dressed in dark blue pants and a tee shirt.

Samuel finished putting new logs on the fire and took a seat in one of the side chairs. Allison joined him in the other one.

"Well, you look refreshed after our hike," said Samuel.

"You too. Where's Peter?" she asked.

"Oh, he's out puttering around in the shop. He doesn't have any customers right now while I'm here, so he decided to clean up a bit. I think he gets restless sometimes and has to feel useful," said Peter.

"I hope I'm not prying too much, but is there anyone special in your life?"

"There doesn't seem to be time. Of course, there are girls backstage always hanging around. When the right girl comes along, I'll be ready to commit," said Samuel. "Speaking of concerts, how would you like to come to the next one in Wyoming as my guest. I would love to have you there."

"I would love it. Seeing you play in person has always been a dream of mine. I'm quite the fan you know. Of course, that was even before I found out you were my brother," Allison said flashing a big smile. "I just have one request. Would it be possible to get two extra tickets? I have a friend and his daughter I would like to invite."

"No problem. I'll send the tickets to you in the mail. By the way, who is the lucky man?"

"Not a boyfriend, just a friend. We will be running the new outreach center our church is having built. The pastor knew I would be looking for a job and offered it to me. Brett also teaches the Bible study group that I'm in. He's a great guy," Allison replied. She was feeling a little uncomfortable talking to her brother about a possible love life.

"Would you like a cup of tea? I'm going to see if Dad left any coffee."

"Sure," said Allison following him into the kitchen.

Samuel busied himself in the kitchen warming up the kettle for Allison's tea as he poured himself a cup of coffee. As it was the last cup and he knew his father would be coming in soon, he put on another pot to brew.

"Samuel, can I talk to you about something that has been bothering me," said Allison fixing her cup of tea. She took a seat at the breakfast bar.

"Sure can," he said taking a seat next to her.

Allison had to think a moment about what she wanted to say. She didn't want to come off as a crazy person or pressure him into agreeing to something he might not want to do.

"You don't know anything about this, but about a month ago, I was robbed at gunpoint. The young man would have killed me except for the fact that the gun malfunctioned. He had rammed my car, knocking me into a tree. They caught him, and I had to identify him at the police department. It was one of the hardest things I ever had to do," said Allison as she waited for his response before going on with the rest of her story.

"What an ordeal? I'm assuming then that you weren't badly hurt," said Samuel reaching over and placing a hand on her shoulder.

"I had some strained muscles and a concussion, but the ordeal of the trauma, took much longer for me to get over. Some of it, I'm still dealing with," said Allison shifting around in her seat facing Samuel.

"I know you are a Christian and I hope you don't think I've lost my mind, but over the past year, I've been visited by several Heavenly Spirits. They all had a special message just for me-lessons I needed to learn about God and his word. Anyway, the other night while I was praying, I heard God speak to me loud and clear. He has requested me to do something. I tried to tell him I wasn't up to the task, but he insisted I was. You're in prison outreach and to do this, I need your help," said Allison, the pain showing in her eyes.

"I don't think you are crazy. My mom used to talk to me about Spirits when I was a teenager. She believed in them. The day she passed away she saw a Spirit motioning for her to come," said Samuel his voice breaking up as he tried to keep his composure.

Allison explained to him about God wanting her to visit Romero in prison. She could see his expression change as she told him the details of what God wanted her to do.

"Allison, what you want to do is admirable, and I'm sure God wouldn't have called you do it unless he was going to equip you for the task, but I don't think you understand how hard it will be."

"I thought since you know the prison system and already have an outreach program in the works, that maybe you could set it up for me to see him," said Allison.

Peter gave Allison a concerned look and then spoke.

"You better give this a lot of thought. You aren't trained for this type of work, Allison. "You might want to leave prison conversions to the professionals."

Chapter 45

The rest of her visit with her new family seemed to pass all too soon. She spent time with Samuel riding the property on a snowmobile, checking out the local businesses downtown, and visiting his church. It was a quaint country church, with whiteboard exterior and a large steeple that rang a bell announcing the starting of church services.

The people of Samuel's community were warm and friendly. He sang and played his guitar for the congregation, which everyone seemed to enjoy wholeheartedly. Allison could feel the Holy Spirit fill the church when the minister preached the gospel. He was on fire and had no problem getting his message across.

Samuel's father hugged her the day she left for home and made her promise to come back often, which she agreed to try to do. She also welcomed him to come for a visit. She understood why Samuel always came back home in-between concerts. He missed the warm atmosphere of home and family.

She would miss them both, but of course, she would see them at the concert in two weeks. She hoped that Brett was free and would accompany her. It would be wonderful to enjoy the show surrounded by people she cared about.

Allison had unpacked her things, placing her laundry in the washer. After starting the load, she decided to call Brett. The concert was on a Saturday, so there shouldn't be a conflict in his schedule. She picked up her cell phone and dialed his number. After about four rings, he picked up.

"Good afternoon, Brett speaking. How may I help you?" he asked.

"Hi, it's Allison. I didn't catch you at a bad time, did I? I know you're working," Allison said.

"No. It's good to hear your voice. Did you have a good time at your brother's?

"The best, I almost hated to come back home," Allison said ignoring another call that was coming in.

"My brother is doing a concert in Cheyenne, Wyoming in a couple of weeks and I wondered if you would like to go with me, Ebony as well. My brother is Evan Storm, the lead singer of Joyful Noise. I'm sure you have heard of him. It's a Christian band," Allison said, waiting for Brett to respond.

"I've heard of him. You have a famous brother that has sold out concerts all over," said Brett.

"I never imagined that my brother was a celebrity. It still seems like a dream. The concert is on the weekend if you haven't already made plans."

"No plans. I'll mark it on my calendar. It's a date," said Brett not realizing the reference he had just made.

"Do you think your mom would like to come too? I don't want to leave her out."

"She would love to, but I heard her talking about going to some Christian retreat that weekend. I'll double check and let you know," said Brett. "Well, I should get off the phone. I have a mound of paperwork staring up at me," Brett said just before hanging up.

Allison hung up her phone, and a puzzled look crossed her face. *Did he just call it a date?* The reference might have only been a slip of the tongue, but she hoped not. She missed him and wanted to introduce him to her family.

Her family, God had blessed her with two of the most loving people she ever met. God's timing is impeccable. Everything seemed to just fall into place, and it was so much better than when she was trying to control everything on her own.

Allison had a godly maturity now. She learned to trust more in God's ways, than man's ways that always let her down. When she went through hard times, there was still peace in the midst of the storm.

Chapter 46

Brett decided to drive to the concert, so Allison rode with him. His mother, Rebecca, decided to join them to help out with Ebony. None of them had been to Cheyenne before, and they were looking forward to taking in some of the sights as well.

Samuel had booked them rooms at the hotel where he was staying, and they would meet up with him after the concert ended.

It was around 6:30 p.m. when they arrived. It was apparent that the concert was filling up fast, by the number of cars and buses parked in the lot. After making a couple of swipes through the parking lot, he spotted a space, pulled in and parked.

After everyone unloaded, Brett, locked the vehicle and they made their way to the concert hall. It was a big building with a marquee out front that read, "Cheyenne Civic Center."

The crowds became thicker as they approached the building. A line had formed, and they joined it. It moved slowly as each person presented their ticket to the cashier. After about fifteen minutes, they finally were at the front of the line. Brett showed their tickets, and they entered the building.

The lobby was brightly lit, with sitting areas on both sides. People were standing around conversing or maneuvering their way through to the main concert hall.

After weaving in and out of the crowd, they were finally inside the auditorium. The concert stubs indicated that they had front row seats courtesy of Samuel.

As they approached the front row, they saw the lighting and sound engineers checking the equipment. Allison had never been to a concert before and had no idea what to expect.

Allison couldn't believe that in a few minutes she would be watching her brother up on the stage in front of thousands of people. She couldn't wait to hear his beautiful voice.

They filtered through the front row and finally found a few seats together. Ebony, of course, wanted to sit between her daddy and grandma. Allison sat on the other side next to Brett. Her heart was so full of joy that she thought it might burst and the man she was beginning to have feelings for was sitting beside her.

Allison glanced around the auditorium and was surprised to see that it appeared to be filling fast. Everywhere she looked was a sea of people, and a multitude of voices echoed all around her.

"Brett, I can't believe how many people are here," said Allison leaning in so Brett could hear her.

"According to what I've read, all his concerts are like this," Brett said as Ebony climbed up into his lap. Brett hugged her and put her back in her seat. "I think the noise is making her nervous."

"I don't blame her. It's pretty overwhelming. I'm not one for large crowds either," Allison said.

Allison was engrossed in her conversation with Brett and didn't notice the man taking a seat next to her. It startled her, but when she turned around and saw who it was, she was surprised.

"Peter, I didn't know you were coming," said Allison.

"I decided to take Samuel up on his offer for front row seats. I don't get a chance to see many of his concerts as they are usually too far away," he said getting positioned in his seat.

"Peter, this is my friend Brett, his daughter, Ebony and his mother, Rebecca," said Allison talking as loud as possible to speak over the voices of the rest of the crowd.

"Nice to meet you," said Peter, his eyes lingered a little longer when he glanced in Rebecca's direction. "We will have to talk more after the concert. I can't possibly hear over this crowd." He no sooner got the words out, then the crowd broke out into yells as Evan Storm, walked out on stage.

Samuel, followed by the other members of the band all took their places, as he walked up to the mic, guitar in hand. He took the mic, looking straight out at the crowd. His eyes locked onto Allison, and his father, and a warm smile crossed his face.

"Welcome, everyone. God has blessed me tonight with a full house, and I wouldn't be here without all of you, my fans. I'm going to be playing some of your favorites and a song I wrote recently in honor of my sister who just happens to be in the audience tonight. This one is for you, Allison.

Allison's eyes begin to fill with tears as she watched her brother on stage. In a matter of minutes, the band struck up a beat, and a beautiful song wafted out into the auditorium.

The song told of a time of wandering alone, broken, hurt by a death of someone close. Then Jesus reminded me of his love and forgiveness. Peace and joy came into my heart, and God gave me someone to share it with. An unknown sister, lost since birth, renewed my faith in you.

Allison is so choked up that it feels like a stone is in her throat. She glanced over at Peter, and he smiles as his hand touches hers. She reached over and put her other hand on his, and for a moment it was like she had her dad back.

She looked over at Brett and his mother, and it appeared that they were enjoying the music also. When the music died down, and Samuel addressed the crowd again, she took a minute to compose herself. She is so touched by the fact that Samuel had dedicated a song to her. God was using him in powerful ways, and he was giving the glory to God.

Samuel and his band struck up another gospel song, and the people in the crowd rocked and swayed to the beat of the music. Lights flickered and flashed behind them, and the audience was lost in the moment.

Allison felt like the air around her was charged with electricity. She could feel the Holy Spirit filling the space, and her eyes began to tear up again. Samuel's voice rang out with passion as he sang praises to God on high.

She looked over, and Ebony was on her feet, clapping her hands to the music. She giggled and smiled at her dad. Allison's heart warmed at the sight of her sweetness. Even with the loss of her mom, God had filled her with joy and love.

It seemed to Allison that the concert ended all too soon. She looked over at Ebony, who had fallen asleep. Brett carefully picked her up and carried her as they made their way back to the lobby.

Samuel was supposed to meet them back at the hotel after he wrapped everything up. There was an autograph signing of his latest CD before he could leave for the hotel.

It was dark when they exited. Instead of waiting to catch a ride with Samuel back to the hotel, Peter had decided to ride with them. Peter, sat in the backseat with Ebony and Rebecca.

Allison could hear Peter as he engaged in a conversation with Rebecca. They were talking about the concert, if Rebecca liked it in Rustin, and if she had ever been to Denver. Their voices were light and cheerful.

Brett drove along the freeway until Peter advised him to turn off at the next exit. A couple of blocks later and Brett was parking the vehicle.

Since it would be another hour before Samuel would arrive, they decided to check into their rooms and then meet downstairs for something to drink. Ebony was already complaining that she was thirsty.

Ebony decided she was also hungry and she gobbled up her food in a matter of minutes. Brett could tell she was exhausted. It had been a long day for her. Rebecca offered to take her up to bed and stay with her.

"It was nice meeting you, Rebecca. I hope to see you again sometime," said Peter as Rebecca stood and took Ebony's hand in hers.

"I would like that," she said. Ebony started to walk and then acted as though her legs were going to collapse. Rebecca quickly grabbed hold of her.

"Maybe I should carry her up," said Brett."

"I'd be happy to help, I'm heading that way myself," said Peter getting up from the table.

"All right," said Brett glancing at his mom.

"Thank you, Peter. Appreciate it. I'll see you when you come up, Allison," said Rebecca.

Brett and Allison were finally alone. Allison took a sip of her tea. She glanced over at Brett who had just finished his coffee and was staring at her.

"What?" she said.

"Oh nothing, I was just thinking how beautiful you are. Not just on the outside, but inside. The light of God just shines from your eyes," said Brett.

"I think that is the nicest thing anyone has ever said to me," said Allison reaching over and placing her hand on his. "Are you sure you just aren't feeling overwhelmed from the concert. It was pretty bright in there?"

"Very funny, I'm trying to be serious, and you're joking. I didn't know you had this playful side to you. What else don't I know?" said Brett.

"Well, I guess if you want to find out, we'll have to keep seeing each other, won't we," she said.

"I'm okay with that. After all, it seems like God brought us together. Who am I to argue with God," he said. He reached over placing his hand on the side of her neck, leaned forward and planted a kiss lightly on her lips.

For Allison, it seemed like time stopped. All she could feel were the taste of his lips on hers and the softness of his touch that sent tingles of warmth through her whole body.

Chapter 47

Samuel walked into the hotel restaurant and looked around. He spotted Allison and Brett alone at a corner table. Since it was going on 10 p.m., the restaurant was relatively empty.

"Where is everybody?" asked Samuel.

"Your dad went up earlier to help Rebecca put Ebony to bed. She was asleep on her feet," said Allison.

"He gets more tired these days. Sometimes I worry about him, but he insists he's just getting older, and it's nothing," said Samuel taking a sip of the coffee the waiter brought him.

"You must have had a lot of fans wanting autographs. Is it always like that?" asked Allison. She wondered how he could stand all the stress of traveling on the road all the time. She knew how much he loved being home.

"Sometimes, it's worse. Tonight, was pretty much what I expected. I'm happy you were here. Sorry, I had to rush off," said Samuel.

"You have a great sound. My mom had a great time, and she seemed to enjoy talking to Peter too," said Brett smiling at Allison.

Allison wondered if Peter ever got lonely. He seemed to be jovial all the time, but she could see the longing in his eyes when he talked about Maggie. She knew that Brett's mom tried to keep herself busy with her Christian retreats, fundraisers, and Ebony, but it couldn't take the place of having a loving partner to share your life.

"A couple of years ago, I tried to get my dad to start dating again, but he just didn't want anything to do with it. He was still hurting from losing my mom. Tonight, when he looked at Rebecca, it was the first time I saw a spark of interest. It warmed my heart to see it," said Samuel.

"I know. I saw something different with my mom too. I was happy she had someone her age to visit with," Brett replied.

"Well, I guess I'll go up and check on dad. I'm wiped out and need some rest, or I won't be any good for anything in the morning." Samuel put some cash on the table to pay for his coffee. He leaned over and kissed Allison on the cheek. "Goodnight, Sis. Brett."

"Goodnight, Samuel," they both said in unison.

"You have a nice brother," said Brett. "I should go check on Ebony before I call it a night. It's been a wonderful day."

"Yes, it has."

They walked to the elevator together and got in. Brett pushed the button for their floor, and they stood quietly as the elevator came to a stop.

She followed him out into the hallway, as they walked toward their rooms. Just before Allison was about to put her key card into the slot, she felt a warm hand on her shoulder.

Bret leaned over and brushed his lips across hers just for a moment before he pulled back. "Goodnight, Allison."

She stood for a moment and watched as he walked away.

Allison stood outside her door mesmerized by the kiss. Every time his hands touched her skin, she would tingle. His kiss was soft and tantalizing. She had never had any man make her feel that way. Not even Tom.

She swiped her card and entered her room. She placed her purse on the nightstand next to the bed and got her nightgown out of her suitcase.

Allison was in the bathroom when she heard the door close. She walked out and got into bed, turned on the lamp on the nightstand, and picked up her bible she had lain on the table earlier when they checked into the hotel. She was just fluffing up her pillow so she could read when Rebecca headed into the bathroom.

"I had a great time today. Thanks for inviting me to the concert. Your brother is quite talented," said Rebecca.

"You're welcome. It was wonderful, wasn't it?" said Allison.

"It was nice to see Brett having a nice time. He spends far too much time working. You are good for him, Allison. He likes you. I've seen the way his eyes light up when you're around," said Rebecca. "A mother knows these things."

"I like him too. I hope we can all become good friends," said Allison. She knew that after tonight it was much more than that.

"I would like that," said Rebecca.

It had been a couple of days since the concert, and it was back to her usual routine. She had unpacked her suitcase, tidied up the house, and spent some time in God's word. Every time she picked up her Bible, she was amazed by the insight the Holy Spirit was giving her. Things that made no sense before were all of a sudden crystal clear.

The police department told Allison that Romero had pled guilty, was sentenced and was transferred to the penitentiary.

Allison had mixed feelings about seeing him. She wanted to obey God, but inside she wasn't sure she could deal with the man that had hurt her. She had forgiven him, but helping him turn his life over to God was a large order and one that would be very uncomfortable. *Can I step out of my comfort zone and help him?*

Chapter 48

Samuel and his father sat in the living room, a crackling fire going in the fireplace, and watched the snow flurries come down outside. Winter was definitely in full force. The light snow that had fallen earlier that day had now left its collection on treetops, roofs, and the driveway leading to the house.

Samuel had shoveled the snow from the front walk leading to the porch, but with the blowing wind, there was twice as much as when he cleared it earlier.

"Dad, I've been thinking about Thanksgiving. It would be nice to have Allison spend it with us. We haven't had anyone to spend the holidays with in a long time," asked Samuel watching his dad thumb through a magazine.

"I'm sorry. What did you say?" asked Peter setting his magazine down on his lap.

"I was asking you about Thanksgiving. Would you mind if I invited Allison?" said Brett.

"I think that would be nice. Why don't we have Brett, Ebony, and Rebecca join us too? We have plenty of room," said Peter.

"That sounds great dad. I'll call them later," said Samuel, getting up to put some logs on the fire.

Samuel could see a friendship building between his dad and Rebecca. She brought out the father he hadn't seen for a long time. There was a light that shone within his eyes when he was around her that he hadn't seen since his mom died. He also seemed to enjoy being around Ebony.

Samuel regretted that he never gave his dad any grandchildren, but he hadn't met the right woman yet. Being on the road most of the time was a lonely life, but it was the path God had chosen for him. He had to use his gift.

"Dad, with the weather being so unpredictable, I sure hope the roads stay clear during that week. Allison isn't used to driving in bad weather and thought I could always go and pick her up a few days ahead. She could ride back with Brett," said Samuel. "I think I'll offer when I talk to her later. Would you like to go with me?" he asked.

"I think I'll stay here. The extra rooms upstairs probably need some straightening up before everyone gets here. I'll be fine."

"Okay. I'll make sure you have plenty of wood and groceries before I leave," said Samuel. "I think I'm going to put a pot of coffee on and start some dinner after I call Allison," he said getting up.

Peter sat on the couch watching Samuel go into the kitchen. He couldn't ask for a better son. Maggie would be so proud of the man he had become. *Maggie, how I miss you.*

He put his magazine down on the coffee table and walked over to the large windows overlooking the front yard. The snow had kicked up and had collected against the walls of the metal shop forming huge mounds.

The sun was just going down, and it was the part of the day that Maggie had enjoyed most. She loved the beautiful pinks and blues of the winter sky, and they had spent lots of time just standing and enjoying the view together. He would wrap his arms around her, and she would lay her head on his shoulder and whisper, *"I love you."*

He missed her so much at first that he didn't know if he could go on without her. With prayer and healing, he finally made it through one day at a time.

And now, he was feeling the urge to be open to love again. He had felt something when he first saw Rebecca. Just a few years younger than he was, she too had lost someone she loved very much, and she seemed to enjoy his company. He enjoyed hers, and they had a lot in common.

Then, the feelings of guilt would creep into his thinking. It was at those times that he had to pray the most. But, Maggie was gone, and he was still here. It wasn't fair, but God knew best, and Maggie was with God in Heaven. He remembered that last night at the hospital when she was nearing her time to leave this earth and go to her heavenly home.

Maggie had looked up into his eyes as he held her hand and said, *"Peter, you know I'll always love you, but you have to let me go. Please, don't grieve too long. You have lots of love to give, and I want you to be happy. Promise me you will open your heart and find love again,"* she said.

Tears ran down his face, and his heart broke into small pieces again. Even after all this time it still hurt. God had forgiven him for the hurt he had caused her during their marriage, and so had she, but at times Satan tried to get a stronghold on his thoughts by punishing him over and over until he finally put it in God's hands and prayed whenever it happened.

He couldn't talk to Samuel even though he would repeatedly ask what was wrong when his face was showing signs of sadness. Finally, the voice stopped inside his head. He had won the battle, and it was only one of many he had fought over the years, but he was never alone. God was with him.

Peter was still standing by the window when Samuel came back into the room. He walked up and placed a hand on his shoulder.

"Well, it looks like we'll have a house full this Thanksgiving, they're all coming. Allison agreed to come early and even insisted on helping me do the cooking," Samuel said, noticing that his dad was wiping tears away. "Is everything all right?"

"I was thinking about your mom. This time of year, it seems to bother me more. Thanksgiving meant a lot to her," said Peter.

"I know Dad. I miss her too, but she wouldn't want you to be alone. I sometimes worry that you are letting your life pass by without enjoying it. It seems that you and Rebecca like each other and I think having everyone here will be good for you. Especially Ebony," said Samuel.

"She is a sweetie. Rebecca told me her grandfather died before she was born. I think she needs a grandpa, so I'm going to fill in," he said joking. "After all, it might be a long time, if I'm waiting for you to give me grandkids," he said.

"Dad, we talked about this. I'm waiting for God to decide when and if I get married," said Samuel as they entered the kitchen. He walked over and filled two cups with coffee.

'I know son. I'm proud of you." said Peter.

237

"Well, I love all the praise, but I think we should eat this chicken casserole I made before it gets cold," he said placing the casserole dish on the table next to their plates.

Peter and Samuel sat down at the table, held hands and Peter said the blessing.

"Thank you, Lord, for this food we are about to eat. We know that you provide for all our needs. We want to thank you for bringing Allison into our lives and for new friends. We pray in Jesus name. Amen.

Peter and Samuel ate their food and engaged in loving conversation. Both their lives had changed due to blessings from God. Little did they know that Gods' plans for them were more wonderous than anything they could ever imagine.

Chapter 49

The Colorado weather had cooperated so that Allison could go to Denver early. It was a special Thanksgiving. She finally didn't dread the holiday's that she usually spent alone.

She was planning on asking Ernest to come share dinner with her keeping her mother's tradition so neither of them would be alone. With her new plans, she had invited him over for an early dinner. They had a wonderful time, and she learned more about the relationship he had shared with her mother over the years. Whenever he mentioned her, she noticed a tear forming in his eye. It was apparent that he still missed her very much.

Allison was just placing her suitcase by the front door when she heard a truck pull up. She walked over to the living room window and pulled the curtain back to get a view of the driveway. Samuel was just getting out and heading for the front steps. She opened the front door and motioned for him to come in.

"Hi Sis, it sure is cold out there. Hopefully, we'll get back to Denver before the bad weather hits," said Samuel rubbing his hands together to warm up.

"Would you like a hot cocoa before we go? I was just heating up some water for some," asked Allison.

"That sounds great," he said.

Allison was just entering the kitchen when the kettle whistled signaling that it was ready. She put cocoa into the cups, filled each one with the hot water, and placed them on the kitchen table while Samuel took a seat.

Allison sat next to him, and they each sipped the hot cocoa that had a touch of mint flavor. Allison's heart warmed just having someone to share even the simplest things with.

Samuel glanced over at Allison. He took a sip of his cocoa and set the cup down on the table. "Do you like living in Rustin?"

"I didn't know at first, but that was because it was so sudden. I didn't know anyone, and there was a lot to take care of after Mom died. I had every intention of selling the house and going back to Collingwood," she said.

"What changed your mind?" asked Samuel taking another sip.

"My best friend encouraged me to pray on it, and God's answer came through loud and clear. I was supposed to stay, even though I had no definite plans of what I would do for a job. Rev. Williams offered me a job, and things just seem to line up for me. Then I found out about you," said Allison giving Samuel a warm smile.

"One of the best days of my life, Dad and I thank God every day for bringing you to us," answered Samuel.

"Stop or you going to make me cry, and when I go outside my eyelashes will freeze shut," said Allison laughing as she walked over to rinse her cup.

"Well, are you ready? I'll grab your suitcase. Get prepared for a cold blast of air," said Samuel. He walked over and picked up her suitcase and headed for the truck.

Allison put on her heavy coat, grabbed her scarf, hat, gloves, and purse. She turned the inside lock on the front door and then put on her gloves.

She shut the door carefully making her way down the front porch steps. A blast of cold winter air whipped around her sending a chill throughout her body. The wind made her face burn as she fought her way to the truck and got in.

Samuel had the heater going full blast, and the warmth thawed her partially cold frame. She removed her gloves, cap, and scarf, placing them on the seat next to her and reached over and buckled up.

Allison looked out the window as Samuel drove along her street and through the middle of town. The store was busy with customers going in and out buying groceries. They were most likely stocking up in preparation for the impending storm.

Samuel merged into the exit, making his way onto the interstate. Allison watched the landscape whizzing by. Houses became small dots along the countryside and then disappeared out of sight, periodically replaced by ranch houses and open fields.

In the middle of the pasture, cattle, and horses alike made their way to barns or whatever structures were available to avoid the harsh wind that whipped blowing snow around them.

Samuel reached over and kicked the defroster up a notch to help keep the front windshield clear. Outside, the weather was worsening.

"Well, our trip just got a little longer. It's going to be slow going the rest of the way unless this lets up," said Samuel. Allison could see the concern on his face.

They had gone a few miles up the road when Allison spotted a vehicle in the ditch.

Samuel braked, pulled over and came to a stop.

"You stay here. I'll check it out," said Samuel.

"Okay. Be careful," said Allison.

Chapter 50

Samuel opened his door and got out. He walked up to the driver's door, brushed away the snow that had collected on the window, and peered inside. The windows were starting to fog up, but he could see a young woman, her age he estimated to be somewhere in her early thirties, with long black hair. Her head rested on the steering wheel.

Samuel moved to the front of the vehicle and over to the passenger's side to see if there was anyone else with her. His boots made a crunching sound as he slushed through the packed snow.

On that side of the vehicle blowing, snow blocked the view. Samuel brushed some of the snow away from the window and looked inside. He saw a young child dressed in leggings and a heavy coat. On her head was a knitted cap that had slid down, covering part of her face. He opened the door as far as he could and felt for a pulse on the side of her neck. She had a strong, steady heartbeat.

He went back around and knocked on the window hoping to get the drivers attention. Nothing. He waited a minute and tried again, still no movement. He checked the door. It wasn't locked, so he pulled it open. He reached in and laid his hand on the woman's shoulder.

"Can you hear me?" he asked.

The woman began to stir, and a couple of minutes later her eyes opened wide.

"Who are you? What happened?" she asked.

"My name is Samuel. My sister and I were driving by and saw your vehicle in the ditch. I'll call 911 and get some help for you. I'll stay with you until they get here," he said.

"Lana," she cried out.

"Your daughter is going to be okay. Where do you hurt?" asked Samuel.

"My head, it's throbbing pretty bad and my vision is blurry," she said trying to focus on his face.

Samuel fished his cell phone out of his pocket and was surprised that he had a signal. He dialed 911 and after checking the mile marker gave them the location. His hands were beginning to go numb and the side of his face burned from the cold.

"Just stay put. Help is coming," said Samuel.

He walked back to his truck and got in. The look on Allison's face was one of concern.

"Was anyone in the vehicle," asked Allison.

"A mother and little girl. I got the mother to talk to me, and the girl is breathing, but she's unconscious. We have to wait for the emergency vehicles to arrive. Hopefully, they get here soon. Its getter colder out," said Samuel trying to get the circulation back into his hands.

Allison and Samuel sat in the truck and waited in-between Samuel's trips to check on the mother and daughter.

On the last trip he made, Samuel put their luggage he had retrieved out of the back of the SUV into the back seat of his truck. He would give it to the ambulance driver so they would have it when they were released from the hospital. If it got left in the SUV, it might be awhile before they would have what they needed.

It had been around fifteen minutes when Samuel spotted the flashing lights from the tow truck and ambulance. Samuel got out and met the ambulance as it pulled up.

"There's a mother and child in the vehicle. The mother was talking to me, but I couldn't get a response from the child," said Samuel moving out of the way so they could assess the situation.

"Are you a relative?" the paramedic asked.

"No! my sister and I spotted the SUV and stopped to help. I called 911 right away," said Samuel. "I'm going to go back to my truck and wait," he said.

Samuel made his way back to the truck and got in. Allison's eyes were riveted to the scene before her.

"Everything is going to be okay now," said Samuel.

"I know, it's in God's hands. I'm so glad that we came along when we did and that you were able to call 911," said Allison. She wondered how long before the woman's family would start missing them.

Samuel and Allison watched as the paramedics removed the child first and then her mother. They were both loaded up into the ambulance, a few minutes later one of the paramedics approached. Samuel rolled down the window part way.

"Well, the mother was able to talk to me. She's going to call her sister when she's released from the hospital. Thanks for stopping and calling this in. A little longer and we might have been facing a different outcome. They will both be fine thanks to you," said the paramedic.

"No problem. Glad to help," said Samuel.

Samuel rolled up the window, started the truck, and slowly pulled out onto the freeway. Allison glanced into the rear-view mirror and saw the ambulance pull out, its lights flashing.

"Well, I feel better now. God led us to help," said Samuel.

"I know. A few minutes earlier and we might not have been there to see them. God's timing is amazing," said Allison smiling at Samuel. Allison wondered what else they might run across on this snowy, cold winter day.

They continued down the interstate, both quiet, lost in their thoughts. Then they both turned and looked at each other and almost spoke at the same time.

"I forgot their luggage," said Samuel.

"They are going to need it," said Allison.

"Are you thinking what I'm thinking?" said Samuel. "I know why I forgot."

"I know too. God spoke to me, and the message was clear," said Allison.

Chapter 51

It was about a half hour later when Samuel and Allison walked through the brightly lit entrance at Denver General. The reception desk was live with people bustling about.

In the corner sat a man with a tightly wrapped shirt around his forearm. His eyes seemed empty as he stared forward, not saying a word. A woman was desperately trying to comfort him.

Across the room, more emergency room patients were waiting to be seen. An elderly woman seemed dazed and unsure of where she was, as a nurse tried to calm her down. A man held in place by a backboard and neck brace on a gurney, pushed by emergency personnel, lie still as they took him to one of the trauma rooms.

As Allison's eyes took in her surroundings, she said a silent prayer for all those who found themselves in need of healing.

Samuel walked up to the reception desk. He stood waiting to get the nurse's attention. Finally, she acknowledged his presence.

"How can I help you," she said.

"I called 911 for an accident my sister, and I came across on the interstate. The woman and her daughter were brought here, and I would like to speak with the doctor," said Samuel. "I just want to make sure she has somewhere to go when she's released. She has a sister here in Denver, but I'm not sure if she is home," said Samuel hoping to get some information on their condition.

"Have a seat in the waiting area, and I'll contact the doctor. It might be awhile. As you can see we're swamped," she said shuffling through paperwork.

Allison and Samuel went over to the waiting area and sat down. The television was on, and a weather update was scrolling across the screen. It looked like they were in for more snow starting tomorrow morning. Hopefully, it would hold off until they got home.

"Looks like it's going to be a long night, I better call dad," said Samuel pulling his cell phone from his pocket. He rang the number and a few minutes later was explaining the situation.

Allison leaned back in the chair and stared at the television. She hoped the weather would calm down enough for Brett to make the trip. Thanksgiving was only two days away.

Samuel completed his call and put his phone into his pocket.

"Dad was going to head to bed but was worried when we weren't there yet. I guess parents never quit worrying about their children," said Samuel shifting his weight in the seat. "Maybe I'll see if I can round up some coffee, and tea for you," he said getting up.

"That sounds great. I'll wait for the doctor," said Allison.

She got up to stretch her legs, making her way over to the front windows and looked out into what was now early twilight. The snow fell in huge flakes and collected on the shrubbery that lined the driveway to the entrance of the building.

Allison spotted a maintenance man bundled in a heavy coat spreading salt on the sidewalk and driveway. He fought the wind as it blew across his back.

Allison was lost in the moment and didn't hear the doctor walk up.

"Are you Allison?" he asked.

Allison turned around to face a man in his late forties of medium build with dark brown hair, dressed in emergency room garb.

"Yes," she said.

"I'm Dr. Metcalf, the ER physician. Sorry, I couldn't get back to you sooner, but as you can see, we are stretched to our limits tonight. We had more cases than usual because of the storm," he said. "I understand you wanted to inquire about the woman and child brought in off the interstate. Are you family?"

"No, my brother and I found them. We just wondered if they are going to be released tonight. She was supposed to call her sister in Estes Park to see if she made it home. If she didn't, she has nowhere to go. We would like to speak with her if that's okay," asked Allison.

"Since you aren't family, I'll have to ask if she wants to see you. If not, there isn't anything I can do," said Dr. Metcalf.

"I understand," said Allison wondering what was taking Samuel so long. The thought no sooner entered her mind, then she saw him approaching.

"Did you think I got lost? I went to the gift shop and bought a teddy bear for the little girl. I thought maybe it might cheer her up," said Samuel handing Allison the cup of tea.

"I just spoke to the doctor, and he's checking with the woman to see if she will see us," said Allison taking a sip of tea.

"I hate to think of her being released and having nowhere to go. The motels may be full up with the blizzard outside. What do you think about taking them home with us if she can't get a hold of her sister? There's plenty of room for two more," said Samuel as he sipped his hot coffee.

"That's a wonderful idea, but we're strangers. What makes you think she will be willing to go with us?" asked Allison.

"I feel God has his hand in this, and I'm convinced it's the right thing to do," he said.

As they were talking, Allison noticed Dr. Metcalf walking towards them.

"I spoke with Katy Marsh, and she would like to see you both. I'm filling out the paperwork right now to release both of them. We haven't been able to reach her sister, so I'm not sure what she plans to do," said Dr. Metcalf.

"We have talked it over, and if she agrees, we would like to take them home with us until she can get a hold of her sister," said Samuel.

"Good. Katy and her daughter aren't in any danger, but Katy may have headaches for a while, and I'm sure she could use some help with Lana," he said. "Trauma room B just past the reception desk to the right."

"Thanks," said Samuel throwing away their cups in the waste can.

The hallway was still bustling with hospital personnel checking on patients in various stages of care. Samuel spotted the placard above the doorway that read B, and they entered a brightly lit room. In front of them lying in bed was Katy, her daughter lay snuggled up next to her fast asleep.

Samuel and Allison walked up to the hospital bed and leaned on the railing. Both Katy and Lana's eyes were closed. Katy had a nasty bruise starting on her left cheek and extending down towards her jaw.

"Katy," said Allison.

The woman's eyes blinked open.

"Do you remember us?"

"You don't look familiar, but I recognize the man next to you. He talked to me after I wrecked my SUV," said Katy turning over to face them.

"That's right. The doctor is getting ready to release you, but they haven't been able to get a hold of your sister. Where will you go?" asked Samuel.

"I don't know. My sister works for an advertising firm, and she went to Estes Park for a convention," said Katy, her voice appearing almost strained. "I have Lana to worry about."

"This may sound strange coming from someone you just met, but I have a large house with plenty of room and my sister, and I would love to give you a place to stay until you can get a hold of your sister. I'll leave my cell number at the front desk so your sister can call you," said Samuel giving her a reassuring smile.

"That's so nice of you to offer. I don't know why, but I feel I can trust you."

"Well, it's settled then. I'll let your doctor know and leave my number at the front desk. We'll wait out in the waiting area until you're ready to be discharged," said Samuel.

As Allison and Samuel were walking away, they heard a small, fragile voice ask, "Who was that, mama?"

Chapter 52

Samuel and Allison helped Katy and Lana into the back seat. They were all shivering after the trek through the parking lot in ankle deep snow and blowing wind.

Lana clung to her mother. Katy rubbed her back to calm her letting her know they were going to be okay.

"Mama, when are we going to Auntie Rita's," asked Lana.

"Aunt Rita isn't home right now. We are going home with Samuel and Allison for now. Aunt Rita will call us later, sweetie," she said kissing Lana on her forehead.

Samuel drove along the interstate and after what seemed like an eternity finally came to the road leading to the house. He drove slowly trying to avoid skidding off the road.

He rounded the corner, and the house came into sight. The lights shone brightly through the tall front windows and smoke churned out of the chimney.

Samuel pulled up in the driveway, put the car in park, and got out. He opened the door for Katy. He picked up Lana and carried her into the house, while Allison steadied Katy. She was still a little uneasy on her feet, and the slick walk didn't make it any easier.

Samuel's dad heard them pull up and met them at the door.

"I thought you were going to bed dad?" asked Samuel.

"I couldn't sleep, so I decided to stay downstairs," said Peter with a puzzled look on his face. "Who are our guests?" he asked.

"This is Katy and her daughter, Lana. She was just discharged from the hospital, but couldn't get a hold of her sister. It was late, and she didn't know what to do, so we brought them here," said Samuel. "She had an accident on the interstate."

"Katy, make yourself at home. Are you hungry? I can rustle up some soup and sandwiches," said Peter smiling at her. "Have a seat by the fire and warm up."

Samuel joined his dad in the kitchen while Allison sat with Katy and Lana. Katy moved over to the chair by the fireplace and Lana settled sleepily in her lap. In the light of the fire, Lana looked like an angel.

"I don't know how to thank you for helping me. I appreciate it very much," said Katy as she brushed the hair out of Lana's face and pulled her close to her body.

"We're glad to help. How are you feeling now?" asked Allison.

"Better. I still have a headache, but it's not as bad as earlier. I'm worried about my sister though," said Katy.

"Were you going to see her when you got into the accident?" asked Allison turning to face the fire.

"Yes. We haven't spent a Thanksgiving together in over two years. She's the only family we have left. Our parents died a few years ago, and my husband was killed overseas a year ago. My sister, Rita, is single and lives alone and wants us to move in with her, but I haven't made up my mind yet," said Katy.

Allison could hear the pain in her voice when she talked about her husband.

"It sounds like it's been rough on you both. Samuel will let you know when Rita calls. After you get something to eat, I'll take you upstairs to your room. I'll be right next door if you need anything," said Allison.

"Everything is ready," said Peter.

Allison, Katy, and Lana followed him into the kitchen where plates of sandwiches and hot soup were waiting. Lana woke up and even though she seemed apprehensive about where they were, she managed to eat some soup.

After everyone ate and had a chance to warm up, they decided to call it a night. Samuel went outside momentarily to get Katy's luggage. He returned instantly, but with snow packed boots and large flakes stuck to his hair.

"Thank you, Samuel. I was wondering what we were going to do for clothing,"

"I figured you would need it after you were discharged from the hospital and I meant to give it to the ambulance driver, but somehow I forgot. Maybe it was meant to be or otherwise, you wouldn't be here. I think God was directing my steps," said Samuel.

"I'm grateful to you both," said Katy shooting a smile at Samuel.

Katy washed Lana up, dressed her in her pajamas, and Lana crawled into the bed snuggling up next to her. Within a couple of minutes, she was sound asleep.

Allison thanked God for the opportunity to lend a helping hand to Katy and Lana. She wasn't sure what tomorrow might bring, but she knew they would have a place for as long as they needed it.

Her heart swelled with pride knowing her brother was such a caring person and knew that the Lord would be using him in some remarkable ways. *Bless Katy & Lana, Lord, and thanks for keeping them safe. I pray in Jesus name. Amen.*

Chapter 53

It was mid-morning when Lana crept down the stairs and wandered into the living room. She clutched the teddy bear that Samuel had given her as she crawled up into the chair by the fireplace.

The snow outside had stopped falling, but the air was still crisp and had a bite to it.

Peter entered the living room, his arms piled high with firewood. He was getting ready to put some more wood on the fire when he noticed Lana sitting upright with her knees pulled tight against her body.

"Hi, Lana, did you have a good sleep?" he asked as he placed the firewood in the fire. It crackled and popped as the flames hit the wood and he could feel the burst of heat.

Peter waited for an answer, but none came. He walked over and stood in front of her and spoke again, "Lana, are you ready to have some breakfast?"

A small, soft voice answered, "I'm hungry."

"What do you say we make us some pancakes? Does that sound good? Peter asked reaching out for her hand.

Lana shook her head yes, took his hand, and walked with him to the kitchen. He helped her up onto the stool at the breakfast bar.

"Do you want to help?"

"Yes, I help Mommy," said Lana smiling at him.

"You can help me stir the pancake batter, okay?"

Lana grinned and shook her head, yes.

Peter got a bowl and the pancake mix out of the cupboard and placed them on the counter. He added the required amount of mix and water and then put it in front of Lana handing her a large mixing spoon. She smiled and took the spoon from his hand and started stirring.

"How about some blueberries? Should we add some?"

Lana was excited and bobbed her head up and down indicating that she wanted blueberries.

Peter opened the refrigerator and took out the blueberries. After rinsing them in the sink, he dropped a few into the batter and helped Lana carefully fold them in.

"I'll fry them up, and then we'll eat," he said placing the batter on the griddle he had warming up.

In a few minutes, Lana's eyes opened wide when she saw the pancakes he set on the plate. He brought them over to the table, along with fresh butter and warmed up pancake syrup.

Peter pulled out a chair for Lana and then sat down next to her. He placed a pancake on her plate, rubbed it with butter, and then drizzled syrup over it. He cut the pancake in small bites so that it would be easier for her to eat and then fixed his own.

He had barely finished fixing his when she had plopped the first bite in her mouth. He could hear a yum sound escape suggesting that she was enjoying her food. She was polishing off the last of her pancake when Samuel came in.

"Hey, looks like someone likes your pancakes," said Samuel.

"It seems so."

"Well, I'll have to try them then," he said taking a seat and placing a couple of pancakes on his plate. "My favorite, blueberry."

The smell of coffee and pancakes lingered in the air making its way upstairs to Allison and Katy's rooms.

Allison was just leaving her room when she met Katy in the hall.

"I hope you slept well," said Allison.

"I did, but I'm missing Lana. She seems to have slipped out of bed without me knowing it," said Katy. It isn't like her to wander around in a strange place.

"She is probably downstairs with Peter. All children just seem to love him. He's everyone's grandpa," said Allison.

"I'm going downstairs to look for her," said Katy as she walked over to the staircase.

"I'll see you downstairs in a bit," said Allison as she went into the bathroom to take her morning shower. It was nice being surrounded by family and new friends.

Chapter 54

Katy walked down the staircase leading to the living room dressed in a pair of designer jeans and a warm pink sweater. From there she could hear giggles and manly voices coming from the kitchen.

When she entered the kitchen, Lana was making funny faces at Samuel. She had the bear that he gave her on her lap and was pretending to feed him pieces of her pancake. When the bear appeared not to want any, Lana pushed the spoon towards Samuel, and he gobbled it up, which made Lana giggle even more.

Samuel's head swung towards the sound of the footsteps. His breath caught as he took in the vision of loveliness. Katy appeared rested and was nothing like the woman he remembered from the night before.

Her long black hair hung in waves around her shoulders and framed her face. Her body was trim, and she filled out her designer jeans well. Samuel immediately thought, model. She flashed him a smile as she took a seat at the table.

Lana got up from the chair and ran over to her Mom and hugged her. "Mommy, Peter made me breakfast. I helped."

"That's wonderful. You're such a big girl." Katy gave her a hug and kissed her on the cheek. Lana kissed her back and then squirmed to get down.

"I hope Lana hasn't been giving you any trouble. She somehow got up without waking me," said Katy.

"No problem at all. We've been having a great time. Haven't we, Lana."

Lana grinned and bobbed her head up and down and took a drink of her orange juice.

"How are you feeling?" asked Samuel.

"Much better thank you, just a little sore. At least my head isn't hurting as bad," she said.

"Can I get you some coffee and breakfast?" asked Samuel.

"I'd love some, but I can get it," said Katy.

"You're the guest. Coffee black or cream and sugar?" he asked walking over to the coffee pot and pouring some into a mug.

"Black with just a teaspoon of sugar. Thanks," she said. "Where is your dad?"

"After he made breakfast for Lana and me, he went out to check the shop. The shop is heated, but he wanted to make sure that everything is working the way it should. He'll be back any minute," said Samuel.

"Has my sister called? She should have called back by now," said Katy concerned that maybe something had happened to her.

"I'm going to call the hospital and see if they've heard from her. Maybe they got busy and haven't had a chance to call," he said retrieving his cell phone from the table.

After a few minutes of being on hold, someone at the hospital finally picked up. Katy's sister had called the hospital that morning, and they gave her Samuel's number. It was just a matter of waiting for her to call his phone.

Samuel had just disconnected the call when his phone rang. It was Rita. He handed the phone to Katy.

261

"Lana and I are okay. I guess I hit a slick patch on the interstate and landed in the ditch. If it wasn't for Samuel and his sister, Allison, I don't know what would have happened to us." Katy glanced at Samuel as she spoke.

"Sure. I understand. We'll be okay here until you can come and get us. God was looking out for us. I know, I'm disappointed about Thanksgiving too, but there isn't anything we can do. There's always next year," said Katy. "Love you too, bye." Katy hung up and handed the phone back to Samuel.

Lana looked over at Katy with a puzzled look on her face. "Was that Auntie Rita? Is she coming to take us to her house now?"

"Not right now, sweetie. The roads have lots of snow on them, and she can't make it. She'll be here as soon as she can."

Lana curled up her bottom lip into a pout and lowered her head and folded her arms.

Katy got up and knelt beside Lana's chair, lifted up her chin, and looked into her sad eyes. "Honey, we'll be all right here until she comes."

Samuel leaned over and said, "We can have fun. We can build a snowman outside when the sun comes out. Your mommy can come too. It will be lots of fun."

Lana's eyes lit up when he mentioned a snowman. She smiled and asked her mom, "Can we?"

"I don't see why not, but you have to be sure and dress in your coat, hat, boots, and gloves, okay?"

"Ok."

Allison walked into the kitchen dressed in warm jeans and a sweatshirt. She had pulled her hair back into a ponytail. Lana ran up to her as she walked over to put water on for tea.

"We're gonna build a snowman. You wanna help?" asked Lana jumping up and down.

"I haven't done that in a long time, but I think I remember how," said Allison.

"Maybe Lana would like to watch cartoons until it warms up outside. What do you say we go find some?" asked Samuel taking her by the hand.

Peter was just coming in the back door. He stopped to take off his coat and placed it on the coatrack. He sat down and pulled off his boots, putting them on the mat before entering the living room.

"We're watching cartoons," said Lana smiling at Peter.

"Wonderful," said Peter. "I think I'll just grab me some coffee to warm up and I'll join you."

Chapter 55

Allison got another cup of tea and sat down at the table next to Katy. Katy seemed preoccupied and appeared worried about something.

"Katy is everything all right? You're not feeling worse, are you?" asked Allison.

"No. I finally heard from my sister. She's still at the conference, and the roads are treacherous which makes it impossible for her to get to Denver. It looks like we can't spend Thanksgiving together after all, short of a miracle. Lana is disappointed and can't understand why Rita can't come now."

"Give her some time, and she'll forget all about it. She's such a joy to have around," said Allison taking a sip of tea.

Katy gave her a smile and took a sip of her coffee. She looked over at the windows facing towards the auto shop. The roof was heavy laden with snow, and the wind had whipped it up against the side of the building where it had collected in huge mounds.

"I feel blessed to have you take us in and made us feel so welcome. I will never forget your generosity."

"Hey, ladies. Are you ready to help make a snowman? The snow has stopped coming down, and the sun is out. Lana wants to play," asked Samuel coming over to the table where they sat.

"We will get our warm gear on and meet you outside," said Allison.

Allison felt so blessed to be able to spend time with Samuel and Peter, and now, Katy and Lana. Even though they had met under strange circumstances, she felt like they were already a part of the family.

Everything would be perfect if only, Brent, Ebony, and Rebecca could somehow make it. She would place it in God's hands.

Katy went upstairs to get her coat, gloves, and boots. She entered the room that was so graciously provided to her and was grateful for having a warm place to be. Of course, she could have gone to a motel, but then Samuel and Allison wouldn't hear of it.

A tear ran down the side of her face, and she walked into the bathroom to grab a tissue to wipe her eyes. Her heart seemed so full of God's love, and for the first time in a long while she felt almost normal again.

She was disappointed that she wouldn't see Rita on Thanksgiving. Things were strained after their parents died. What used to be a close relationship seemed to slip away from them, especially after Scott died.

Scott, why did I have to think of him? Her heart ached every time the memories crept in. She tried to keep busy with her job and Lana. *Why Lord? Why did you have to take him from us?*

Katy's faith had been tested, and when the rough times came, she wasn't strong enough to trust in God to see her through. In her heart she knew that he was still with her, but why couldn't she feel him? She had prayed, even pleaded for the pain to stop, but her heart always felt as though it was breaking.

Many a night, she went to bed with Lana crying her eyes out. How could she comfort her when her heart was breaking too? Where was God then?

Now she had to deal with the accident. Yes, God had spared them, and she didn't know what she would have done if anything would have happened to Lana.

She finished putting on her warm clothing and carried her boots down to the front door and sat on the bench to put them on. She stood up and opened up the front door, and a snowball came flying by hitting the door with a splat.

"I almost got you, Mama," said Lana picking up another snowball to throw.

"You sure did," said Katy crunching through the snow as she made her way over to where Lana stood.

"See, what we built. Isn't the snowman big?" asked Lana. She helped place a couple of buttons for eyes and a large carrot for a nose. The snowman also sported a long blue woolen scarf and hat to complete his look.

"You did a great job. It's the best snowman I've ever seen," said Katy giving Lana a hug and kiss as she pulled her towards her.

As they were all enjoying their time outside in the crisp morning air, Allison spotted a familiar vehicle heading up the driveway.

Chapter 56

Brett, Ebony, and Rebecca got out. Brett walked up to the front of the yard where everyone was gathered.

"Well, we made it," said Brett. "Who do we have here?" he said looking over at Lana.

"That's Lana and her mom, Katy. They are staying with us for a few days," replied Allison.

"Hi, Katy and Lana. It looks like you've been having a good time. Awesome snowman," said Brett as he walked up the driveway towards the house.

Rebecca came over to Allison and hugged her. "It's so nice to see you again, dear. I wasn't sure we were going to make it, but the Lord was with us," she said.

Brett was carrying a suitcase in one hand, and Ebony clung to the other. Her eyes were fixed on Lana and the snowman.

"When the forecast called for the impending storm, I thought we should go ahead and leave a little early. I was afraid if we waited, we might not make it at all. We spent last night at a motel in town and missed the worst of it," said Brett.

"Well, I'm glad you did. Let's get everyone into the house and settled into their rooms. It's going to be a wonderful Thanksgiving," said Peter as he walked next to Rebecca. He placed his arm on her shoulder as he guided her into the house. "It's nice to see you again," he said.

Rebecca smiled and replied, "Nice to see you too."

With everyone settled into their rooms and introduced to Katy and Lana, they all relaxed. Samuel stoked the fire in the living room, and the place was filled with warm chatter.

Lana and Ebony were on the floor in front of the fireplace, their eyes fixed on a cartoon show. Their giggles filling the room.

"Can I get everyone some hot cocoa?" asked Peter. The answer seemed to be a resounding yes from everyone.

"I'll give you a hand Dad," Samuel said getting up from the sofa.

Samuel followed his dad into the kitchen. Allison was close behind.

"I'll put on the water while you get the cups," said Peter. "It's so nice to have so many to share the holiday with."

"It sure is. That's what Thanksgiving is all about. Spending time with family and friends," said Samuel.

Samuel and Allison filled the cups with cocoa and Peter poured the water into them. After giving the cups a quick stir, Allison walked into the living room and passed them out. Samuel followed behind her with the rest.

Lana and Ebony were instructed to go into the kitchen for cocoa. Katy and Allison sat with them.

The two girls brought their mugs to their mouth and after a quick blow on the cocoa, took a long sip. They both in unison licked their lips and made a smacking sound. When Allison and Katy looked their way they giggled, their mouths sporting a chocolate mustache.

"Girls, let's act like little ladies now. Take small sips," said Katy giving them both a stern look. "Soon it will be time for your bath and then to bed."

"Momma, can you read to us? I want Ebony to hear my favorite story. Please momma," asked Lana giving her mother a pouty face and sad eyes that she knew her mother couldn't resist.

"We'll see. If it's okay with Ebony's dad, she can come into our room until I'm finished with the story," said Katy. She saw Lana's expression change to a smiley face.

"I can put her to bed afterward. Her room is right next to mine," said Allison.

All finished with their hot cocoa, the girls were taken upstairs for their bath. They insisted on bathing together. They splashed and giggled while they played. In the end, there seemed to be more water on the tile than there was in the tub.

Katy dried them both off and dressed them in clean clothes. Allison had helped Peter and Samuel with dinner preparations, and the house was beginning to fill with the smell of baked chicken. With the addition of asparagus and a green salad, there was plenty to go around.

Everyone gathered around the dining room table and joined hands for a moment of prayer. They had a lot to be thankful for this year.

Samuel had found a sister he didn't know he had.

Katy and Lana had new friends that had come to her aide when she needed help most.

Brett had found what seemed to be the healing of his broken heart and was beginning to believe he could find love again.

Rebecca, for the first time after her husband died, felt that maybe she could love another man.

And Peter felt a twinge of romance budding inside of him.

Allison had a whole new family, friends, and found her way back to the Lord. Brett was her inspiration and the feelings that she felt deep inside, she knew was the beginning of a powerful love. One sent from God.

Chapter 57

Everyone enjoyed the meal, especially Ebony and Lana who voiced that chicken was their favorite. When it came to asparagus, they both pushed it around on their plate but weren't in any hurry to place it in their mouths.

After the dishes are done, they all retired into the living room for a bit of television. The girls were coloring in color books at a table adjoining the couch. It was all that Katy could do to make them put them away and get ready for bed.

Samuel went outside. The darkness of evening had settled in on the landscape, and he could hear the familiar night sounds as he opened the door to gather some wood from the wood box.

Rebecca tired from the drive had went to her room, after giving Ebony a good night kiss.

The others, one by one, had made their way upstairs to retire for the night. Tomorrow was Thanksgiving and a busy day ahead.

Allison and Brett were the only ones left downstairs. They sat next to each other on the sofa. Allison was also feeling tired, and before she knew it, her head was resting on Brett's shoulder, and she fell asleep.

Brett glanced over to see if Allison was awake. She hadn't moved or spoke for a while.

Her eyes were closed, and he could hear her soft even breathing. He leaned over and placed a kiss on her forehead waking her.

"I'm sorry, I must have dozed off. I promised Ebony that I would put her to bed after Katy finished reading to both girls. That is unless you would rather do it," asked Allison.

"No. Go ahead. I'll check on her before I go to bed. Ebony seems to have warmed up to you, and it's nice to see her coming out of her shell. She's been so withdrawn since her mother died."

"She's a sweet girl, and I enjoy spending time with her. It's a challenge though since I didn't have any brothers or sisters growing up," said Allison wondering if she would learn to be a good mother when the time came.

Brett sat on the sofa deep in thought. He enjoyed sharing Ebony with another woman. His mother, of course, was a big help to him and he didn't know what he would have done without her to pick up the pieces after Vicky died.

Since the day he met Allison his life had begun to change, and he found himself thinking about her a lot.

He felt guilty raising Ebony alone. She needed a mother so that she could feel more secure as a family. But, until recently, he couldn't imagine sharing his life with anyone again.

He still thought of Vicky often. Especially, when Ebony would do that little pouty face and look at him with her big dark eyes. He would give her the moon if he were able.

His mother was always warning him of being too soft on her, but his heart would break every time a look of sadness appeared in her eyes, and he would cave. Most of the discipline came from his mother, which he was glad for. Regardless of the circumstances, Ebony needed correction and guidance to grow up into a loving, young lady.

Allison was a joy to be around. She was a loving, caring person who would go out of her way to help anyone. Her faith in God was an attribute that he admired.

The person he was with had to be a believer. If he ever decided to commit to someone, he had to be equally yoked with his partner. Yes, Allison could very well be that person.

When Allison got to the hallway upstairs, she could hear the sound of Katy's voice as she read to the girls. She approached the doorway that was left ajar and stood quietly watching.

The two girls were under the covers snuggled up together listening intently to the story that Katy was reading. When she changed her voice to act like another character in the story, the girls giggled, and Allison could see the sense of wonder and magic on their faces.

Allison entered the room and stood beside the bed. Katy was just finishing up the last page and closed the book to the protest of the girls.

"Mommy, can't you read more. We're not tired yet," said Lana.

"I'm sorry girls. It's getting late, and you have to go to sleep now," said Katy placing the book on the night table beside the bed.

"I'm going to take you to your room, Ebony, like I promised," said Allison as she walked over to the side of the bed where Ebony lay.

"Can't I stay here with Lana?" asked Ebony.

"Your daddy will be coming up soon, and you need to be in your own bed. You can play together in the morning."

"Okay," said Ebony giving in, but it was apparent that she didn't want to.

Allison uncovered Ebony and carried her to the doorway and then turned around and said goodnight to Katy and Lana.

They each called out, "Goodnight."

Ebony's arms were wrapped tightly around Allison's neck with her face snuggled against her shoulder. She was burrowed in, and it would be hard for Allison to pry her loose. Allison was also enjoying the closeness.

Allison opened the door to Lana's room that she shared with her father and put her in the twin bed next to his. As she laid her down and tucked her in, Ebony looked up at her.

"Are you going to be my new mommy?"

"I know it's been hard because your mom is in Heaven, but she is still with you in your heart. Your dad and I are friends, and I want to be your friend too." Allison's voice began to quiver, and she could sense a tearing starting in her eyes. "You're a special girl, Ebony, and if I had to choose someone to be a mommy too, it would be you."

Ebony sat up and wrapped her arms around Allison's neck and kissed her on the cheek. "It's okay if you want to be my mommy," she said smiling up at Allison.

"Your dad will be up soon to tuck you in. Goodnight, Ebony. See you in the morning."

Allison turned out the light. She took one more look at Ebony before leaving. The thought of possibly someday being her mom filled her with joy. It would mean that she would be married to Brett. He was the first man that made her trust again, gave her a sense of belonging, and made her feel happy inside about the woman she was becoming.

She left the door ajar so the light from the hallway would bathe the room in dim light and continued down the staircase to the lower floor. The house was quiet, except for the crackling of the fire. With the setting of the sun, the room had taken on a soft glow.

As she entered the room, Brett, Samuel, and Peter were engaged in a warm conversation.

"Have you looked at the weather forecast this evening? It's supposed to kick up again tonight and dump a couple of feet of snow. The roads will be messy. I hope you don't have to rush back to work," said Samuel shifting positions in the chair and crossing one leg over the other.

"No. I've got plenty of holiday leave, and we packed extra clothes in case we couldn't get back right away. I can't think of a better place to be snowed in," said Brett.

"Well, I for one, feel blessed to have so many friends to share the holiday with," said Peter rising from the couch. "Now if you will excuse me, I think I'm heading up to bed."

"Goodnight," said Samuel.

"Goodnight," said Allison giving him a warm smile.

"Goodnight," said Brett.

Peter gave everyone a slight wave and headed down the hall and into his room.

Peter knelt down by the side of his bed to talk to God the same as he did every night. But tonight, it was different. Loving people surrounded him, and his heart was so full that it felt like it would explode.

"Lord, I know at times that I might not have shown you that I am grateful for everything you do for me, but without you, I know that I would not have the joy I am feeling in my heart. You have blessed me with a fine son and now a daughter who means everything to me. I know that for a short while I was mad because you took my darling Maggie from me. I had to have someone to blame, and I lashed out at you. I know you love Maggie, and I'm happy that I'll see her again someday."

"Lord, if you have sent Rebecca into my life to help me heal, I feel my heart is ready now. She is a godly woman, and I feel like I don't' deserve her, but I promise that if we are supposed to be together, that I will do my best to honor her. I pray in Jesus name, Amen."

Peter rose from the side of the bed. Turned off the table lamp and crawled into bed. Somehow, he didn't feel like an old man. His heart was light, and a smile crossed his face. He had a second chance to do things right this time, and he was determined to walk the path of obedience.

Allison opened the door to her room. She went into the bathroom to brush her teeth and get ready for bed. She felt at home here.

With the addition of Katy and Lana, who she was becoming very fond of, they were beginning to feel like a part of the family too. She would hate to see them leave and would make a point of staying in touch after they went to her sister's.

Her mind wandered to Brett. While she was cuddled up next to him on the sofa and had fallen asleep, she dreamt of him. When her eyes first opened, she saw him looking at her. *Had he been watching me sleep?*

It gave her a warm feeling knowing that maybe his feelings for her had deepened. She knew that hers most definitely had. He was everything she wanted in a man, even though she didn't realize that she was ready for a relationship yet. And then there was sweet Ebony.

It threw her when Ebony had presented the question about being her new mom. She didn't want to confuse Ebony, so she downplayed her relationship with her dad.

After all, she wasn't sure where it was heading. The last thing Ebony needed was more disappointment in her life. It was up to Brett now. Did he think about a long-term relationship? Maybe marriage?

Chapter 58

Allison awoke to the sound of children's voices. Ebony and Lana were up and were outside in the hallway. She could hear Katy telling them to quiet down as they passed by her door.

She pulled herself to a sitting position and turned to look out of the window at the view of the backyard and the mountains in the distance. The sun was just peeking out from behind the clouds overhead. It would warm up, but the sun would be blinding against the newly fallen snow.

A movement in the yard below caught her attention. Brett was heading for the house, his arms loaded to capacity with firewood. She could see a puff of what looked like steam escaping his lips as he approached the house. Samuel had finished clearing the walkway and was spreading salt.

Allison eased herself out of bed and headed to the bathroom for her shower. When she finished, she dried off and pulled out a warm gold sweater and a pair of black leggings from the closet. She dressed and headed back to the bathroom to brush her teeth and style her hair.

Allison thought about the day. It was Thanksgiving. This time she wasn't alone. She had family and loving friends to share Thanksgiving with.

She walked down the stairs and entered the kitchen where she could hear voices. Peter, Samuel,

Rebecca, and Katy were busy with breakfast and greeted her as she entered the room.

Ebony and Lana were seated at the table with Brett. They were patiently awaiting their French toast which Rebecca was kind enough to fix for everyone. The room smelled of freshly brewed coffee and maple syrup.

"Need more help?" asked Allison as she walked over to where Samuel was pouring coffee.

"Nope I think we have it covered," replied Samuel grabbing a plate of food and sitting down at the table. "Are you ready for some of Rebecca's special French toast?" he asked.

"Sounds great, it looks like the girls are enjoying it," said Allison as she grabbed a plate and joined the girls.

"Good," said Ebony.

Lana looked at Allison and smacked her lips and then put a big bite into her mouth.

Allison joined everyone at the table. She bowed her head and silently said grace before putting a bite of French toast into her mouth. It was delicious. There was a distinct taste of a spice she couldn't quite distinguish.

"Rebecca, these are delicious. You'll have to give me the recipe," said Allison. She continued to eat while watching the girls. It was nice seeing them getting along so well.

With breakfast out of the way, and the kitchen cleaned up, it was time to prepare some of the dishes for the Thanksgiving meal later that day.

Rebecca was busy preparing her Gingerbread Bundt Cake, and Katy was making a pumpkin pie. They worked side by side in the kitchen with Ebony and Lana eager to help. Katy let Lana stir the pumpkin mixture in the bowl and Ebony was helping stir the Bundt cake with her grandmother.

Allison helped Peter and Samuel get out the Thanksgiving decorations that were stored in the closet in the dining room.

There were candle holders with red and white candles. Fall leaves in browns, yellows, and reds entwined within large and small silver pinecones made up the centerpiece. A green linen tablecloth would complement the table well. Allison saw a smile cross Peter's face as he handed each item to her.

"It's been a long time since these have been used. Maggie loved the holidays and went all out with the decorating," said Peter. His expression changed as the memories rushed in on him. "I'll help Samuel get the dinnerware and glasses out if you want to set up everything else," he said.

Allison placed the tablecloth on the table and then put the centerpiece in the center of the table. She was just setting the candle holders on each end when Samuel and Peter entered the room, their arms loaded with dinnerware.

Allison grabbed a couple of plates from Peter and start placing them on the table. The plates complimented the centerpiece wonderfully. Each white dinner plate had engraved fall leaves on them. Samuel handed her the mugs and glassware for each place setting.

In a short time, the table was all set for the afternoon meal and Allison was amazed at how beautiful everything looked.

"I think our work is done," said Peter giving Allison a look of approval.

"It's beautiful," said Allison. "I think I'll see if Maggie needs any help in the kitchen.

"Why don't we see if the girls are up for a sled ride," said Samuel.

"I'll go see if I can pry them away from Maggie and Katy," said Peter walking towards the kitchen. As he got closer, he could hear laughter.

Peter entered the kitchen with Samuel right behind him. "Girls, how would you like to go sledding? You need to bundle up though," said Samuel.

The two girls starting jumping up and down, yelling, "Sled, Sled."

"Let's go get you dressed," said Katy. Allison followed close behind.

The girls followed them upstairs and put on their coats, hats, and gloves before going downstairs to sit on the bench to pull on their boots. Allison could see the excitement building. Samuel and Peter waited patiently for them to get ready.

Once they were done, Samuel and Peter took each one by the hand and led them out the front door. The air was crisp, but the sun was shining. The landscape had accumulated new powder.

Samuel walked over to the shop building, his boots sinking into the fresh snow, and a few minutes later came back with two red sleds. Peter grabbed one of the ropes and pulled it along with Ebony by his side. She looked up at him and smiled.

Lana sitting proudly on the other sled as Peter pulled it along, held onto the sides tightly. Peter glanced back to make sure she was holding on.

They approached a small hill just to the right of the shop building. Samuel put Ebony in front of him and held onto her. Peter and Lana did the same.

With one big push off, they were soaring down the hill. Flashes of the countryside and the wind rushed up around them. Squeals of delight rang out from the girls.

When they reached the bottom, the girl's said, "Again! Again!"

They were going down for the second time when Allison spotted them through the living room window. Memories came flashing back to her.

Every winter Allison's father would take her up to Falls Meadow just outside of Rustin, and they would spend the whole day playing in the snow. It was a magical time, and Allison knew that Ebony and Lana would have beautiful memories of their own to recall later. *Would I be with Ebony to enjoy more of them?*

Chapter 59

Everyone was seated at the dining room table. Samuel and Peter were seated at the head. Candles glowed at each end of the table, and the lights were turned down.

There was a feast before them. Roast turkey with all the trimmings, mashed potatoes, green bean casserole, rolls, and two different salads. There was even homemade ice cream which the girls had helped make.

Peter had led them in prayer, and they were just about to eat when they heard the doorbell.

Samuel excused himself and went to answer it. As he approached the door, the bell rang again.

When he opened it, a woman in a knit cap, coat, and boots was standing there. Her long black hair hung down around her shoulders, and she appeared to be in her early thirties. Her trim body made him think that she worked out. In the driveway sat a Cadillac SUV.

"Hello, I'm Rita. I'm looking for my sister, Katy. I hope I have the right house," she said. Rita stood mesmerized, the man in front of her looked strikingly familiar.

"You sure do. Please come in. We are just sitting down to dinner. There's more than enough for one more," said Samuel.

Rita entered the hallway and sat down on the bench. She put her gloves in her coat and hung it on

283

the rack. She pulled off her hat, scarf, and boots. Peter saw her shiver.

"Would you like some coffee?" asked Samuel. "The kitchen is this way."

Rita started to follow Samuel into the kitchen when Lana spotted her. She hopped down from the table yelling as she ran towards her.

"Auntie Rita, you came!" said Lana.

"I wouldn't let my favorite girl down, now would I?" said Rita grabbing her up into her arms and embracing her in a big hug.

"Momma, Momma, Auntie Rita's here," yelled Lana, as she fought to get down.

Katy got up from the table to greet her sister. There were a lot of tears from both of them and then a long hug. Lana crowded in between both of them.

The three of them walked over to the table, and Rita took an empty seat next to Katy and Lana.

Katy introduced Rita to everyone and then began eating. Lana was so excited about Rita showing up that she hardly took time out to eat. Katy finally had to tell her to finish her food.

When the feast was over and dishes cleared away into the kitchen, they all gathered around the fireplace while Samuel sang. When he first started to sing, Rita realized why he looked familiar.

With the onset of late afternoon, Katy went upstairs to pack her things for the trip to her sister's.

With the weather being so unpredictable, Rita didn't want to take any chances that they might hit some flurries. It was still cold outside, but it had warmed a little. But, that would all change once the sun went down.

Katy made her way down the stairs carrying her suitcase. Her stay had been enjoyable. But now she would have to concentrate on settling her insurance claim for the damage to her vehicle, getting settled into Rita's, and the big decision of whether they would move there permanently. She didn't know if she was ready to make that decision.

She still missed Scott. A year had passed since she found out he had died, but it was as fresh as yesterday. *How am I supposed to go on with my life without him?*

They had met at college and had fallen deeply in love and were married six months later. Then when Lana came along, life was complete. Lana was Scott's special girl. There was nothing he wouldn't have done for her.

Now it was just the two of them, alone. Katy had tried throwing herself into her work but then found herself neglecting time to spend with Lana.

The past few days with the Evans family restored her hope in a new future. They were supportive, loving people that had become like family to her. She would make a point of keeping in touch.

When she stepped off of the staircase, her sister was there waiting for her. Lana was standing by her side, her hand grasping Rita's.

"Ready, Momma?" asked Lana.

"Have you said goodbye to everyone?"

"Yes. Momma, can Ebony come visit us?" asked Lana.

"That's up to her dad, but it's okay with me. I'm sure Rita wouldn't mind," said Katy.

Lana looked up at Rita waiting for a look of approval.

285

"Sure, honey. Well, we better get going before the weather kicks up again," said Rita walking towards the front door.

Samuel grabbed the suitcase from Katy and carried it out to Rita's SUV. Allison and Peter were close behind.

After lots of hugs, and promises for another visit, Rita put Lana in the back seat and buckled her in. She got in, and the SUV's engine fired up.

Katy stood outside the SUV with Samuel. Samuel gave her a business card with his private number.

"Katy, please stay in touch and know that you are welcome here anytime," said Samuel, a look of sadness in his eyes as he hugged her.

"I will. Your family has made this Thanksgiving the best one in a long time. I'm going to miss all of you, and I know Lana will miss Ebony very much. They have become such good friends," said Katy and she walked towards the SUV.

She waved as she got in and looked away. Tears streamed down her cheeks leaving a trail of hot liquid that burned into her heart.

"Are you okay, Katy?" asked her sister.

"Yeah, I'll be fine," said Katy. She tried to concentrate on the landscape. She watched in the rearview mirror as the house faded out of sight.

Chapter 60

With Katy and Lana gone, the house seemed amazingly quiet. Samuel, Peter, and Allison sat at the kitchen breakfast bar sipping on a cup of hot cocoa. Brett, Rebecca, and Ebony had gone into town to pick up a few things.

"Anyone else here feeling a sense of loss since Katy and Lana left?" asked Samuel waiting for a response.

"I sure am. Katy and I became good friends. She is like the sister I never had and Lana, well she is just unforgettable," said Allison taking another sip of cocoa.

"Who would have imagined under the circumstances, that they would seem like family in such a short time. It was as if they were always meant to be here. God sure works in mysterious ways," said Peter. He got up from his stool and moved over to the windows glancing out at the landscape before him. "It's almost like what happened to me years ago," he said.

"What do you mean, Dad?" asked Samuel.

I guess I never told you about it. It was a long time ago," said Peter.

"It was the night before Christmas Eve. I lived in an apartment over an auto shop. We ran a towing service, and a call came out that there had been an accident on the highway."

"Well, I jumped into the tow truck. I didn't know what I would find but hoped that it was just a slide off into a ditch or something.

"When I arrived at the scene, the car sat just off the road, a beautiful woman was leaning against the side of her car. She was cold and shivering so I took off my jacket and put it around her shoulders. The woman smiled up at me with the most beautiful blue eyes I had ever seen. I took her over to my tow truck, got her settled in the seat, and offered her a cup of hot coffee from my thermos.

"I loaded the car on the tow truck and drove her back into town. She left the car to have the repairs done, so I drove her home. There was something about her. I couldn't get her off my mind. That woman was your mother, Samuel."

"Wow, I had no idea," said Samuel.

"Do you feel God brought the two of you together?" asked Allison as she walked up beside Peter.

"Yes. God had a hand in our lives from that point on," said Peter. His voice was softer, and it was apparent that the memories were closing in on him.

Allison knew he was hurting and felt she needed to do something to take their mind off the subject.

"Anyone up for cake and ice cream?" asked Allison.

"Sure," said Peter.

Samuel walked over and picked up the covered cake dish that housed Rebecca's famous Bundt cake while Peter got out the ice cream. Allison placed a piece on each plate while Peter added a couple of generous scoops of the homemade ice cream.

They were enjoying their dessert when they heard the front door slam and footsteps approaching the kitchen.

"Allie, grandma bought me a new movie. Will you watch it with us?" asked Ebony all excited.

"Sure," said Allison in between bites of cake. "Are you ready for cake and ice cream first?" she asked.

"Yeah, ice cream!" yelled Ebony.

"What's all the yelling about?" asked Brett as he entered the kitchen.

"I'm gonna have cake and ice cream, and then Allison's gonna watch my movie with me," said Ebony.

"You're not eating cake and ice cream without me. Move over," said Brett taking a bite of her cake. "Boy, that's pretty good," he said.

Rebecca entered the room and smiled seeing that everyone was enjoying her Bundt cake. "Did you save a piece for me?" she asked.

Samuel cut her a piece and put some ice cream on top. She took her place at the breakfast bar next to Peter. He smiled at her as she sat down.

"Did you have a good time in town?" he asked.

"It was pretty. All the new snow hanging off the branches, and loading up the roofs of the town buildings. We even found Ebony a new movie which I'm sure she has told everyone about by now," said Rebecca.

"Yeah, we are all required to watch it with her after we finish our dessert," said Samuel.

Ebony gobbled up her cake and ice cream in a matter of minutes and was ready to watch the movie. Her favorite movies were, of course, Disney, and she couldn't wait to watch The Little Mermaid.

They all gathered around in the living room to watch the movie. Allison sat next to Brett with Ebony between them. Samuel took a chair next to the fireplace. Peter opted for the other corner of the couch next to Rebecca.

This is a family at its best. A family joining together to embrace what a young child feels is important to her. She loved how Brett and Rebecca always put Ebony first and tried their best to be there for her. They couldn't take the place of her mother, but they could bring a little joy into her life and make sure she knew she would never be alone and would always be loved.

Chapter 61

It was around 8 p.m., and Ebony was sound asleep. It wasn't an easy task, as she was wound up from all the day's activities.

Samuel was gathering some firewood and Peter had gone into the kitchen to collect the trash to take to the dumpster outside. He was just heading out the back door when Samuel was heading out for another armload of wood.

"Dad, let me get that for you. No need for you to go out in the cold. I'm heading back out anyway," said Samuel.

"Thanks, I appreciate it," said Peter heading into the living room.

Allison was sitting in one of the armchairs next to the fire. She was lost in thought and didn't hear him come in.

"Is everything okay Allison. You seem especially quiet," asked Peter.

"Have you ever got a message from God to do something you had a hard time with?" she asked.

"You bet. Many times," he said.

"What did you do?" asked Allison.

"I prayed a lot and remembered the scripture that said that God doesn't call unless he equips," he said walking over placing a hand on her shoulder.

"Do you want to talk to me about it? I'm always here to listen," he said.

291

"God placed it on my heart to go and see Romero, the man who robbed me. I'm just not sure I can handle it," said Allison. "I mentioned it to Samuel, and he suggested I leave it to the professionals."

Allison got up from her chair and paced in front of the fireplace, stopping only to glance up at Peter.

"You're right. Samuel won't want you to go alone, but I understand that this is something you have to do. We all have to obey God. It's our duty," he said. "But, why not talk to Samuel and let him drive you to the prison. You're going to need support when you leave there. You have no idea what you're facing. Samuel has experience with these things, and so does Brett, let them help you," said Peter.

"You have a point. God did tell me to have my brother help, but Brett, that's a tough one. He has all this training, and I don't know a thing about what I'm walking into. I'm sure he will try to talk me out of it." She knew that Samuel was protective, but she had to bring him around.

"Talk to Samuel. I'm sure he can help," said Peter as he hugged Allison. "You are family, we stick together no matter what."

"Talk to Samuel about what," he asked placing the last armload of firewood into the box.

"Sit down, Samuel and I'll tell you," said Allison taking a seat in one of the chairs by the fireplace.

"What have you been hiding?" asked Samuel teasingly.

"Don't laugh. God has placed something on my heart. I've tried to dismiss it, but I've been called to do it. I mentioned it to you before. I have to go see Romero," said Allison.

All the color drained from Samuel's face. "You're still considering going by yourself?"

"I tried to argue with God about it, but the message was pretty clear. I have to see him. I've been called by God to do it," said Allison.

Samuel got up from his chair in an agitated state. She could see his irritation building.

"Allison, you don't know what you are saying. Romero is a felon. He has no respect for anyone and even less for you. You are one of his victims. He will eat you up and spit you out. Dad, tell me you tried to talk her out of this," asked Samuel.

"I told her she would need her family to lean on and that she needed to have you go with her. I understand why she has to do this. God has laid it on her heart, and he will equip her to follow through," said Peter.

"Why on earth would God want her to go see someone who has brought her so much pain? I can understand my working with them because that is what I've been called to do, but Allison. No way!" said Samuel.

"Samuel, please don't be upset with me. I didn't choose this, but God told me to have you help me. He has chosen you to be a part of this. Please, tell me that you'll help me. I can't-do it without you," she said. Tears were beginning to fill her eyes. Since she first met Samuel, she had never seen him like this. Why was he fighting her on it?

Chapter 62

Brett drove along the interstate with his mother in the seat beside him. Allison was in the back with Ebony, who was sound asleep, her head resting on Allison's shoulder.

The ride home was maneuvered in silence, except for the occasional comment in regards to the scenery. The mountains started to fade away in the distance and were replaced with the flatter landscape of the meadows.

Allison rode along, her gaze fixed on the landscape that rushed by as they covered the short distance between Denver and Rustin. Memories of the past few days filled her head.

She couldn't help but feel saddened by Samuel's change towards her. She hoped that he would come around as Peter suggested he would. She could only pray he was right. It was the first rift they had since they met.

Allison looked over at Ebony as she slept. She reached over to straighten her head a little, and she stirred but didn't wake up.

An hour later, Brett, was pulling up in front of Allison's house. He turned off the engine, got out, and helped Allison carry in her luggage in.

Allison thought she was composed until Brett looked down at her with those eyes of his. "Allison, you've been quiet all the way home. Is something wrong?"

That's all it took for the waterworks to start.

Brett gathered her into his arms and let her get it all out before pulling her away from him. "What's wrong?"

"Samuel and I had our first argument. He barely said goodbye to me. Can I ask you a question?"

"Sure."

"Samuel is upset because I'm going to go see Romero. He doesn't want me to go alone, even though I asked him to drive me there."

"I can understand his concern. Prison isn't somewhere I would want you to go either. Why are you going?"

"It's something God called me to do, and Samuel is supposed to help me turn Romero around. Bring him to God. I can't do it alone," said Allison taking a seat on the sofa.

"Give him time. He'll come around. I have to get Ebony and my Mom home. It's been a long day. Call me anytime if you need to talk. Pray. God is listening," he said as he walked towards the door.

Brett gave her a soft kiss and wiped away the tear that had slid down her cheek. Moments later she watched as his truck backed out of the driveway.

She was alone with her thoughts. She bowed her head and said a prayer that God would soften Samuel's heart. She wanted to call him so badly, but he probably wouldn't be ready to talk about it yet. It was too soon.

She picked up her suitcase and unpacked. She left her room with a few articles of clothing and headed for the washer. Soon, the lull of the washing machine replaced the quiet.

Peter had sent her home with quite a few leftovers which she placed in the refrigerator. She put the kettle on for tea and sat at the kitchen table.

The clock on the wall said 4:30 p.m. Carol should be off work since it was a Friday afternoon, so she picked up the phone, dialed the number, and waited for her to pick up.

Allison spent the next hour filling Carol in on all the details of what took place over the last few days. Carol suggested having Brett set up the meeting with Romero and then call Samuel to see if he changed his mind. If not, maybe Brett could take her.

What Carol said made sense, but then God gave her explicit instructions for her brother to help. Maybe God meant differently. She had to be patient, and perhaps it would be revealed to her in time.

After the call to Carol, Allison heated up a plate of Thanksgiving leftovers and watched a Christian movie on television. In the movie, a man in prison was led to Christ. *Was it a coincidence? Allison didn't think so.* She watched as the counselor in the movie began reading the Bible. Maybe there was a message there that could help her.

After watching the movie to the end, she found it to be inspiring. With God's help, she might just make a difference in Romero's life. Maybe he just needed someone to care about him. After all, he was still God's child even if he didn't believe it.

That night as Allison lay in bed, the nightmares started, with Satan trying to fill her mind with fear, doubt, and insecurity.

Just as she got to the most vivid part of the dream, a heavenly spirit appeared.

Calmness came over her, and the spirit warrior filled her with strength, and in the end, she was victorious. The spirit warrior crushed fear, doubt, and insecurity with one swift blow.

It had all seemed so real. God had given her the power to fight against all forces of darkness and be victorious. She knew she was capable of dealing with any vicious comments that came out of Roberto's mouth by using scripture.

She knew it wasn't going to be easy, nor immediate. Romero would fight her, but she would be relentless. With her brother or Brett helping, she would fulfill God's directive.

She grabbed her pillow and fluffed it up, rolled over in the bed, and pulled up the covers. She would sleep a peaceful sleep wrapped in the security of her Lord.

Chapter 63

It was early afternoon when she heard a vehicle pull up in the driveway. She looked out the living room window and saw Brett getting out of his SUV.

Allison walked over to the door and opened it. The crisp, brisk winter air slammed her with its bitter wind, and she quickly shut it. A couple of minutes later, she heard a loud knock and opened it.

"It's brutal out there. It looks like snow is going to start falling any minute," said Allison ushering him inside and quickly shutting the door behind him.

"The wind does have a bite to it."

Allison wondered what had brought him over. Brett usually didn't just drop by without calling.

"Have a seat. Would you like some hot tea?"

"Sounds great," he said taking a seat on the sofa. "I have some news for you."

Allison placed the tea kettle on the stove and lit the burner under it. She joined Brett on the sofa while she waited for it to signal that it was ready.

"I hope its good news," she said.

"I have an appointment set up at the prison for you to see Romero, next Tuesday at 3 p.m. Have you heard from your brother yet?"

"No."

"If he doesn't get back to you before then, I'll go with you," he said smiling at her. "I wouldn't want you to go alone. It's a rough place."

"I know it won't be easy, but I trust God to give me the words I need to say," said Allison getting up to retrieve the kettle that was whistling and sending steam out into the air."

Allison poured the hot water into two cups and added a tea bag. Brett got up off the sofa joining her. They carried their tea over to the kitchen table and sat beside each other sipping the hot liquid, talking in between sips.

"Allison, I had a wonderful time spending Thanksgiving with you at your brother's and having a playmate for Ebony made a world of difference to brighten up her day," said Brett taking a sip of tea.

"Katy and Lana were a great addition to the holiday, I'm going to miss them. I do hope Katy keeps in touch," said Allison.

"I noticed Samuel exchanging phone numbers and addresses with her. I think he's smitten with her," said Brett getting up and placing his cup in the sink. "Well, I guess I better get going. I have to get home to Ebony. We have a movie night tonight."

"Tell her I said hello and I'll see her soon."

He walked over to where Allison was standing and placed his hands on her shoulders.

"Allison, I feel like we have the start of a great relationship. We have a lot in common, and Ebony seems to like you a lot. What would you say to making it official and start dating?" asked Brett.

Allison had thought of exactly this conversation many times, but now that he had asked her, she was speechless. It took a couple of minutes for her to get the words out.

"I'd like that very much."

"Great. How about dinner tomorrow night? Around 6:30?"

"It's a date," said Allison.

Brett gave her a soft kiss on the lips and a hug before letting her go.

"I'll pick you up around six," he said making his way towards the door.

Allison stood in the middle of the living room stunned. *Am I dreaming or did he ask to start dating? Even more remarkable, did I agree?*

God was about to do something unbelievable with her life. She smiled thinking about Ebony and how much she adored her. Maybe her dream of a family of her own was more than possible. She smiled to herself and started concentrating on what to make for dinner. Tomorrow was planned. She had a date with a Christian man that she was very fond of.

The next morning the phone rang. It was Samuel.

"Hi, Allison, before you say anything, let me speak. I know I over reacted and I'm sorry. I just couldn't bear the thought of you having to look at the person who hurt you. I know how hateful felons can be. I just wanted to spare you. If you still insist on going, I'll take you," said Samuel.

Allison could hear that he was genuinely sorry and she felt terrible for him. Now it was up to her to extend a hand of forgiveness and accept his apology.

"I was hoping you would say that. God intends for us to do this together. I've thought about it, and I want you to go in with me. Do you have an extra Bible or magazines we can bring to him? I realize he may not want them, but I have to try," said Allison.

"I can gather a few things up. When do you want to go?"

"The appointment Brett set for me is on Tuesday at 3 p.m. Is that going to work for you?"

"Sounds fine, why don't I drive up on Monday and spend the night at the house with you if that's okay," he asked.

"Sounds great, maybe you can talk Peter into coming too. We can have dinner here at the house. Maybe have Brett, Ebony, and Rebecca too. I know your Dad, seems to get along with her well," said Allison.

"I'll see what I can do. It's hard to pull dad away from the garage sometimes, and he doesn't like to travel if the weather is bad. Hopefully, it won't get any worse. It's coming down pretty good here."

"See you Monday. I'm happy you called. I wanted to call you, but I was afraid it was too soon," said Allison.

"Have a good weekend. We both miss you," said Samuel.

"Me too. See you soon."

Chapter 64

Allison and Samuel are led along a brightly lit hallway and into a secure room at the end of the hall. Romeo sat cuffed at a table, dressed in a typical orange jumpsuit.

It was stark and cold, and Allison shivered just realizing the sense of hopelessness that it brought within her. Her pulse raced and her breath caught in her throat.

Allison and Samuel took a seat across from Romeo. His eyes stared directly into Allison's with a look of hatred that she had a hard time dismissing. It made her skin crawl.

A guard stood by the door, a reminder that they weren't alone.

The cold, hard walls seemed to close in on her. She felt her hands tremble. She said a silent prayer. *Lord, please help me. I don't know if I can do this.* Her throat was dry, and when she swallowed, she felt as though a stone was lodged in her throat. *What can I say, Lord?*

Samuel sat trying to size Romeo up. He shifted in his seat, his eyes not leaving Romeo's. Silence filled the room with a deafening fullness.

Then, as if by no will of her own Allison spoke. "Why did you want to kill me, Romeo? I was a stranger to you," she said. Her voice seemed to shake, but she was sure of what she said.

"Wrong place, wrong time, bitch. You should have died," said Romeo giving her a look that made her squirm.

Samuel held his tongue even though everything inside of him wanted to lash out at Romero. He wanted to come to his sister's aid, but God told him to sit still.

"Only, God decides when my time is up. He saved me for a reason," said Allison.

"Your, God doesn't exist. The gun jammed," said Romero. "Why are you here anyway?"

"I wanted you to know that my God is a God of forgiveness and I forgive you. Your life doesn't have to end this way, Romeo. You can turn your life around. God loves you and wants to free you from this life," said Allison looking directly into Romeo's eyes.

Samuel took it as his signal to pass the Bible and other Christian tracts over to Romero. "Romero, my sister is trying to reach out to you. She wants to help," said Samuel.

"I didn't ask for her help. Where was her God when my father almost beat my mother to death? I sure don't need him now!"

Romero glanced down at the Bible, and a throaty laugh that seemed non-human escaped his throat. "Go back to your life, I don't need your God."

With one broad swoop of his hands, he swept the Bible, and other tracts from the table and they hit the floor with a bang, which made the guard react. He walked up to Romero.

"The meeting is over," said the guard jerking Romero from his seat and pushing him towards the door.

Samuel gathered up the books and pushed them into the guard's hands to send back to Romero's cell. The guard grabbed them and continued on his way.

Allison's encounter with Romero was more emotional than she could have imagined, but then Samuel had warned her that it would be hard.

The memory of the day when Romeo robbed her, and she almost died weighed heavily over her like a massive anvil. She had to remind herself that this was just the first step towards fulfilling God's request. He didn't say it would be easy, only that he would be there with her every step of the way. Allison sobbed as she left the coldness of the building.

Samuel walked alongside her on the way to the truck. The silence only broken by the sound of the crunching of the gravel beneath their feet.

"I'm sorry, Allison. I didn't want you to go alone. Young people in Romero's situation become very hardened to anyone or anything after their incarceration," said Samuel. "We just need to give him some time."

"You're right. Maybe sooner or later Romero will read the Bible," said Allison, a tear escaping her eye and running down her cheek. "I just don't feel like I accomplished much today."

"You planted the seed. It will grow from that. Maybe that's all God intended for you to do. I'll call Brett and see if he wants to visit him with me. He is trained in outreach work, and between the two of us, we won't give up on him. I've worked with far worse felons than Romero," said Samuel opening the door for Allison. Allison got in and put on her seat belt.

Samuel got in, buckled up, and started up the engine. In a few minutes, they were headed to the gate and after a quick check of their truck, they were waved on through.

Allison glanced out the side mirror and saw the massive building with its guard towers vanish into the distance. She wondered how the prisoners could ever come out of an experience like that without being changed for the worse. Allison knew their only hope was in finding Christ.

At that moment, she knew how vital Samuel and Brett's outreach work was in saving lives. She wanted to be a part of that change, even if she had to go through some unpleasant times. Through God, the experience would change her too. She would work to become more like Christ through love and forgiveness.

Chapter 65

Samuel and Peter showed up early Monday afternoon. Allison was glad that Peter came.

Allison was convinced that there was a spark starting between Peter and Rebecca which could end up being something more. She hoped so. Peter and Rebecca both deserved to be happy, and maybe God meant for them to do that together.

A knock on the door broke her train of thought. She opened the door, and Ebony ran up and grabbed her by the waist giving her a big hug.

"Hi, honey. Don't you look nice," said Allison checking out Ebony's pink dress that made her eyes sparkle.

"Dad said we're going to eat dinner with you. Is grandpa here too?"

Peter walked up to Ebony. "Hey, squirt. How's my favorite girl?"

Ebony hugged him and gave him a big smile. Peter smiled back at her, took her hand and led her over to the couch. She immediately crawled up into his lap snuggling in close.

Just seeing the two of them together made Allison's heart fill with joy. She knew that he always wanted grandchildren and Ebony loved pretending he was her grandfather.

Rebecca walked over and took a seat next to Peter. He smiled and Ebony leaned over and grabbed Rebecca's hand trying to pull her closer. She gave her a quick squeeze and got up to see if Allison needed any help with dinner.

Brett and Samuel were talking about their experiences with their outreach programs. Allison could hear Samuel asking Brett about going to visit Romero. She hoped that eventually, Romero would be open to accepting the Lord.

Brett crossed the room entering the kitchen. His Mom was helping Allison dish up the food.

"Brett, could you give me a hand with the leaf for the table. We're going to need extra room," asked Allison.

"Sure," he said picking up the leaf that was tucked away against the wall and installing it on the table. "That should handle everyone nicely."

"Thanks," said Allison as she placed the food in the middle of the table. Rebecca was doing the place settings for each person and was humming as she worked.

With everything ready, Rebecca called everyone in to eat. They all gathered around the table, and Allison felt blessed that her house was filled with the love of family and close friends.

With heads bowed, Samuel said grace.

Ebony sat between her dad and grandmother. She looked from one person to another grinning before taking a bite of food.

"Grandma isn't it good," she said as she took bites of her fried chicken and mashed potatoes. The broccoli she pushed from side to side indicating it wasn't one of her favorites.

"Ebony, you need to eat your vegetables too. I know they aren't your favorite, but you need to eat some," she said giving her a stern look.

Everyone continued to enjoy the food. Allison made a pot of coffee and put on the tea kettle. She had made a banana cake for dessert. I was her mom's recipe and was one of her favorites.

Her cake was a big hit with everyone, especially Ebony who tried to get a second piece but was stopped by her dad. Too much sugar- not a good thing before bed.

With the dinner over, dishes done and put away, everyone gathered in the living room to visit. Ebony snuggled in between Peter and Rebecca and was watching cartoons on the television.

Allison, Bret, and Samuel were discussing the new wing of the church and how it was coming along. The structure was built, and the contractors were working on the inside rooms which were coming together well. They had so many extra volunteers from the community that provided their time to help finish in their area of expertise that they were ahead of schedule.

If things kept progressing as they hoped, it looked like they would be ready to open by Christmas. Carol had consulted on some of the choices for the interior and had saved them a ton of money due to contacts she had with suppliers.

"Allison, are you ready to start training on Monday? Rev Williams wants me to walk you through everything that your job entails," said Brett.

"Nothing I would like more. I'm sure there is a lot to learn, and I can't wait to start working again," said Allison. "What time on Monday?"

"Around 10 a.m.," said Brett.

"I'll see you then. Can't wait to see how the new building is coming along," said Allison taking a sip of her tea.

"I hope you enjoy the outreach part of the church as much as I do," said Samuel smiling at Allison.

A few months ago, Allison, would never have thought of outreach being a part of her career choices. But then, God had other ideas. Would she learn to approach this part of her life with a willing heart?

Chapter 66

Peter couldn't take his eyes off of Rebecca. She was a striking woman, and the love of Jesus was evident within her. He was struggling with the urge to ask her out on a date.

Part of him was hesitant, even though Maggie had been gone for a long time. It was hard putting his life with her behind him and moving on. His mind didn't want to let go of the memories, but his heart ached with the urge to find love again. Samuel was right, he needed to go on with his life. Even Maggie wanted that. So then why was he having such a hard time with it?

Rebecca realized he was looking at her and smiled at him. It made his heart melt a little every time she smiled. Her smile was infectious, and it brought such a joy to his heart. Ebony's eyes were closed signaling that she had fallen asleep in his arms.

He got Rebecca's attention, and the words just poured out. "Rebecca, I hope you don't find this too forward, but I enjoy your company very much. Would you consider going out on a date with me sometime?" asked Peter.

Peter saw the look on Rebecca's face change to one of surprise. She waited a couple of minutes before answering. Peter waited with anticipation.

"Peter, I didn't think I would ever date again, but then you came along. I enjoy your company too, and I would love to go out with you sometime. It's going to be a little difficult though since we live in two different towns," said Rebecca.

"We can work that out. We'll take it slow and see where it goes," said Peter. He reached over taking her hand in his.

"Okay," she said placing her hand on his. "I look forward to it."

About that time, Brett entered the living room.

"Well, Mom, are you ready to head for home. It looks like Ebony needs to get to bed," said Brett as he put on his coat. He carefully lifted Ebony from Peter's lap. She stretched but didn't wake.

"I'm a little tired myself. It's been a wonderful evening," said Rebecca as she got up from the couch and retrieved her coat from the coat rack by the front door.

Allison walked over and gave Rebecca a hug and kissed Ebony on the top of her head. Brett reached down and planted a kiss on Allison's lips before she even realized what happened. Everyone in the room was taken by surprise.

"Okay everyone, Allison and I have agreed to start dating. Now you know," said Brett finally relieved that it was out in the open.

No one said a word, but the smiles on their faces said everything.

Brett and Allison had been working together at the church for a couple of weeks. Everything was going well, and she was learning quickly. Of course, Allison felt it was because Brett was a good teacher. He had provided her with some workbooks entailing all the center's programs. She had asked numerous questions which he had answered and went into vivid detail to make sure she understood completely.

Carol had shown up unexpectedly, and Allison spent time filling her in on all the things that had been happening in her life and how they had changed her.

The old Allison from the past was fading away and being replaced with a new Allison filled with faith, hope, trust and lots of love. Her life was so much fuller now and each day seemed to present itself with unique opportunities to shine for the Lord. She was happy and filled with joy.

Allison's feelings for Brett had deepened. Brett had started out as a good friend and now was someone she wanted to live the rest of her life with. She loved Ebony with all her heart, and Ebony got excited every time Allison was around.

Rebecca seemed to be happy about their relationship also. She went out of her way to make Allison welcome and was pleased with the change in Brett since they met.

Allison and Brett had many dates over the next couple of weeks, some alone and some with Ebony along. When they ate out, the restaurant staff and patrons always thought they were already a family.

There were trips to the movies, visits to the zoo, and dinners at Brett's house. Their kisses became more passionate and lingered longer and love blossomed in Allison's heart.

Chapter 67

Allison was straightening up the house when she heard a knock on the front door. She went to answer it and to her surprise, was greeted by Peter.

"Oh, my goodness, come in," said Allison.

Peter knocked the snow from his shoes and slipped them off before entering the house. He placed his coat on the rack by the front door.

"Samuel didn't come with you?" asked Allison.

"Samuel's out of town doing a concert, and the house just seemed so empty. I decided a road trip is what I needed," he said.

"Well, I'm glad you're here. Can you stay for a few days?"

"I was hoping you would say that."

Allison got Peter all settled into one of the guest rooms, and she put on some coffee and the tea kettle for her.

"How was your drive? Were the roads slick?" asked Allison.

"Not bad. That's why I decided to leave today. There's no snow in the forecast for the next few days," said Peter. "I do have another reason for coming," said Peter.

"Oh, you sound so mysterious. Now, you have my curiosity going."

"The last time we were all here for dinner, I finally got my nerve up and asked Rebecca out. It was one of the hardest things I've ever done," he said.

"I'm not surprised. I could see that the two of you seemed to get along really well. I know it will make Brett happy. He has wanted his mom to find some-one. She's too sweet a lady to spend the rest of her life without someone to share it with," said Allison as she got up and hugged him.

The kettle whistled, and she went to make her cup of tea. "Coffee is also done if you would like a cup."

"Sounds good," he said.

Peter called Rebecca and made a dinner date at Allison's favorite Italian restaurant. He hung up the phone and gave Allison a quick smile indicating it was a date.

"You'll have a wonderful time at Geno's. The food is delicious, and the atmosphere is so romantic. It's where Brett and I went on our first unofficial date," said Allison.

"I'm going to go unpack and maybe take a short nap. I'm a little tired from the drive. I don't do much out of town driving anymore," said Peter.

"Just make yourself at home," said Allison.

Allison sat down on the sofa and decided to get out her Bible to spend some time with God. She said a prayer for God to bless the relationship of Peter and Rebecca. If they decided to get together, Rebecca would, of course, move to Denver with Peter. It would mean a lot of changes for Ebony too.

Allison realized at that moment that change most likely would start a domino effect. Even if it were for good, it would bring about changes for the whole family. She wondered what changes tomorrow would bring for her?

Chapter 68

It was the first week of December and Christmas was right around the corner. Allison felt like the year had flown by and with all the changes in her life, sometimes it seemed like a blur of fleeting moments.

Ever since her encounter with the Heavenly Spirits, she had continued to walk in her faith and felt closer to God than she ever had. Only a few months ago, she felt alone, and her future seemed bleak. This year, she would spend Christmas with family.

Samuel and Peter had invited everyone to their home for the holidays. Samuel had called Katy, and she agreed to join them. Her sister, Rita, was bringing her. It had been awhile since Katy's accident that had brought her and Lana into their lives, and Allison was looking forward to seeing them again.

It was a Wednesday morning. Allison awoke around 6:30 a.m. and was standing in front of the kitchen window watching the winter snow falling against the window pane. Some stuck to the window making intricate patterns.

It was a typical cold winter day. Winds blew the falling snow around outside, and Allison wondered about heading out to work. The snow plows had whizzed by earlier, but the roadway was most likely still slick. Driving in the winter in Rustin was a challenge.

The phone rang breaking the silence of the room.

"Hello," said Allison wondering who it could be.

"Hi, Allison. I'm sorry to call so early, but I wanted to catch you before you headed to work. The roads are a mess, and Rev. Williams wants all the staff to take time off today. He's closing up and transferring the phones to his house for the day," said Brett. "He wants to keep everyone safe."

"Actually, I was just sitting here wondering how bad the roads were. The snow plows have already been by my house early. I can't say I'm not relieved that I don't have to go out," said Allison placing the tea kettle on the stove.

"Schools have been canceled, so Ebony is home today too. When she found out I wasn't going to work, she had the day all planned for us. Color books, cartoons, and getting her grandmother to bake her some cookies," said Brett.

"Sounds like a day of fun. Wish I could join you," said Allison.

"We would love that. Maybe if the weather lets up over the weekend, we can do some Christmas shopping together. Since we will be at Peter and Samuel's this year, I would like to pick up a gift for them as well. Also, for Lana. Ebony is so excited about getting to see her again. I could hardly get her to sleep last night," he said.

"I can't wait to see them either," said Allison.

"Well, Ebony will be up soon wanting her chocolate chip pancakes. I'll call you later if I hear anything from Rev Williams about work tomorrow," said Brett. "Enjoy your day off."

"You too, give Ebony a kiss for me," said Allison.

She hung up the phone and smiled. Brett was such a good father. He reminded her of how her Dad used to be with her, and the memories of all the good times they had together while she was growing up put a smile on her face. But it seemed so long ago.

The kettle let out a shrill whistle, and Allison walked over and poured the hot water into a teacup. She added a tea bag and let it steep.

The snow was coming down in large flakes now, and visibility was so limited that she couldn't see across the street. The lampposts were still on emitting a golden glow creating a strange eeriness to the landscape.

Allison's mind was filled with her conversation with Brett. She knew he cared deeply for her, but she wanted to hear those three words-I love you. She came close to saying them to him the last time they were together, but she was waiting for him to say them first.

She was headed into the living room to watch a Christian program on the television when the phone rang again. She answered it on the second ring.

"Hi, Sis, I wasn't sure if you would be home or not," said Samuel.

"Brett just called, and everything is shut down because of bad weather. The roads are pretty bad. How is it there?" she asked.

"About the same, I was afraid my flight was going to get canceled, but some flights were shut down right after I landed in Denver," said Samuel. "Dad said he drove up to visit you for a couple of days while I was gone."

"I was missing you both, so it was a nice surprise. Do you think you will be down before Christmas?" asked Allison.

"If the weather lets up, I plan to. Brett, and I want to go see Romero again before the holidays. He's going to try to get him into his outreach program at the church. Sometimes it takes a while before they will even listen to what we have to say. But then if they don't have any visitors, they will be more open to seeing anyone. Even us." said, Samuel.

"I'm glad you are trying. God works in his time, not ours," said Allison.

"I talked to Katy and Lana yesterday. Lana is so excited about being able to see Ebony again. Those girls act more like sisters," said Samuel.

"I know. Brett said he could barely get Ebony to go to bed after he told her they were coming for Christmas," said Allison as she adjusted the heater's thermostat. She was feeling a little chilled. Evidently, the temperature outside was dropping fast.

"How are things with you and Brett?" asked Samuel.

"Everything is going well. I thought maybe it would be strange having Brett as my boss, but he's a great teacher. I'm learning a lot," said Allison.

"Do you love him?"

Allison wasn't ready for that question. She took a moment to regain her composure and answered.

"I think I'm starting too, but he hasn't told me he does yet?"

"I see the way he looks at you. It's just a matter of time. I think he has fallen for you big time. I see all the signs," said Samuel.

"This is coming from my single brother who isn't even dating," said Allison.

"Yeah, well. I know more than you think," Samuel said. "Well, got to run. I hear Dad rattling around in the kitchen. I might have to go rescue him."

"Okay. See you soon. Love you," said Allison.

"Love you too. Take care," said Samuel.

Allison never grew tired of Samuel and Peter's words of endearment. It felt good to hear them tell her they loved her. Now, she had to wait patiently to hear those same words from Brett. *But would he say them to her? Was he really the one she would spend the rest of her life with?*

Chapter 69

Everyone made it to Samuel and Peter's house for Christmas in spite of the weather. There was a lull, and the only window of opportunity was on Christmas eve, and they all took advantage of it.

From the moment you stepped into the foyer of the Evans home, you noticed that Christmas had enveloped the entire house. The staircase going to the top floor was wrapped in green and red garland topped off with silver and gold bows.

In the corner of the living room stood a fresh Noble Fir that looked as though it reached the top of the high ceiling. The tree was decorated with country ornaments of various shapes and sizes. Underneath the tree were Christmas presents wrapped in colorful paper to entice the Christmas, curiosity seekers.

The mantel above the fireplace gave a resting place for fresh pine boughs and candle holders with tall taper candles of white, green and red. Even the end tables by the couch were adorned with Santa figurines and snow globes.

As Brett, Ebony, and Rebecca entered, the fragrance of pine and spice enticed their senses'

Ebony broke loose from Brett's grasp right away and headed for the tree. She stood in awe of its gigantic size until she spotted the packages underneath.

"Can we put our presents under the tree too, Daddy?" asked Ebony jumping up and down.

"Sure honey. We have to leave room for Santa's presents though," said Brett.

Samuel kicked off the snow from his boots and entered with an armload of firewood. In a matter of minutes, he had a crackling fire going.

"How was your trip?" asked Samuel.

"Not too bad. Just a couple of slick patches as we got closer to Denver," said Brett.

"Need any help with your luggage?" asked Samuel.

"Sure. I have some packages to bring in too," said Brett heading for the front door. Samuel was right behind him.

The bitter cold blew wet snow across their face as they fought their way to Brett's SUV. He pushed the lever on the back hatch, and it popped open. He grabbed an armful of packages while Samuel retrieved the luggage.

Brett glanced toward the mountains and the massive accumulation of snow already gracing its peaks. It was going to be a record snowfall this winter.

Brett and Samuel scrambled up the walkway onto the front porch of the house knocking the snow from their boots before entering. They were just walking into the foyer as Peter was coming out of the kitchen.

"Hot coffee is ready. You two look like you could use some warming up," said Peter.

'I'm going to put our luggage upstairs, and I'll be ready," said Brett.

"Hi, you made it," said Allison walking through with a laundry basket. She followed Brett upstairs, and they visited as they climbed.

Allison took her clothes into her room and put them away. She was just coming out when Brett entered the hall.

"Where's Ebony and Rebecca?" asked Allison.

"Ebony spotted the tree. Mom was unable to pry her away from it. I can't imagine how she is going to be when the lights are turned on," said Brett.

"I remember how much I loved Christmas as a child. Still, do," said Allison.

Brett took Allison's hands in his and pulled her close to him. His lips found hers and enveloped them in a sweet passionate kiss that made her tingle all over. When their eyes met Brett said, "I love you."

Allison thought she was dreaming. It took a few minutes before she realized what he had said. She kissed him back and said, "I love you, too."

"Allison, this is a special Christmas for me. Being able to spend it with you and your family means the world to me. I've never seen Ebony happier than she is today. I never thought that I could love again, but then I met you. You're everything to me, and I want us to have a life together," said Brett as he pulled Allison close to him.

As Allison was being held in Brett's arms, her head resting on his shoulder, she saw a bubbly Ebony yelling, "Allie, Allie!"

Allison pulled away and gathered Ebony into her arms planting a big kiss on her cheek. Ebony hugged her back and then struggled to get down and pulled a small blue velvet box from her pocket.

"She knelt down on one knee, opened the box and repeated what her father had told her to say.

"Will you marry us?" she asked.

Allison looked over at Brett. He was patiently waiting for an answer. Ebony smiling from ear to ear got up from the floor.

Allison is so overwhelmed that she is speechless. There were tears of joy streaming down her face. *Could it be true?*

"Will you be my mommy?" Ebony asked waiting for an answer.

Allison scooped Ebony up and said, "I sure will."

As she held Ebony in her arms, Brett put the engagement ring on Allison's finger.

She stood looking at the diamond as it sparkled in the light, knowing that the rest of her life was just beginning. God had given her the desires of her heart, and it was so full of love that she thought she might not be able to contain it all.

"Well, should we go tell the others," asked Brett as he took her hand. But before they hit the bottom of the stairs, they could hear Ebony downstairs yelling.

"Gramma, Gramma I'm getting a new Mommy!"

Chapter 70

Allison and Brett decided on a New Year's Day wedding. Rebecca was happy beyond words and offered to help with the planning. Rev. Williams agreed to marry them at the church, and after some coaxing, they decided to have the reception at Peter's house. Samuel would be the best man and Peter would give her away.

Allison called Carol, who wholeheartedly agreed to be her maid of honor, along with Katy and Rita. Ebony and Lana would be flower girls.

Christmas with the Evans was terrific, with an afternoon of sledding for the girls, followed by hot chocolate around the fireplace. Lana and Ebony were inseparable. Their laughter could be heard throughout the house and Peter beamed. The once quiet house was now filled with love, laughter, and children.

Brett stood quietly looking out into the darkness of the night. The lights from the stars and moon cast a glow onto the snowy landscape, his heart filled to the brim with more joy than he had felt in a long time. He sipped his mulled cider and reflected on his past life.

His life with Vicky had been perfect from the beginning, and when Ebony came, he felt like God had given him an angel. Then when Vicky got sick, he felt as though he couldn't breathe and his beautiful life crumbled.

It happened so fast. One day, Vicky was bubbly and filled with life and then she was gone. Brett never thought he could ever love again. He was too afraid, and he didn't want to feel that kind of pain again-Ever.

He was angry at himself for a long time and with God.

Then slowly he turned back to the one chance for hope and peace for his life, Jesus. Things gradually began to make sense again. Some of the joy started to return. It happened slowly and not without lots of prayers.

He prayed for the hurt to stop, to be a better father, and to be able to hold onto what was left of his family. When he felt he was at his lowest, that's when God picked him up, dusted him off, and placed him on the road to recovery.

He thought of Allison. God sent him another angel. Allison was a loving, compassionate person who he loved with all his heart. He was taken with her almost immediately, even though his heart wasn't ready yet.

He knew he probably loved her from the moment he saw her. God knew what was in his heart and hers and there was no doubt that he had brought them together.

Ebony loved her so much, and he knew that Allison would be the best mom she could be. She could never replace Vicky, but then no one could, but Allison would be there to answer all the questions little girls needed to ask their mother growing up. Together they would watch her grow into a young lady, watch her attend her first dance, observe her first crush on a boy, graduate from high school, then college, marriage, grandchildren. They would watch what God would do in Ebony's life.

Brett didn't know what the future would bring. There were no guarantees, but with his soul mate and God by his side, he knew the future would be one of challenge, opportunity, and growth in God.

There were many things to work out. *Where will we live? Would Allison feel uneasy living in the same house I had shared with Vicky? What about my mother?*

He heard soft footsteps coming up behind him. A pair of arms wrapped around his waist and soft breath traveled down the side of his neck making his body burn with desire. Warm lips caressed the side of his neck and a whisper of three of the most beautiful words he thought he would never hear again fell upon his ears.

"I love you."

He turned and wrapped his arms around Allison and kissed her on the lips and then on her neck traveling down until he reached her shoulders. Allison pulled herself tighter into his embrace, lost in the passion of the moment.

It was the first time she had felt so sure of anything in her life. She couldn't imagine her life without Brett and Ebony. A tear of joy slid down her cheek as Brett pulled her from him.

"What's wrong?" he asked.

"Nothing. I'm just so happy," Allison said looking up into the eyes of the man she loved with all her heart.

"I promise. It is only the beginning. God brought us together, and he has great plans for our life. Together we will walk the path he has chosen for us, and we will honor him together," said Brett kissing her on her forehead. "I love you now and forever."

Chapter 71

Allison stood in front of the mirror in a room set up for the bride at the back of the Rustin Baptist Church. As she glanced into the mirror, she was having a hard time believing that it was indeed her. Her hair was swept up on top of her head, and curls framed her face which glowed with love.

Her wedding dress fit her petite frame beautifully. She chose a simple, yet elegant gown with an old-fashioned look. The bodice and front of the flowing skirt were trimmed in vintage lace and on her head, was a matching train that flowed perfectly onto the floor.

She stood there looking at herself in the mirror, feeling blessed. Today was the beginning of a new life with a man that she trusted, loved, and knew in her heart that God had chosen for her.

This time, she would follow God's path. She would walk proudly, with confidence, as a child of God and become the woman God intended her to be.

Allison grabbed the bottom of her gown gathering it up in her right hand and did a twirl. She is not only becoming a wife but a mother to a beautiful little girl. Ebony's mother.

Katy entered the room with Rita.

"Wow, you look gorgeous," said Katy.

Just then the door opened, and Rebecca got her first look at Allison in her gown.

"Allison, you look stunning," said Rebecca hugging her. "I am so happy for you both. You will be a wonderful wife for my son and mother for Ebony. I'm so happy that you found each other," said Rebecca kissing Allison on the cheek.

"I will do my best to make them both happy," said Allison. "You know, we didn't just find each other. God brought us together."

"I'm sure you're right," said Rebecca.

"Speaking of God bringing people together, what about Peter? It seems that love might be blossoming there as well. Am I right?" asks Allison.

"Who knows, Peter's a sweet man, and we are taking it one day at a time. Of course, at our age, we don't plan on waiting too long,"

There was a light knock on the door.

"Ladies, are you ready? It's time," asked Peter.

The bridal party followed by Allison shuffled to the door. Peter was standing on the other side looking very handsome dressed in his pale blue suit.

He put out his arm, which Allison proudly accepted and they continued down the hall stopping at the entrance to the door leading into the church. Rebecca quickly entered and took a seat in the front pew..

The church was filled with members of the congregation, family, and close friends. Up front, there were vases of floral arrangements on each side in bright blues and pinks.

Rev Williams patiently waited. Katy and Rita dressed in powder blue dresses carried lovely bouquets of flowers and joined Rev Williams.

Ebony and Lana entered scattering flowers from the baskets they carried. Both were smiling as they threw the petals. The wedding march began, and the doors opened. Peter and Allison walked down the aisle.

Next to the minister, stood Samuel on the left, with Brett on the right. Allison could see Brett, and her heart caught in her throat. He was so handsome. She couldn't take her eyes off him, and his eyes locked on her too.

As she got closer to Brett, her heart began to race, and her knees felt weak. Soon she faced him, and she hoped when it came time to recite her vows, that she didn't lose her voice.

Peter stood next to Samuel and waited for the ceremony to begin. His eyes searched out Rebecca in the front row, and he smiled at her.

"Dearly beloved we are gathered here in the sight of God and this congregation to bring together Brett Victor Collins and Allison Lynn Stevens in holy matrimony. What God has joined together, let no man put asunder. Since Brett and Allison have written their vows, I will let them recite them to each other." Rev Williams's eyes met with Brett indicating it was his turn to start.

Brett took both of Allison's hands in his and looked deep into her eyes.

"When you came into my life, I was still a broken man and afraid of living life again. I was afraid to care about anyone again. I was afraid to take a chance to love again. As I got to know you, Allison, my heart changed, and I knew that God had sent you to me and it was okay to give you my heart. I think Ebony knew before I did that you were the one," said Brett.

"I promise to love you, to cherish you in good times and bad, knowing that God will see us through whatever rocky road might be ahead. Allison, I love you with all my heart."

Allison looked into Brett's eyes and spoke her promise.

"Brett, when I first met you, there was a spark that made my heart flutter. I think I knew at that moment that something wonderful was about to happen. Like you, I had been hurt in the past and had guarded my heart for so long that I was afraid to share it with anyone. Through your loving spirit, tenderness, and patience, I learned to take a chance and fell in love with you. I promise to love and support you always."

Ebony stood just behind Brett and Allison. Allison let go of Brett's hands for a moment and took both of Ebony's small hands in hers. She leaned over facing her.

"Ebony, you are a bright ray of sunshine in my life. I promise I will always love you and be there for you when you need me. I will rejoice with you in good times and cry with you when you feel like crying. I will support you and be there for you as you grow into the young lady I know you will become."

Ebony kissed Allison on the cheek and said, "I love you, Mommy."

Allison's choked up by those few words from her new daughter. She let go of Ebony's hand and stood facing Brett.

Rebecca left her seat and took Ebony's hand, leading her to the seat next to her, and then used a tissue to dry her eyes.

With Allison's promise to Ebony, there wasn't a dry eye in the church. She had moved everyone to tears, including Rev. Williams who had to clear his throat before he continued on with the final vows.

Allison and Brett exchanged rings, repeating the final vows and then came together for a kiss. Rev Williams introduced them to the congregation as Mr. & Mrs. Brett Collins.

Brett and Allison walked down the aisle as everyone looked on. As they exited the building, others followed to shower them with rice.

Brett's SUV was parked out front with a "Just Married" sign on the back.

Allison turned her back to the crowd and threw her bridal bouquet. When she looked to see who caught it, she was surprised to see Rebecca holding it.

Brett picked Allison up and carried her to the SUV. He opened the passenger's door and carefully sat her on the seat, then went around to the other side, got in and started the engine. They both looked at each other and almost at the same time said, "Are you ready for the rest of your life?"

Chapter 72

Everyone was gathered at the Evans house for the reception. Thanks to Rebecca, Katy, and Rita, the house was beautifully decorated for the occasion in a combination of wedding and New Year motif.

The dining room table was filled with petite sandwiches, salads, and the most beautiful wedding cake Allison had ever seen.

Friends and family were conversing in various parts of the house. As Allison watched the joy of family all around her, she was reminded that someone very dear to her was missing-Her mom.

It was a new beginning for all. Ebony was surrounded by people that loved her. But, there were still some things to work out yet. Where would they live? Would she sell her house and move into Brett's? She could be comfortable living in Brett's house. After all, it might be too traumatic for Ebony to move from the place she had lived all her life.

Allison thought about selling her house and putting that money into the outreach fund at the church. In her heart, she knew that her Mom would approve. She would discuss it with Brett after the honeymoon.

Honeymoon... A week in California. She would create new memories. She would walk the surf with her husband knowing he truly loved her. No insecurities and no doubts.

Samuel walked up behind her.

"What are you thinking about, Sis?" he asked.

"About how blessed I am. I'll never be alone again," said Allison smiling up at Samuel.

"You and Brett make a wonderful couple. I only hope to find the happiness you have someday," Samuel says placing an arm around Allison.

"It might be sooner than you think.," said Allison.

"Well, we better get back to the party. You still have to dance with your husband and cut the wedding cake. And then there are photos," he said grabbing her hand as they walked towards the dining room.

The air had stilled outside, and everyone had bundled up and gathered on the deck.

Music streamed through the outdoor speakers, and a slow waltz was playing. Everyone moved to the outer edge of the deck and made way for Brett and Allison.

Brett took Allison's hands, and they danced locked in each other's arms. A couple of minutes later, they were joined by Ebony who decided to stand on her father's feet to complete the dance with them. The air was filled with joyous laughter and of course giggles from Ebony and Lana.

Samuel looked on. Katy and Lana stood beside him.

"I believe they are the perfect family," said Samuel.

"I hope someday to find their kind of happiness, but it seems a long way off," said Katy.

Samuel lifted her chin and looked into her eyes.

"It might not be as far off as you think." He leaned down and pressed a soft kiss to her lips.

Lost in the moment with her eyes closed, she felt Samuel slip away from her, and when she opened her eyes, he was gone.

Allison stood in front of the living room windows looking at the sky. A figure caught her attention. She realized it was a Heavenly Spirit looking back at her and she received a message that didn't require words.

Well done, my child. God is well pleased with you.

The Heavenly Spirit let her know that being equally yoked in their marriage, they would be able to withstand any trials that came their way.

Allison receives a glimpse of her future. Ebony growing up into a young lady, Romero living for the Lord, and then the scene switched to a hospital room, and she heard a baby cry just as the vision begins to fade.

"Wait, is that my child?"

Sorry Allison, but the future is lived out according to God's timing. You must trust him.

Allison smiled to herself. She did trust God. She learned first-hand that God was the restorer of broken lives. People that crossed her path were not there randomly but placed there by God in a most profound way that was beyond understanding. Not only was her life changed in surprising ways, but the lives of all those around her.

That particular Christmas they had all learned valuable lessons in forgiveness, charity, compassion, generosity, and most of all, how to LOVE again!

J.E. Grace

If you enjoyed this novel, please leave a review on Amazon.

http://www.amazon.com/dp/B0773FWP45

ABOUT THE AUTHOR

J.E. Grace was born in Northern California where she managed a Campground and RV Park for many years. In the late 1960's, she lived on a 4,000-acre horse ranch situated along the Pacific coast, which was used for the setting of her Pacific Cove series.

She has a background in Retail Management and Property Management which she worked in until relocating to the State of Missouri in 2000, where she now resides with her husband, Joseph.

From 2005-2012 she worked as a Real Estate Agent and then retired to pursue her passion for writing and painting. Her artwork is showcased in Fine Art America, Zazzle and Society 6. She creates art in traditional oil/pastel, as well as, digital art and has expanded into e-book cover design.

She writes in the Christian fiction, science fiction, and mystery/romance genres. Her first novel was a science fiction novel entitled, The Zarion-Saving Mankind. She is also author of the Pacific Cove series of books: Haunted Visions and Testament of Faith and is currently working on "Pacific Cove-Love's Enduring Legacy" Book 3 and a new mystery/suspense novel.

Amazon Author Page
http://amazon.com/author/jegrace

CPSIA information can be obtained
at www.ICGtesting.com
Printed in the USA
LVOW10s1638010218
564918LV00009B/776/P

Chapter 33

Carol had left for home with instructions to call her immediately after her meeting with Mr. Benson. She couldn't wait to hear the details on Allison's brother.

Her brother. She wondered what he was like. A million questions rattled around in her head. She would find out some answers soon, but she would just have to trust God and be patient. Patience was something she would have to work on.

Allison decided to fix an early dinner, as she was tired from the day's activities and would soon call it a night. She lay down on the sofa, turned on a Christian movie, and before long dozed off and began to dream.

She was walking along with a broad-shouldered man, with black shoulder length hair, and gray eyes. He had a deep, but soothing voice and Allison couldn't help but think that they had met before. "No, don't leave! What's your name?" Allison asked.

The man turned and looked back as he was walking away, "I'm Samuel. I have a good life, and I don't need any more family."

"Please, stop! Let's talk about this," Allison pleaded, but he kept on walking. She watched as his form faded into the distance and she began to cry. "Mom, why did you give him away?

A few minutes later, Allison, woke in a cold sweat. Her blanket had slid off the sofa into a heap on the floor. It had all seemed so real. *What if this was a vision*

J.E. Grace

of what was to come? She tried not to take her dream too seriously as it had to be a torment from Satan.

She reached down and picked up the blanket. Her muscles ached. She needed to crawl into her comfortable bed and quit over-thinking the situation. Everything would be fine.

Allison shut off the living room light, and as she entered the bedroom, she turned on the lamp next to her bed, grabbed the gown that was lying on the foot of her bed and put it on. Allison pulled the covers back and got into bed shutting the lamp off.

As she lay in bed, her mind wandered. She thought back to how different her life was now compared to just a couple of months ago. The journey wasn't easy, but it seemed that with God's help, she was finally getting her life together. She realized that she had a long way to go, but at least the path was clear. The bumps in the road just made her realize that the journey wasn't without some lessons.

She had just turned over on her side, tucking her pillows tightly around her head when all of a sudden, the room took on a glow, and even with her eyes closed, she could feel the warmth on her face.

Allison opened her eyes. A Heavenly Spirit was across the room. It moved in a fluid motion, not touching the floor as it approached the bed.

"Allison, I'm Blessing. I help administer words of comfort, praise, and peace to those in need. I can sense that you have some reservations about finally meeting your brother. Remember, God is in control, and everything works for good in the end. You are starting on a new journey in your life, and it's one that will change you forever. Don't be afraid. God is shaping you into greatness. You and your brother both need healing."

"Why did my mother hide the fact that he is alive? We lost precious years," asked Allison. Her heart weighed heavy, and she couldn't understand why she didn't find out the truth until after her mother had died.

"It's not my place to tell you why, but I can tell you that building the relationship between you and your brother will be worth the effort. Give things a chance. Remember forgiveness brings about healing. Start there."

Allison's eyes began to tear up. She loved her mom and wanted nothing more than to understand why things happened like they did. She might never get the answers she desperately needed. But, there was one person who might be able to give her some answers-Peter Evans.

Chapter 34

Allison pulled her car into the lot, parked and turned the ignition off.

Her Heavenly Spirit had told her last night not to worry. God had this. She believed in her heart it was true. Satan was trying to get a stronghold again and use her moment of weakness against her. *No, I'm stronger than that!*

She pulled her purse towards her from the passenger's seat, opened the car door and got out. She gathered her coat inward to keep out the brisk wind that was now blowing. Storm clouds were gathering on the horizon, and she reached in and grabbed her umbrella from the back seat.

She walked, half-ran to the front of the building, and entered closing the door quickly behind her. Inside of the brightly lit lobby, in one corner, was an autumn display, reminding her that Thanksgiving was around the corner. *What would I do this year?* Everything in her life was changing so fast.

She walked up to the counter and was greeted by the receptionist.

"Hello, Allison. I'll let Mr. Benson know you're here," she said. She picked up the phone, spoke a couple of words, and signaled her to go in.

Allison walked across the room to the office.

"Allison, please have a seat," said Mr. Benson pointing at the chair. "Allison, I know you are probably nervous about this meeting. I have some